The Girl in the Summerhouse

"A hugely enjoyable blending of fact and storytelling with a fresh perspective on the forgotten WWII Intelligence War in Southern Africa. A recommended read."

Dr Stephen Dorril
Author of *MI6: Inside the Covert World of Her Majesty's Secret Intelligence Service.*

The Girl in the Summerhouse

William Paterson

The third novel in the Kirkwood trilogy

FISH EAGLE BOOKS

Typeset by Amolibros
www.amolibros.com

Printed by Ingram Spark worldwide

For my son Kirkwood

About the Author

William Paterson, a journalist and author, was born of Scottish-Cornish parentage in Durban and grew up with his sister in an old colonial clifftop house, surrounded by virgin bush, with views of the Umgeni River and the Indian Ocean. He was educated at Michaelhouse, then the Durban School of Art in Natal and the University of Westminster, London. Upon his return to South Africa he spent most of his working life in the media. He is now settled with his Irish wife Patricia in Co Wexford, Ireland, where he continues to write.

Acknowledgements

I am indebted to the kind people who provided a wealth of background material and guidance, without which this story could not have been told:

Francoise Anthony, widow of Lawrence Anthony, the "Elephant Whisperer", for permission to use the name Thula Thula, which now occupies what was part of Ntambanana in this book; Anna Baggallay, who combined her enquiring mind, honed at Trinity, her love of Africa and her meticulous punctuation to knock my untidy manuscript into shape; Dr Bill Bizley, author of the article 'Unsung heroes: the trek ox and the opening of Natal' which appeared in *Natalia* #34 upon which my description of oxen and wagons is based; likewise for permitting me to draw from his article 'U-boats off Natal' which was published in *Natalia* 23 and 24; Jan Bezuidenhout, Webredakteur of Landbouweekblad and his colleague Koot Louw of Cotton South Africa for expert information about cotton cultivation; Alec Bozas, Chairman of T M Loftheim (Pty) Limited, for his permission to use the store name of Loftheim's in these pages. Loftheim's is arguably the oldest company in Zululand and still going strong, nowadays as a property-owning company. Nadia Connolly, for providing vital technical assistance to my editor, Anna Baggallay, during the editing process; Peter Croeser, Trustee & Administrator of the Natal Society Foundation in Pietermaritzburg, for his ready help in locating elusive information on matters-Natal; Reverend Michael Fourie, Rector of St. Thomas Anglican Church, Berea, Durban, and Sheryl Roberts, Parish Secretary, for providing invaluable historical insights on the Old St Thomas Church, which still stands on the corner of Julia and Ridge Roads; Mark Henderson, owner of the *Zululand Times* printing company, and Arthur Ashburner; the late Allan Jackson and Gerald Buttigieg of *Facts About Durban*, an interactive website, who provided a lot of information and who continues to mine the rich seam of Durban history; Brendan Lillis, retired banker, for cutting through the mysteries of local banking. The Reverend Sally Muggeridge, International President of The Malcolm Muggeridge Society, for insights into Malcolm Muggeridge's activities in Lourenço Marques during the Second World War, and allowing me to use Muggeridge's name in Book Three, although the narrative in the novels strays from the actual facts; Professor Donal McCracken, University of Kwa-Zulu Natal, College of Humanities, for providing invaluable insights into the limited educational facilities available to Indians and Bantus between 1927 and 1930; Emeritus Professor Howard Phillips, Department of Historical Studies University of Cape Town, for his wealth of information about the ravages of Spanish Flu in South Africa; Nicky Rattray and her kitchen staff at Fugitives' Drift Lodge for helping with Zulu forms of address – the Lodge overlooks Isandlawana and Rorke's Drift, two famous battlefields in the Anglo-Zulu war of 1879 – their battlefield tours have become legendary; David Savides, Editor, and Kyle Cowan, journalist, *Zululand Observer*, who helped to track down Ashley Peter, co-author of *Centenary of the North Coast Railway*, who had the facts at his fingertips about the Mtubatuba railhead in 1919; Goolam Vahed, Professor of History, University of

Durban, for information on the Moharram Festival, Islam, and Indian transnationalism in South Africa; Jane Tatam of Amolibros for her seasoned professionalism in making ready this novel, despite encountering some formidable snags and pitfalls along the way. Emerson Vandy, Papers Past Service Manager, National Library of New Zealand, for news material on Bolshevist atrocities in 1919 and the influence of Bolshevism in Natal; Dr Johannes Christiaan van der Walt, author of *Zululand True Stories* for allowing me to pluck and transmogrify some material from his fascinating book; Dalene Worrall for sending me a magnificent fistful of anecdotes gathered from her Zululand relations, many of whose memories have found their way into these pages in disguised form.

The book cover is by Áine Boland, ThINK, Wexford.

Foreword by Albie Sachs

The final novel in the Kirkwood Trilogy leads readers to recognize the importance of South Africa's role in World War II and the troubling contradictions between impulses of liberation and practices of oppression. As the Kirkwood family settles into their new home in Natal, all is not well. The bucolic landscape that surrounds the Kirkwoods is quickly overshadowed by chatter about World War II and the looming possibility that South Africans will soon need to join the fight against Nazism. Conversations about the immorality of white supremacy weigh heavily against restless constructions of how the official policy of systemic Apartheid would soon further divide South Africa. Paterson weaves the story in a way that considers the impact of war on both national and familial levels. The result is a historic and personal telling of how World War II impacted South Africa. The central character of the book – Ewan – memorably emerges as being both a good soldier yet a "bad" South African, according to his white contemporaries.

This book traces history across southern Africa in a way that vividly recreates how Africa was part of World War II's battlegrounds. Within a story about war, a story of forbidden love also unfolds with bleak honesty. The tragedy and ripples of suffering that result from this love demonstrate the way that a person can escape from the brink of catastrophe only to quickly find oneself in a new and unmanageable disaster. As the fates of the characters become increasingly uncertain, the predictability that a bougainvillea will bloom or a hadeda will call out in the morning hours, stays constant. This honest description makes for a story that offers a stirring recognition wherein the joys and beauty of life in a verdant land are neatly contrasted with the debasement of persecution

While South Africans will surely have a special appreciation for how their native country is represented, the saga ought to appeal to an international audience. The book is written with a coarse honesty that anyone who has attempted to stare down injustice will find relatable and touching.

For me personally, the book had a special resonance. I grew up a thousand miles away in another spectacularly beautiful part of South Africa, the Western Cape. This book reminds me of how every weekend in the apartheid days when I climbed past the distinctive fynbos [fine flora] of Table Mountain and reached the summit, I found myself hating the beauty I saw below. All the glorious parts of the landscape had been legally reserved for white ownership and occupation. Something terrible happens when you feel compelled to hate beauty. This book, through a family saga, shows why it would be necessary for people like Ewan eventually to take up arms and join a wider struggle so that all in our wondrous country could enjoy the beauty. May the days of war never return. May beautiful love never be destroyed.

Albie Sachs
Cape Town

Anti-apartheid activist lawyer, and writer, Albie Sachs was the son of Lithuanian Jews who had fled the pogroms of the early 1900s to settle in South Africa. Born in 1935, he joined the African National Congress and the fight for justice in a society governed by openly racist laws, where native Africans and descendants of Indian labourers were exploited by people officially classified as Whites of European origin.

After being arrested and held in solitary confinement for prolonged periods, he went into exile, firstly in England and then in Mozambique, where in 1988 a bomb was placed in his car by apartheid security agents, causing him to lose his right arm and the sight of one eye. On returning home in 1990, he helped draft his country's new constitution on the principles of human dignity, equality and freedom, and was later appointed by Nelson Mandela to his country's first constitutional court.

The Jail Diary of Albie Sachs was dramatised by David Edgar for the Royal Shakespeare Company and the BBC. Two other books of his were awarded the Alan Paton Prize in South Africa. He was the first recipient of an Albie Award, created by the Alma and George Clooney Foundation to recognise the exceptional courage of lawyers and journalists fighting for human rights.

Characters

Donald Kirkwood
Sisters Winnie and Jean
Ntambanana settler, 1919

Prue Kirkwood, neé Jardine
Librarian,
Daughter of Keswick Jardine, Durban Harbour
Master and his wife Cordelia;
Donald's wife

Ewan Kirkwood
Donald and Prue's son, joined the Air Force.

Emilia Kirkwood
Donald and Prue's daughter

Toby Strafford
Good friend / co-farmer/ Anglo-Irish

Sonya Strafford, neé Broccardo
Good friend of Emily Bell, married Toby
Mother of David, Andrew and Olga

Masheila Reddy
Daughter of indentured Indian at Bells
Trained as Accountant, worked for Sonya
Member, Natal Indian Congress

James (Jim) and Edna Bell
Neighbouring Empangeni farmers

Emily Bell
Their daughter
Andrew and Nigel Bell
Sons
Arthur and Lucy Reed
Empangeni farm manager and his wife
Eric and Marie Schnurr
Ntambanana cotton man / American, wife Mauritian
Paolo Broccardo & his wife Bianca
Parents of twins Zeno (killed in shark attack) and Sonya, married to Toby.
Joy Broccardo
Sonya's younger sister
Jean-Pierre Meyer and wife Caroline
Dinghy sailor friends (Madagascar)
Keswick Jardine
Durban Harbour Master, Prue's father
Cordelia Jardine
Prue's mother
Kim Logan
Logan's Import & Export
Hubie von Weldenburg and wife Frieda, Braille teacher
'Swiss' farmer
Deepika
Employed as maid by von Weldenburgs
Ivan Cohen and his wife
Musical instrument shop owners
Layani
Donald's loyal Shangaan assistant in "Yonder", continued at Chelmsford
Chinnamama
Donald's cook, transferred to Chelmsford with them

Jeevin
Known as Jeeves – Jardine's cook/ servant
Luitpold Werz
Frieda von Weldenburg's nephew, son of her sister Anna
Ardent Nazi supporter
Winnie Kirkwood /Russell
Donald's sister, married to Kim
Kim Russell
Geologist, married Donald's sister
Jean Kirkwood
Donald's younger sister
Muller Brothers
Owners of Oceanic Hotel, Durban; suspected Nazi sympathisers
Miss Wainwright
Keswick's secretary
Pierre van Ryneveld
Ewan's Airforce boss, founder and first Head of the South African Air Force
Dr. Monty Naicker
Activist for Indian Rights, Director of Natal Indian Congress
Malcolm Muggeridge
British Vice-Consul in Mozambique in WWII
Journalist and broadcaster
Umberto Campini
Italian Consul, Mozambique, WWII
Fulvio Manna
Campini's assistant
Harry Grimes
Special Operations Executive for British, in Mozambique

Rosa and Lucia

Bar girls, Penguin Club, LM., working for the Brits, under Harry Grimes

Preface

On Christmas Day, 1479, strange clouds might have been seen moving along the eastern seaboard of southern Africa. They would have come into view when rounding a long grassy bluff. The strange clouds were the sails of the galleons of Vasco da Gama, the Portuguese explorer, who named the region 'Natal', derived from the Portuguese word for Christmas.

This bountiful land they were passing, rich in subtropical foliage, bordered in the south by the Great Kei River and stretching from the Lebombo mountains in the north, the mighty Drakensberg Range to the west, 100 miles inland, and its eastern border was the Indian Ocean abounding in marine life. Centuries later the bay inlet protected by the bluff came to be known as Port Natal and later, Durban, after a Governor of the Cape Colony, Sir Benjamin d'Urban.

This is where our story begins in early December, 1927, to the end in 1946, during which time life in Natal changed utterly.

This is neither a historical novel nor an accurate description of historical events. It could be described as a farrago – a mixture of facts and myth; nevertheless, the many scenes are accurate enough. There never was a grand Oceanic Hotel, yet a glimpse remains of a very real funicular from the beach to the top of the Bluff. The Masheila in the story is a figment of the author's imagination, as are most of the characters in this book – except for some public figures, long gone.

Utterances of such figures and actions are entirely imaginary, although based on research. Any resemblance to persons living or dead or events connected with them is purely coincidental. The portrayal of Nazi meddling in the years leading up to and including the Second World War is accurate.

By November of the year 1927, a small community of white farmers in the Ntambanana area were obliged to abandon their farms after two disastrous years. The first catastrophe was when millions of locusts destroyed their crops and all other vegetation. After efforts to recover in the second year, the topsoil and all the crops were swept away by cyclonic floods. The farmers and their families were left near-destitute and were forced to disperse – many to Durban.

This is not a war story, but rather one set before the backdrop of conflict part of the time. For this reason, not much attention is given to ranks and campaigns, but there is no intention to diminish the sacrifices and heroism displayed in the East African campaign and later, further north, by South African soldiers and airmen. There are many fine books on the subject.

Chapter One

"Come quickly, Daddy, Mummy," cried Emilia. "Quick, Grandad and Granny! Bring a tablecloth to wave!" shouted Ewan as they raced down the garden to the summerhouse overlooking the Umgeni Valley.

The children had heard the sound of the steam engine far below and across the river, as the driver signalled his intention to pull away from the small Umgeni railway station. As they crowded the rail of the summerhouse, the passenger train began to chug and clunk its way across the level crossing and head for the railway bridge, slightly further west. The train driver was in the habit of sounding frequent steam chords as the engine thundered onto the metal bridge. On that day he caught sight of the little group, high up on the hilltop, waving their tablecloth, and responded by unfurling a white flag and waving back. It became customary for him to do so whenever he saw the children waving; they would go on waving until the train to Zululand disappeared towards Red Hill.

The summerhouse was perched at the very edge of the clifftop over 300 feet above sea level, with a view across the wide Umgeni Valley to the Berea hills opposite. Immediately below the summerhouse the quarried cliff revealed a history stretching back millennia. Below the topsoil was ancient schist, a jumble of boulders, rocks and gravel created by the steady withdrawal of the glaciers. Below the schist was shale,

1

and, many feet down, quarrying had revealed the important granite, which, when crushed, provided the foundation for new roads and concrete. The Umgeni River had worn its way to the edge of the continental shelf, before plunging into a deep ocean. Rising sea levels had tamed the salt-laden river over the millennia to where it was in 1927. A few feet below the summerhouse railing, a huge relic of the schist, a wide and flat stone, projected out into space. Cordelia, Prue's mother, was quick to name it 'Lover's Leap'.

A few days before, a lumbering railway man had laboured up the narrow Buttery Road and turned left, with much manoeuvring, into Mount Argus Road, past the mission tree, and had come to rest beneath the giant fig trees in the Chelmsford drive. The screech of Christmas beetles was so loud that it almost overpowered normal conversation. Packing case after packing case was unloaded by sweating railway workers as they carried them through the front door. Next to be unloaded were the clanking pieces of the windpump, followed by the Ferguson plough. Delivered separately was the farm tractor, which was stowed temporarily in one of the stables.

With the unloading of the packing cases came questions from the supervisor about which room of the vast house he was to deposit them in, overseen by Donald relaying shouted questions to Prue, such as, "Where do we put all the books?" and "What about the grandfather clock; where shall we put that?" The crated, boxed clock was lowered to the floor in the front hall. Soon, there were endless crates of books cluttering up most rooms… even the ironing room. Clearly, Prue was in domestic command, and had a very clear idea of where objects and possessions would find their permanent place for the years to come. Her stammer had faded away, at least for the time being, and the birthmark on her neck had become almost imperceptible with the years.

Separate packing cases, marked Layani and Chinnamama, were directed to the appropriate stable outbuildings, where the servants were also going through the procedure of having to decide what should go where.

The next few days were a child's paradise of packing cases being emptied, the doll's house being put into Emilia's bedroom, and a mountain of old newsprint used for packing, which the children could jump on and scrunch up, as new games of hide and seek developed during the organised chaos. Then, one day, when all the packing cases and paper had been collected by the railway's truck, the furnishings, crockery, signboards, dresser, the old toaster, crateloads of books overflowing in every room in the house, and drawerfuls of teaspoons and cutlery had their permanent place. Many years later, it was all still fixed in the collective memory of the two children.

The sun was setting to the melodic sound of the starlings and returning Indian mynahs, replacing the screech of the Christmas beetles which had died down in the late afternoon. By that time all was unloaded, and the railway truck disappeared down the drive, after the workers had been fed with doorstep sandwiches and sugary mugs of milky tea, during which bonselas were distributed by Donald.

The grass on the neglected lawns had grown so high that the children disappeared as they raced around on them. They had already discovered a Wendy house near one of the front lawns and had to be persuaded that, for the time being, serving tea and cake for the family inside the Wendy house would have to be put off for a day or two. They had also discovered the bell pushes suspended from most rooms in the house, which would sound in the bigger of the two kitchens, once the electric power had been switched on. Much excitement could be had in selecting the room, squeezing the bell push, and waiting for the staff, based in the big kitchen, to work out which room it was.

That night, being high summer, there was an enormous electrical storm and the family discovered that the magnetite in the Umgeni heights rocks was very attractive to lightning strikes. The very first crash and bang of lightning blew all the fuses and most of the lightbulbs. Strangely, split seconds before the flash the lightbulbs gave of a ringing sound before expiring. The family's first night was spent huddled together in the very wide double bed which Donald had managed to erect. Candles were lit and Donald got out of bed to stumble through to the main kitchen where he recalled seeing a very large row of fuses. To the crash of another electrical strike very close to the side of the house, his fingers discovered a reel of old fuse wire. Rewiring a fuse was a cumbersome fiddle of loosening nuts and winding the fuse wire around to terminals after tracing the path of the fuse over the ceramic plug. Donald realised it would be a hit-or-miss affair to decide which strength of fuse wire was required – given that he could only find one little roll, he had no choice.

After working his way through half a dozen fuses he decided that was enough for the night. Then he had to pull the powerful main fuse box lever down. A moment later, some of the rooms were flooded with light again; he then shuffled the long way back to bed to comfort the children, who were imagining that something awful had happened because of the length of time all this rigmarole had taken. After turning off all the lights except the one in the bedroom, they cuddled under the blankets together and listened to the first drumbeats of heavy rain, punctuated by thunder rolls. Five minutes later the Wagnerian orchestra was expanded to include the sound of hail.

"I suppose the servants are used to all this, but I will visit them early in the morning, just to give them reassurance."

"What took you so long?" asked Prue. "The children were not frightened, but it was I who was wondering what had happened to you."

"I'll have to get in an electrician to improve the wiring – or otherwise this kind of drama will be played out every time there is a storm... and, of course, we are in storm season. I'll ask the Esse stove man from Henwoods to bring an electrician along with him tomorrow. Thank goodness the telephone is still working!"

"Oh, good lord! I forgot he was coming to install the Esse. He'll be here for hours. But what time is he expected?"

"His name is Bill Cameron – and he has a strong Scottish accent, so my guess is he will be here punctually at noon. Let's get some sleep. Goodnight, everyone."

"Daddy and Mummy are coming as well!" Prue added. She said that Jeeves was aching to see the new house, and was bringing across a roast lunch. 'Jeeves' was not his real name, but Jeevin, the Jardine's house manager and cook, enjoyed being called such, as he loved the writings of P G Wodehouse, and he could sometimes be heard chuckling in his quarters when he was off-duty.

Mrs Cordelia Jardine, Keswick's wife, was a reformer at heart, ever since she had battled with the Singapore authorities to stop allowing the Singapore labourers to smoke the scrapings from the opium factories. Her husband had been deputy harbourmaster there at the time, before he transferred to accept the position of harbourmaster in Durban.

Prue was the only child of the Jardines, and was nicknamed by them 'Dodo' due to her childhood stammer. She had enjoyed being read the stories of Lewis Carroll, whose real name was Dodgson; he suffered from a similar stammer, leading to his Cambridge colleagues nicknaming him 'Dodo' as he would introduce himself, stammering, as 'Do-do-dodgson'.

Prue's stammer faded over the years but tended to surface during moments of stress, and Donald continued to call her Dodo, with fondness. Likewise, the servants called her 'Missy Dodo'.

Donald suddenly remembered that a man from North & Sons was due to arrive and establish in which direction underground the hilltop aquifer ran, in order to position the windpump borehole. "It will be an interesting day tomorrow… especially if it keeps on raining."

They awoke as early as the children, to a sunlit and rain-washed morning. The Christmas beetles were still asleep – they only started tuning up for their daily earsplitting racket at about 10 o'clock. The whole family wakened, however, to an extraordinary dawn chorus of Natal's rich birdlife, assisted by the sound of Indian mynahs welling up from the Umgeni valley.

The borehole man knocked on the door before breakfast and drew Donald, still in his dressing gown, away to discuss the possible positioning of the windpump, subject to the location of the underground aquifer. Donald took him around to the valley side of the house and pointed to a position so that the pumped water would flow down into an elevated tank. Soon, the children could hardly contain their excitement at the breakfast table, hearing the clatter of activity outside.

"There's no guarantee that we'll find water. You'd better sign these papers before they start," said the borehole man, whose name was Fred, "but looking at the richness of the grass up against the tree, my guess we will find water pretty close to the surface."

The rest of the day was a jumble of borehole clatter and shouts, new technicians arriving to install the Esse, the arrival of the Jardines with a turbaned Jeeves in tow, wild racing around the enormous garden by the children, and Prue's unpacking, calling for Donald to assist from time to time; and in due course the start-up of the Christmas beetle racket.

Jeeves had excelled himself, and took over Layani and Chinnamama to help with the finalising of the roast, and the laying of a trestle table to cope with seating the family and many visitors. He had anticipated that the stove would not be functioning so had brought a multiple of Primus stoves and a griddle to put over the fire in the servants' kitchen. The soup would be cold vichyssoise, but roasting beef on an open fire would have proved a problem – so he had pre-roasted it ahead of time; likewise the roast potatoes and Yorkshire puddings. The rest was mere child's play to cook the pumpkin, beans and gravy. Jeeves was diplomatic enough to seek Layani and Chinnamama's specialised cooking knowledge and participation.

The next course was pre-made jelly and cream, followed by traditional cheeses and water biscuits.

"How are you going to make the food stretch?" asked Prue, with concern.

"Simple, Missy Dodo," he said, "we just fill up with vegetables and gravy!"

There were not enough chairs to go around, so most of the men sat on packing cases. Lunch was just about to be started when a hooter announced the arrival of Donald's sailing friend, Jean-Pierre, his wife Caroline and two young teenage daughters. There was a scramble to unpack more plates and cutlery, and a scraping of more packing cases being drawn up to the trestle table. Ewan and Emilia became momentarily tongue-tied upon the arrival of these older children – but not for long, as they excitedly told them about the wonders of the summerhouse and the Wendy House – and that they were getting a donkey to feed off the long grass of the lawns. They could hardly resist the desire to drag the visiting children away from the luncheon table before the meal had even begun.

"We've something for the house to show you after lunch," announced Jean-Pierre mysteriously, winking at the children.

"What a wonderful old house!" Caroline exclaimed to Prue. You must show us everything after lunch."

"But meanwhile I have brought some wine from my parents' estate in Madagascar, and some fizzy drinks for the children," said Jean-Pierre. "Where are the glasses?" – which caused Donald to scramble through a packing case, calling for Layani and Chinnamama to help wash the glasses for the table. Donald noticed that Jean-Pierre was weighing up Prue and seemed satisfied with what he saw. He had last helped Emily onto a Cape Town-bound Union Castle ship when Emily was returning to the University of Cape Town. He had learnt by letter from Donald that Emily had died of Spanish Flu, and thus he was interested in meeting the girl that Donald had eventually married.

After glasses were charged, Jean-Pierre rose and said, "My dear old friend, Donald, and the lovely Prue, whom we've just met, and Ewan and Emilia, we drink to your good health and 'bon chance' in this beautiful old house, for many, many years to come!"

Fred, the borehole man, had slipped away, and on Jean-Pierre's closing words the clatter of the borehole machinery had started up to compete with the shriek of the Christmas beetles, in full chorus and drowning out the arrival of latecomers Toby and Sonya Strafford. She entered, bearing an armful of summer flowers.

The children were released to explore and Cameron excused himself to go and tinker remotely with the Esse stove's innards. After the coffee, Prue took the women away on a grand tour of the house and gardens, winding up, for a while, at the cliff summerhouse, which now boasted the garden benches from Yonder.

"That windpump beside the house is going to act as a magnificent lightning conductor, unless you set a lightning mast a few yards away from it, and taller than the pump," Toby said.

"Good point," said Donald, "I'll see if North's offer them, otherwise I'll have to make one myself.

"I see the papers are full of the French leaving the Ruhr, and the Krauts have been let off the hook, not being able to repay reparations over fifty years. Here's betting that they never will pay much of the rest, with that madman in charge... Give them another ten years and they'll be at it again."

"Oh, I don't know as much," said Keswick. "They were brought to their knees, deservedly, and there are marked efforts to rebuild their economy. Mind you, they are an untrustworthy bunch, as proven before. I keep on receiving disturbing letters from a friend in Munich, reporting the STP's mad notions of Aryanism, building racial purity and all that rot, suggesting that anyone who was not a blue-eyed blonde is in for a very rough ride in the years to come... And that includes the Jews, Slavs and cripples. It seems hardly believable that Jewish citizens' rights are being whittled away and that there is talk of shunting them into resettlement camps for indoctrination."

Toby said that he had received similar information coming

from Jewish professional friends in Berlin. "One such friend was an eminent physicist, in charge of an excellent team of theoretical scientists, when he was suddenly discharged and found that it was impossible to find employment elsewhere. I wrote back to him and suggested that he got the hell out of the place, before it was too late, and considered emigrating to South Africa... At least he would be welcomed with open arms at one of the country's young universities."

With a greater insight than Donald cared to reveal, he said, "Of course the Krauts claim that they are developing a bulwark against the Bolsheviks."

"They have a point, but I have received other reports about building up a standing army, far greater than the Treaty of Versailles permits," said Keswick. "The clever trick is to recruit the minimum specified by the treaty, train them like crazy, then release them from their duties, and replace them with new recruits for the same treatment, ad infinitum. Likewise, because they cannot build up an air force, they are training airmen on gliders, and now have the best gliders in the world... I believe there is a particular exceptional trainer glider, for example called the Rhoneschwalbe [Rhone Swallow]. I saw them at a glider base of enthusiasts last time I was in Germany."

Jean-Pierre said, "There is a certain element here, among some of our Boer friends who are susceptible to right-wing propaganda flowing out of Germany... I have seen them, all dressed up in grey shirts and badges, marching down West Street on Sunday afternoons and saluting some idiot in uniform with the Nazi salute...right arm extended. This is ominous, my friends, if no action is taken to dismantle such craziness. I believe a group of men from the printing trade union had a garden gathering a couple of weeks ago."

"Perhaps our society should just make provision for the

eccentric section of the community to dabble in such silly ideas, unless they get completely out of hand." Privately, Donald was wondering what Prue's 'Pickering Street regulars' were making of it, and suggested to Prue that they invite her contact to visit them, realising however that he might not say much. Keeping his thoughts to himself, he said, "I think a greater danger at the moment might come from America, where the world and his wife are buying shares in risky enterprises, with excessive claims and highly overpriced stocks and shares. As an ex-banker, I predict there will be a very painful crash, sooner or later, and a lot of people will lose all their savings. The drop could be so catastrophic, that it could affect economies around the world – including South Africa."

"Do you really think so?" asked Jean-Pierre.

"Yes, I do, and you can understand how sensitive I am to catastrophic events, after what happened to our farms. Forgive me if all this sounds very gloomy."

"Your words of caution are well noted, Donald; but while you were away digging up Zululand for these past few years, you might have noticed that a bright blue white and yellow cenotaph has been planted in Farewell Square, complete with a couple of snarling art nouveau lions, and a brass soldier at rest…tin hat and all, with the slogan, 'Tell the next generation.' What do you think of that, Donald?"

"It's not a bad effort for the pigeons to perch on, but I maintain that most members of the population will walk past it with eyes wide shut; it's becoming so commonplace and invisible that pedestrians will not even notice it. I am against such memorials, and a huge waste of money is spent on such glorification around the world. I would far prefer to see the Durban municipality spending spare coppers on a working monument such as an educational or training institution.

They could stick a prominent display at the entrance of such an institution so that students will really get the message."

"You are not so terribly far off the mark, Donald. Your next-door neighbour but one on the hilltop is a fella called Bill Hirst who won an Emma Smith travelling scholarship to study at the Architectural Association in London. His dissertation was the design of a University College in Durban with a copper dome in the centre flanked by two double-storeyed wings. It was such a good design and so well-timed that his plan has been accepted and will be built on the ridge of the Berea, the uplands overlooking the city of Durban."

"Of that I approve," said Donald, "and so, I know, will Prue. Speaking of whom, shall we find the ladies?" Saying so, he pointed his group of friends to the summerhouse, where the women were still seated. He excused himself for a while, to inspect the borehole and also have a discussion with Bill Cameron in the main kitchen.

With sharper hearing than the adults, the Kirkwood and the visiting children heard the Zululand train whistling down at the station; so, after telling them what to expect, they all rushed down to the summerhouse with their old tea cloth, shouting, "Watch the train driver! Watch him how he waves back to us!" They all waited, amused to see if this was true, which it certainly transpired to be… At the appropriate moment, everyone in the summerhouse started waving.

Chapter Two

The downstairs phone was jangling in the Jardine household, long before Keswick realised that he was not dreaming and made his way downstairs to answer it, his eyes still full of sleep.

"Mr Jardine, sir?"

"Yes, that's me. Is that you, Neil?"

"Yes, sir. A body was found near D Shed early this morning by a harbour policeman, so perhaps you should come down? It had been almost sliced in half by the rails of a crane... Went right over it, the driver said, without noticing it. Something very odd, sir, the body is dressed in the uniform of a Grey Shirt...you know, those pro-Nazis that gather and shout slogans on the City Hall steps. That is a long way away, sir. My friend who watched the most recent demo tells me that they were attacked by a gang of Bolsheviks, but that doesn't explain how this man was found on the dockside, doesn't it, sir? My friend said that they all belonged to the Printers' Union... And all they did was to break up the Grey Shirts with their fists and a few kicks. They had them running away, eventually – quite the thing for the natives to see, sir, a bunch of us Europeans fighting in front of them. The natives just squatted on the opposite kerb, exclaiming and laughing loudly. That's bad, sir."

"Have you told the harbour police, Neil?"

"Only some men from the water police, sir... There was no one else stirring at this time of the morning. The lieutenant said he would report it to them, sir. The body is still there, waiting for the district surgeon to arrive. It's on the dockside beside the German East Africa Line ship, the 'Kroonprinz' – the ship with the red, white, black and yellow funnel."

"Yes, yes, I know that very well. Perhaps the man was visiting a friend on the ship, but that doesn't explain what happened to him. Tell the police, I will be down there as quickly as I can. Have the police been able to identify him yet?"

"I don't know, sir."

"What's up?" asked Cordelia, after Keswick had trudged sleepily up the stairs and into the bedroom.

"I'll have to get to the port. A body has been found of one of those pro-Nazi types near a German East Africa Line ship. Looks like a murder... But I can't tell until I get down there."

"Oh, dear, what a way to begin the week! What about breakfast? Is it really necessary – surely the police can attend to everything?"

By the time it took Keswick to get to the docks, the police surgeon had arrived with the Chief Inspector. The small group gathered about the body included the gantry crane driver, who was standing beside Neil, the assistant dock master.

The docks police corporal, who had found the broken body in the dim light before dawn, said "I saw some rats... It was them that attracted me to the body, sir."

Jardine grunted an acknowledgement, and said to the police inspector, "If you're thinking what I'm thinking, I presume we'd better ask the ship's master if we can come aboard so your men can interview the crew. Have you asked permission to come aboard?"

They found the captain, Franz Kohlrausch, in his quarters. Leaving the police sergeant and corporal cooling their heels outside the door for the moment, they were offered seating at the board table as strong German coffee was produced. Silver framed photographs of his wife and three children were on his writing desk. Kohlrausch was a seasoned mariner who was clearly distressed to have learnt about the discovery of the body near his ship. "Yes, yes of course," he said, "You must know that some of the men had permission to take short shore leave for a few hours, but I will order the rest to assemble in the crew's canteen, and instruct my officers also to be present. Some might have to be called as needed, as you will understand some are performing essential services?"

The Inspector thanked him and left the quarters to undertake the interviews, leaving Kohlrausch and Jardine alone. The ship was a regular visitor to the port, so the two of them knew each other quite well. As soon as they were alone, Kohlrausch said, "I'm not supposed to tell you, but you and I know each other well enough for me to speak openly. Coming from Austria, I can't stand the present regime in Germany and the implications for the Deutsche Afrika Lijn. This incident, if it becomes serious, will only be a black mark just at the time when these bloody Nazis are planning to nationalise all shipping – meaning our independence will disappear. Until that happens next year, please keep this information to yourself – but privately, you might 'accidentally' drop a hint in the right quarter? Otherwise, how you say, 'mum's the word'."

"Officially, 'mum's the word', now that Austria is the last bit of the Habsburg influence remaining, leaving Austria with diminishing stature. What are your feelings about the possible unification with Germany, which the Nazis are beginning to rant about?"

"There is a strong feeling in the Sudetenland in favour

of unity, but, for myself, I would rather be seen dead than linking up with this German regime. My wife and I come from Graz, we have three lovely children," he said, gesturing at the family photographs, "and we would rather get out of Austria, before that happens... God forbid that it might!"

At that point, there was a knock on the door, and the police inspector put his head round it, and said, "Excuse me, sirs, we have completed our interviews and have asked a couple of the crew to accompany us to the station, with your permission, sir, merely to take routine fingerprints."

"Certainly, but get back in time for the sailing. Have you discovered anything?"

"Nothing much, sir, except that the two crewmen I mentioned had one helluva party last night, and would seem to have let it get out of hand. This does not incriminate them in any way, and our enquiry is merely routine. However, it appears that the dead man was present at the on-board party, because he was a distant relation and was thus taking the opportunity to make contact while you were in port. We have theories of our own on who the guilty party or parties were, and will be pursuing several lines of enquiry, not connected with your crew or the visit of your ship. Thank you, sir."

"Well, we had better depart. But, before I go, I would like to have a small dinner party at our house, with you as an important guest, along with the docks master, your shipping line representative and the master of the stevedoring company you use in Durban."

"Why, thank you!" Franz said, rising. "I'll cable you ahead of our next visit...should be in six or seven weeks' time."

As the Inspector and Keswick walked down the gangplank, the Inspector said, "He seems a pleasant enough fellow, and his ship's so clean you could eat your breakfast off any deck! I'm glad he didn't click his heels."

"That's a Prussian habit – full of sabre scars and the like. This kind of Austrian is more wedded to Mozart than army gymnasiums. Did you uncover anything?"

"I don't think anyone on board had anything to do with the death. The dead man is a local – yes, we have identified him as a member of the pro-Nazi Greyshirts movement, and I will be surprised if it wasn't some kind of plot to get rid of a troublesome ringleader by some of those Bolshies. We'll see. The crewmen accompanying us to the police station will be released immediately we have their particulars and have taken fingerprints. We're creating a red herring to allow the Bolshies to lower their guard."

"You spoke to the crane driver, of course?"

"Yes…Only that he came on duty at seven the morning; that's two hours after the body was discovered; and, according to the police surgeon's rough estimate, before the body was removed. He could have been slain in the early hours of the morning. Someone must have climbed up to the crane driver's cabin much earlier… Someone who knew enough to operate some of the controls. No one heard anything, but that is quite possible."

"So what now?"

"Well, sir, it's routine police work from now on and the pursuit of several lines of enquiry… The usual stuff. We've let the newspapers know, and it's my guess that the Natal advertiser will issue a 'stop-press' edition, with its front page plastering the news… And so will the evening paper, no doubt with far more background stuff."

"Then there's nothing more than I can do. Inevitably, I'll be receiving calls and I'll refer all reporters to you. I won't speculate to the press. It will be funny (funny peculiar, I mean) if it turned out to be one of the passengers."

"We know the victim's name… Waldemar Verhagen,

twenty-three years old and an apprentice printer at (wait for it) the *Natal Advertiser*. Of course, he has every right to belong to the right-wing Greyshirts: the members of the Printers' Union are far more likely to belong – if they wish to belong to anything like that – to the Communist Party – not the Nazi crazies. Unmarried. Parents divorced. I still have to break the news to them and to his newspaper. All a bit odd. Next step is the inquest." He sighed, raising his eyes heavenwards.

"Just an afterthought… Would you please take into account the possibility of it being by black dockworkers?"

"Unlikely, in my opinion, although we will snoop around as part of our enquiries."

"You dashed off in such a hurry this morning. Trouble at t'mill?" Cordelia asked, as they settled for their usual sundowners on their Nimmo Road front verandah, way up in the Berea. They sat watching the ragged flight of hadeda ibises returning home to roost, in a poor imitation of a vee formation.

"Durban wouldn't be the same at sunset without the maniacal cries of the hadedas and the nesting calls of the Indian mynahs," said Keswick, without immediately answering her question. "These are the moments I treasure most when I come home… Just sitting here with you in the remains of the day, and listening to the birds winging home for the night. Yes, there is always some kind of trouble at the docks, but this one was serious – a mutilated body was found on the dock, close to the German ship. What was odd was that the body was dressed in one of those pro-Nazi Greyshirt uniforms. One of the cranes was operated without permission overnight, and just about sliced the man in two. The police are investigating it as a suspected murder.

"The Austrian captain is distressed that such an incident might be associated with his ship. Decent fellow... I am getting to know him quite well; he views the goings-on in Germany with great concern."

"Well, it's out of your hands," she said. "When we visited Chelmsford the other day, did you notice how our daughter's Indian maid Chinnamama behaved when Jeeves was around?"

"Can't say that I did."

"She disappeared for a while during lunch and returned with her long black hair freshly brushed, with a small ornament in it. She had changed her sari too. I think Jeeves caused quite a stir below stairs, but Layani's nose might have been put out of joint by them seeming to take over his kitchen."

"I did have a few words with Layani but had great difficulty in understanding him... Seems to speak a mangle of Portuguese and Zulu. Donald and Prue and the children seem to understand him perfectly, though. They all seem very happy, given the circumstances, but there is a degree of sadness about Donald. I sense a certain feeling of failure to make a go of the farm."

"Perhaps, but I think they made the correct decision in not throwing more good money after bad. He still has his investments, and I would imagine he'll capitalise on his banking and farming knowledge to land a pretty good job in the city... Has Prue said anything to you?"

"I believe he is in contact with the Cane Growers Association... Prue did mention that there was an opening for a manager of their Equalisation Fund, whatever that is. I think it's something to do with paying the small farmer a higher rate for his cane. The post requires liaison with the farmers, the Mount Edgecombe research station, and then there are the banks."

"That could suit him down to the ground, and it removes all the worry that he and his fellow farmers had suffered at Ntambanana. He's not the kind of bloke to let the grass grow under his feet for long. Dodo seems very happy...and so she should be. Have you noticed that her stammer has just about disappeared? There she is, with complete ownership of her own house...No mortgage to worry about, huge garden to improve and surrounded by books – her love and joy."

"There's the dinner gong... It's been almost seven years since she left for Zululand and her present life. Just thinking... we've been sitting at the big dining table, just the two of us, for all those years. I suppose that's why I made a habit of inviting dinner guests so often, just to fill up the empty chairs. It will be lovely to have our extended family here again."

"Don't pressure them too much; after all, they've developed their own traditions in the meanwhile; but it would be pleasant if we could encourage them to come over on Friday nights – whenever they found it convenient."

"I noticed Prue has kept the tradition alive of keeping the children's pronunciation in line by getting them to blow out the dinner candles with 'what', 'where' and 'when' and all that. Weekly dinners and debates will give you plenty of time to turn the children into left-wing liberals, like you!"

"Darling, you know that description of me is wearing a bit thin. All I am is a believer in rescuing the downtrodden...I suppose it started – remember – when I managed to get the manager to ban the selling of the opium factory sweepings to the rickshaw men."

"I remember that very well. You made yourself highly unpopular with a corrupt Chinaman in Singapore... I encountered many difficulties in getting things done as assistant harbourmaster there. Nevertheless, you're quite right."

"Thank you, Keswick, for that correction," she said ringing the dinner bell for the main course plates to be cleared away and the pudding to be served.

Chapter Three

Prue had woken in the middle of the night when Donald spoke in his sleep. He was back, in some jumbled-up form, in East Africa, and muttered, "We can't get through all that with no food." He fell silent again and Prue could tell by his breathing he was still fast asleep. During the first years of marriage, she became familiar with his frightening wartime nightmares, often waking them both up with some shouted words. As prosperity grew on the farm, these occurrences dwindled away, but he still occasionally spoke in his sleep. The children sometimes experienced childhood nightmares, and when these occurred one or the other would find their way from their bedroom into the comforting warmth of their parents' bed. Usually, it would be Emilia.

That night Prue lay awake for a while, listening to the distant thud of the windpump – more felt as a faint vibration than a sound itself. During the installation of the pump, Donald had discovered some ancient waterpipes leading down to the fountain and fish pool in one of the lower gardens at the front of the house. He and the plumber discovered that the ancient pipes terminated in an underground well, which had been covered up by many years of fig root growth. When they peered inside their faces were reflected by ancient water. As they spoke their voices echoed up again.

This discovery was a godsend, as the efficient windpump

was rapidly filling the associated tank and the plumber was scratching his head as to what to do with the overflow. He could now channel the water into the underground well, and, in turn, to the pipes leading down to the fountain which had been dry for as long as the previous tenants could remember. Child curiosity being what it is, the plumber clamped and sealed the well opening, making it fast from the children.

A gentle fountain started continuously, refilling the dry fish pool, and the overflow was allowed to flow into the lowest garden flower bed, with the water diverted at many points, thus allowing flowerbeds to flourish without becoming muddy.

Prue could hear the gentle splash of the fountain floating up through the bedroom windows, now securely covered with mosquito netting. There had been some debate with the children concerning the type of fish for the fish pool; Donald was all for black bass but was overruled by both the children, who plumped for conventional goldfish. The first family of goldfish soon vanished down the gullet of a heron which made an occasional appearance. The second lot had to be protected by chicken-wire over the pool, through which water plants were encouraged to grow.

There was a third faint sound, barely discernible, of the gravely slow ticking of the grandfather clock. All these were comforting sounds that helped to lull her back to sleep. On the farm, the children had attended Mrs. Siedle's school, with extra tutoring provided by Prue at home; but this was no longer practical, so they were enrolled respectively, for the next year, at Durban Preparatory High School and adjacent Gordon Road Girls' School. Uniforms were something entirely new for the children, and Emilia and Ewan were full of wonder at the hats each would have to wear – Ewan's basher bordering on the absurd, they both agreed. As they ran around barefoot most of the time, they did not look forward to the prospect of having to wear shoes and socks every day. Ewan's snake clasp belt, resplendent in DPHS colours, was a thing of great pride to him – and would always bring it through to impress visitors. The thought of the children getting to and from school every day occupied Prue's dozing mind, before she fell asleep again.

The dawn chorus half woke her again, and for some semiconscious reason her mind filled with thoughts of her mother and her reforming zeal. She likened her to a miniature Pericles, a nobleman introducing democracy and rule by the people – viewed by some as a traitor to his class, encouraging mob rule. She wondered how her mother would react if democracy were to rule in South Africa. She thought of the Indian zither player, who played at their wedding – much to the surprise of their conservative guests – and imagined him as president, and smiled. She wondered if such an unthinkable society of universal freedoms might implode, to be followed by despotic rule. She wondered if the Weimar Republic was surely heading that way.

Some days later, at breakfast, Donald mentioned that he would have to go into town to settle up with Henwoods and to keep an appointment with the Cane Growers' Association. "It seems pretty positive that I'll get the job, but there are still some details that they would like to go through with me – pension fund, sick fund, leave and so on."

"Let's go in together and take the children. I'd like to pop in to the Children's Library to say hello, and then take the children to Adams to buy penholders and G-nibs and pencil boxes and all the other excitements ahead of going to school. I'd like to ask Mummy to join us and cart the children off for chocolate ice cream at the Royal, while I pop over the road to the library."

"Well, my visit to Cane Growers will be over before lunch, so perhaps we can all meet up at the Royal for lunch. Agreed?"

"Marvellous; I'll try not to be late."

After greeting her former colleagues at the library, she walked up the stairs to the museum floor, paused at the dodo skeleton, remembering that first kiss with Donald beside the dodo which eventually led to their marriage and the farm, before knocking on the door of Dr James Scobie, ornithologist.

Scobie had lost his wife to Spanish Flu in 1919. His children were now young adults and off his hands. Never marrying again, his waking days focused more and more on his scientific studies. His political views he kept to himself, and what friends he had might have been surprised to learn of his covert occupation. He was a rather sad man, sitting behind an enormous desk littered with several piles of books and correspondence, a microscope and a glass-boxed weighing scale – the kind found in school chemistry labs. The walls were covered with framed drawings and paintings of birds, a rather good, romantic painting of *The Fair Maid of Perth* by Robert Agar, accompanied by several engraved views of Perth, Scotland. A posed group photograph of his wife and children stood beside his telephone. A small table stood in the corner, supporting a slanting drawing board, and a short china vase of watercolour brushes and several pinned specimens of butterflies on a cork mat.

He shared his home and, occasionally, his office, with his younger sister, Annette Scobie, a lepidopterist of some note, having published *Scobie's Butterflies*.

Scobie brightened visibly when Prue came into the room, and said, "What a pleasure it is to see you again. Annette is away for a few days, so we have the office to ourselves. Would you like some tea?"

"I'll make it…where's the kettle? Oh, no water. Where is the tap?"

"Down at the end of the other building – but if you don't mind ducking into the 'ladies'… There's a tap in there, I am told by Annette. She's off chasing butterflies again, with someone called Pennington… or was that the Labour place? She did mumble a name as she went out of the door."

"I think Donald and I have outserved our usefulness, haven't we?"

"No, not at all! Persuading that Indian girl to remain on von Weldenburg's estate proved very useful indeed – as was your husband's technical knowledge, in spotting those hidden shortwave aerials and the transceiver on von Weldenburg's farm. We have been monitoring him ever since. He is German, and not Swiss at all, but it is true that he spent most of the Great War in Switzerland in one of the banks.

"You know, of course, that 'Captain Stoughton', his friend who was visiting at the same time as Donald and Toby Strafford, has left the area and changed his name again to François du Buisson. He has moved to Bloemfontein, to start recruiting members of what is called the Ossewa Brandwag, the 'Oxwagon Sentinel'…entirely German funded through Switzerland. Von Weldenburg channels instructions from Germany to du Buisson (we'll call him that, in future, until he changes his name again). The money to fund his new organisation and his travels around the country, still under the cover of being a brandy salesman, is sent to a Swiss optometrist in Bloemfontein (yes, he really is Swiss… German Swiss, that is). The two of them have quite a cosy relationship, chasing girls. In addition to fitting spectacles, he is the South African agent for new Swiss lenses of great purity. Funding for marketing the product to fellow eye-specialists all over the country provides the perfect cover for the channelling of covert funds as well. What dear old François does not know is that he is a double agent, keeping us informed.

"Please stay in touch, you and Donald, with the Weldenburgs, who make buying trips to Durban quite regularly. Apparently his wife, Frieda, patronises the ladies fashion shops. We know that Frieda is vaguely aware of what her husband is up to, but is under the impression that his contact with Germany is merely a wireless hobby. She is, however, a skilled Braille teacher, and this we might exploit at some time in the future. Could you, perhaps, invite the couple to visit sometimes and perhaps express sentiments and attitudes about the local 'Untermenschen' (the Bantus and Indians). One might throw in the occasional anti-Jewish remark as well."

"Well, all right, we'll do our best to shake the tree and see what falls out. Did you – of course you must have – hear about the Greyshirt who was found, apparently murdered, near the German ship some time ago?"

"Of course. For a horrible moment we wondered if it was our man, but it wasn't – just a gullible fellow who seems to have got caught up in a fracas. The police are having great fun trying to work it out…The Greyshirts are a troublesome, lunatic fringe lot, also secretly funded by Germany – or at least some Nazi source in Germany – like the British New Party idiots in Britain. It's a dangerous game they're playing. The Big Picture is, as I know you fully realise, evidence of powers in Germany laying the ground for some future anti-British conflagration.

"Are you thinking of going back to work at the library, or are your hands full? I would imagine you're quite happy to let things settle down a while. Am I right? Perhaps you might be one of Annette's butterfly hunters? Your hilltop is one of the last remains of original bush, flora and fauna, not properly investigated or recorded – and it will be a great pity if the whole lot disappeared under development in the years to come."

"Dr Scobie, I really must depart. My family is waiting for me across the road at the Royal, and if I don't get there soon, my children will be overstuffed with chocolate ice cream. Here is our telephone number and do, please, pass it on to Annette. Perhaps she might like to come to tea? I know that you would prefer that our working relationship should be discreet as usual, otherwise I would welcome your visiting us as well! I would love to help Annette explore the flora and fauna of the hilltop, but, for the moment, I am all tied up with the home, school preparation, servants…You know what it's like. But keep well, and convey our good wishes to Pickering Street. Donald knows you as my 'Pickering Street Irregular', you know."

Scobie smiled and chuckled, as he rose to say goodbye. But his expression suddenly changed when he said, "Warn Donald that there could be a huge stock-market crash in the United States. I know he's a shrewd investor, with his past banking experience, but he has been out of the financial world for some time, and unless he has the time to read between the lines of financial reports coming out of America, he might not have been alerted in time. From the usual grapevine, I am led to believe that they will be huge financial losses which will overflow even into South Africa… through a substantial drop in product purchasing – perhaps even gold and silver. He will know that the best insurance policy, in such circumstances, would be to invest in strategic land. Now, I have heard that there are plans to build an aerodrome at Stamford Hill, near the Umgeni River, but out of the floodplain, and it might be a wise move to speculate on purchasing, before the municipality decides to go ahead. Quite honourable…This is not insider trading in the stock exchange. Just useful knowledge."

After she was gone, he thought, "What a pretty and intelligent thing she is!"

The Pickering Street office to which she referred was a shipping company operated by a Willie Logan. Howard Creighton, ostensibly his overseas manufacturers' representative, actually worked for the Admiralty out of Room 40, in their offices, the headquarters of SIS, which later evolved into MI6. While the Western world watched with growing concern the spreading tentacles of the Comintern (Communists International), lulled into believing that a powerful Germany would act as a part of an effective barrier, Room 40's gaze was also elsewhere, at growing Nazi domination of the political scene in Germany and the rising threat of fascism spilling out of Germany and Italy to such places as South Africa, Paraguay and the Argentine...

"What took you so long? We had to go ahead and order," Cordelia said. "Ewan, at the age of six, has ordered a child's portion of hot Durban curry. I tried to dissuade him, but he was insistent. Emilia and I have ordered something far more sensible – fruit salad."

"Yoogh!" said Ewan, squishing up his nose in distaste, as Cordelia said to Prue. "I have asked the waiter to bring some paper tissues, just in case Ewan finds it unbearably hot. What are you ordering, Dodo?"

"I'll be daring, like Ewan, and order curry too – and we can share the sambals. May we have some bread and butter, please?" she asked the waiter.

"I've already ordered. It's curry for me too – with sambals and grated coconut on top," Donald said to Prue. "For Ewan, it could be a baptism of fire."

Chapter Four

A sub-tropical Christmas in postcolonial Natal was celebrated dining on traditional British fare. At Chelmsford, the make-do for a Christmas tree was a limb from the Scots pine rescued from the Yonder farm. The humid Durban climate was not ideal for the Scots pine's survival, but survive it did in its tub, in a sheltered part of the garden, to be brought in every Christmas until it became too large and had to be planted. The Scots pine is the emblem of the MacGregor clan, to which the Kirkwood surname belonged – the seeds for the tree had been sent out from London by Donald's older sister Winnie, and the sapling which grew from them was cherished by Donald and Prue in turn, in empathy. It was an important day when the tree was brought in by wheelbarrow as close to the entrance as Prue would allow, then with much grunting and strenuous effort carried the rest of the way into the house by Layani and Donald.

After its significance was retold to the children, the pine was decorated with tufts of cotton wool, resembling snow; then strips of tinsel, and a glittery papier maché Christmas star wired to the top. Keeping the star standing upright was usually an art, as it was inclined to flop over sideways. The tub holding the tree was concealed with old Christmas wrapping paper artfully held together with glue, and a generous red paper sash. The tree stood in the drawing room, and accumulated mysterious boxes over the days leading up to Christmas morning.

The presents were chosen only after careful enquiries about what the family member truly yearned for, and this list was slimmed down to what was within the family's budget. The children knew that they would be getting books, in addition to other year-end objects of desire, and there was always a surprise present allowed for each member of the small family which extended, at Christmas time, to the servants, and not least the Jardines and their head servants. All presents were kept modest, though meaningful – something for the doll's house, a small metal Schuco car, and so on – with the important big presents reserved for the children's birthdays. As servants' birthdays were not celebrated, their presents were somewhat more important; for Layani's wife, a good pair of new shoes; for Chinnamama, a nine-yard sari (selected by Prue and her mother, based on strategic hints dropped by Chinnamama); for Jeeves, a very good hat from Natal Hatters (he was going bald and complaining about the powerful effect of the Durban sun).

This recognition of the important role of servants was not necessarily typical, but Cordelia had inculcated into Prue, from an early age, her liberal disposition, and this in turn infused into Donald's thinking. This approach was not universal in Natal society, but was far more frequent than a bloody-minded overseas journalist might be tempted to suggest. The class barrier remained firmly fixed in the Jardine and Kirkwood households, nevertheless.

The children were encouraged to share the excitement of making the Christmas pudding and Christmas cake, rather beyond the skills of Prue or her servants. In previous years spent on the farm, Prue had had access to good friend and neighbour Marie Schnurr's chef, who had been hotel-trained in Stanger, before being charmed to serve as the Schnurr's outstanding cook, Johnson. It was inevitable that a call went out to Cordelia and Jeeves to take command of the kitchen, and soon the children were allowed to take turns at licking the spoons used to prepare pudding and cake mixtures. Cordelia introduced the time-honoured custom that every member of the family and the head servants should take turns in stirring the plum pudding mix with a wooden spoon. Prue introduced small tokens into the mix which included a silver sixpence, a thimble, a button and a ring. When Ewan and Emilia were absent, two more tokens, small silver representations of books, were secretly added. Although the discovery of one of them by a diner was to be taken lightly, the books would land up in the children's bowls. Donald would express delight and explain to them that serious pupils at school who worked hard would do very well in their education. Although the servants would be eating their Christmas fare in the big kitchen, the family Christmas pudding would be served to them as an important event, with Prue explaining the significance of the tokens, which might or might not turn up in their serving.

The main pudding and the servants' puddings were steamed in bowls each covered with a piece of linen, tightly secured with sturdy string.

In this first year at Chelmsford, Jeeves, assisted by Chinnamama, slightly a-flutter, was responsible for making the cake, rich in sultanas and raisins, although Prue's responsibility was for the icing which Jeeves had taught her many years ago in the Jardine household. The decorations were the same, even in Yonder – a white china Eskimo and two little reindeers. She remembered them from her very earliest childhood in Singapore, years before the family transferred to Durban.

During sundowners, while the children were busy expending their surplus energy in playing 'Bumble Puppy' (tag) in the garden, during the dying embers of the day, Prue said to Donald, "What are we going to do about schooling for Layani's son? I have done as much as I can to introduce him to reading simple text, but from here on he must go to school. There's an important primary school for natives near Somerset Road but his getting back on his own at his tender age might be hazardous."

"Have you made enquiries?"

"Yes, and they are full, but I suspect that Mother could charm a place for him, if we asked her – you know what she's like."

"Only too well! This Cane Growers position is open to me, and I have a good mind to accept as it utilises a lot of my experience in both banking and farming. It would require someone travelling to remote farms – meaning that I could be away for days at a stretch. Would you be happy about that?"

"It might be a bit lonely, with the children away at school during the week, but no more lonely than I could have been at Yonder when you were away. I could always ask a friend from the library, or perhaps Danielle – that girl who teaches braille (perhaps you may remember her from that meeting about the League of Nations?). It seems like a good opportunity for you, and will bring you into contact with a lot of reasonably powerful people, which could do neither of us any harm. If you take the job, when would they like you to begin?"

"In about seven days from now – well ahead of when the children will be starting school. I broached the subject because I daresay I could drive Layani's child to school, but he would have to make his way back. He couldn't possibly walk that distance and you know how difficult it is for a black child to get onto a tram – there are so few places at the back upstairs for them, and he could be pushed out of the way in the scramble for the few seats there are. Mindful of this, and taking into account that we have received some mumbled complaints about having a black family living on the premises, and also mindful that the municipality is tightening up on such practices, it might be an idea if we could get Layani's wife a domestic position at Adams College, with the condition that the son could go to school there. I've heard very good reports about their standards of education and, by some miracle, if he makes it to the matric, he would be able to go on to greater things, even in this restrictive society."

"Adams College – but that's miles away at Amanzimtoti; and who would pay for all this?"

"With his mother working there, education and accommodation are likely be practically free. I dare say we could cover the costs of books and uniforms. It all seems pretty radical, but far better than allowing the authorities to banish them to an out-of-town shack somewhere. I know the municipality proposes building accommodation out-of-town for married nationals, but Layani's family wouldn't qualify for obvious reasons – if we were forced to let him go, which is about the last thing in the world I would like to happen after all these years, I should be most upset, and I am sure that Layani feels the same. I think we had better make some enquiries, assisted by the charm of your mother if necessary, before we raise the subject with Layani."

"All right, I'll do that right away. Of course, there's always Marianhill Monastery – don't know anything about them, though – but they run a school. The place is full of nuns, isn't it? Get the child genuflecting in no time. How would Layani take to that idea, I wonder?"

"By the way, our reliable source asks me to warn you

that a huge financial crisis is coming, you remember. Is our money secure?"

"There is very little likelihood of our bank folding. It's a branch of the main bank in Threadneedle Street in London. Nevertheless, I have moved a substantial chunk into government bonds, with some into Union Loan Certificates. As for the rest – I'm investigating the sale of Yonder land. We can't expect anything much, with the land ruined by floods, but the dream might be to get something for it. It's difficult to get anything moving at this time of year... You know, better than I do, that everything closes down, except in shops, and everyone goes on holiday to the Drakensberg, to escape the hordes of Freestaters clogging up our beaches. As for talk about building an aerodrome at Stamford Hill – the land is owned by the municipality, so that's that, but there is talk of establishing an airship station at Compensation... Much wild talk about linking Durban with Frankfurt and Rio de Janeiro. All that hydrogen just waiting for the single spark. Too risky... Still, it's all very ambitious."

"And all very romantic! I wouldn't mind flying down to Rio – just fancy!"

"Let's fly into bed for the time being, but before that, let's look at your Christmas tree again."

Whether it was by chance or manoeuvre, Prue stood beneath an inviting sprig of mistletoe hanging below a lampshade. Looking at the tree, their arms about each other, Donald gently swung her to him and kissed her lovingly, saying, "I love you, Dodo, more and more. Thank you for reawakening this dear old house. I am sure that the first owners, the Butterys, are smiling down on our little family. Do you know that Mrs Buttery had their carriage buried near the summerhouse after they bought their first car? This is going to be a very sweet Christmas."

They stole through to the children's bedrooms, on their way to bed. Even though Emilia was nine years old, the raggedy Dodo doll still slept on the pillow beside her.

While it was still dark, Ewan was woken by the melodic call of a bird heralding the Christmas Day dawn chorus, accompanied by the sound of crickets and the final calls of bats returning…too high a pitch for adults to hear. He stole into Emilia's bedroom and touched her awake, whereupon they both tiptoed through the house to see what new parcels had accumulated mysteriously overnight, under the Christmas tree. It was with difficulty that the Emilia restrained him from touching the small pile, and then, with mounting excitement, they got into their parents' bed, to snuggle up until their parents awoke.

The family had attended an early Christmas Eve service at the little chapel in St. Thomas Road, where they were married. It was the cattle and sheep which shared the manger with the holy family which most fascinated Ewan. Tucked back into their pew seats, the rest of the service after the entrance hymn followed in a sleepy blur, culminating in Ewan being carried back to the car by Donald, fast asleep, with a drowsy Emilia dropping off to sleep immediately she reached the back seat of the car.

After the Jardines arrived with further mysterious boxes, Christmas lunch, served in the middle of the day at the height of the Durban summer, was a humid affair, but an exciting, wonderful feast, nevertheless – with their parents and grandparents wearing funny paper hats. Before lunch began, however, Donald stood with a charged glass after Prue had rung the dinner bell to summon Jeeves, Layani, Chinnamama and their underlings to cluster at the kitchen door, when Donald wished everyone the happiest of Christmases –

despite the fact that Jeeves and Chinnamama were Hindu and Layani practised ancestor worship; after which they were invited to depart to enjoy their lunch in the servants' kitchen, with Prue and Cordelia serving the family. Towards the end of the feast the dining room curtains were drawn and Donald lit a spoonful of brandy and poured it over the Christmas pudding and lit it, for Prue to bear aloft to the table.

Plum pudding, cream and brandy butter revealed the mementoes – the children's bowls revealing silver book tokens and Keswick discovering a button, much to everyone's laughter – when he said, "Well, it's a bit late now!"

"But..." winking at the children and glancing with raised eyebrows at Prue and Donald, "We have a surprise for you – Prue, if we may leave the table?" – whereupon they all rose and Keswick led them to the stables – where two Shetland ponies, a gelding and a mare, were munching away at hay bags. Layani, who had long been in on the secret, had carefully combed their manes.

"You will have to allow them to get used to you first, but Donald will show you how to hold your hands flat when offering them a quarter of an apple or a piece of carrot. What are you going to call them?"

"Magic and Treasure!" Emilia said quickly. She had just read a girls' adventure book called *Pony Tracks*, in which these names appeared.

Ewan, who worshipped his older sister, said, "I like those names too," jumping up and down, during which Layani appeared and Donald said, "Layani is in charge, and he will show you what you have to do to care for them. Your jobs are to clear out the stable on Wednesdays when you get back from school – and that means during the holidays as well – and Layani will report on how well you do the job every week. If he gives you both a good report, we will pay you a shilling every Friday. If you don't do the job properly… no shillings."

"And if your father tells me that you have been doing a good job for the year, you will each get a guinea at Christmas time. It will be up to you whether you spend it or save the money in the post office savings books you found under the tree – Prue has already taken you to the Umgeni Post Office to see how it's done."

"What's a guinea?"

"It's one pound and one shilling," said Donald, smiling at Keswick. "The ponies have joined the family to do their part of the work. During the day, Treasure will be tethered on a long rope in the top lawns, and Magic will keep the lawns at the front half of the house in good trim. Thank you, Layani, you must go back quickly to your lunch before Jeeves and Chinnamama eat the lot!"

"I think it's time to open those big boxes we brought, which you weren't allowed to open," Cordelia said. After the leather contents, all to go with the ponies, were revealed, she said, "You can't use these yet until Layani, Daddy and Mummy teach you how to ride."

Upon which, Emilia burst into tears. When asked what the matter was, she replied, "There's nothing the matter, I'm so happy!"

Chapter Five

A letter arrived from Empangeni addressed to Mr and Mrs Kirkwood, the letterhead blind embossed with a cornucopia and dated 15th of January, 1933. It was from Hubie von Weldenburg, and read:

Dear Donald and Prue,

I trust this letter finds you in good health? Jim Bell kindly gave me your address and asked me to send the family's best wishes. (Privately, Jim is really beginning to age visibly — and that deterioration started, I think, with news of Emily's tragic death from Spanish Flu. Edna remains optimistic, but her health is also deteriorating due, we suspect, to those Turkish cigarettes she continues to smoke. Their two sons have taken over much of the responsibility of running the farm in conjunction with the farm manager, who does a good job.)

All is well on our farm, or at least as best as can be expected — allowing for the usual labour problems, which get progressively worse, like weeds we have to battle with. I don't have to tell you about the financial crash affecting world prices of sugar — as I believe you now work as a manager in the Cane Growers'

Association, so encounter this problem at first hand. Nevertheless, we are reasonably insured against the disaster, for the time being. Donald, you will know that this area enjoyed good rains and sunshine, so the sucrose content of the cane is at its best. All it now needs is local and international customers! The mills and the refineries are expecting a surfeit of sugarcane and a there is a warning about a traffic jam of supply. The reason for this surprise letter is that we plan to visit Durban from Friday, 27 January, and will be staying at the Royal Hotel for much of the time, although we will be travelling up to Pietermaritzburg and staying at the Imperial for a couple of days also. We have also been invited to stay for two nights at the Oceanic Hotel on the Bluff, which you will know is owned and managed by the Muller brothers, who are distantly related to Frieda and her sister, who remains permanently with us.

The main purpose of the visit is to lodge my nephew, Luitpold, who matriculated quite well and has been accepted by the University of Natal, in Pietermaritzburg. He is enrolled to study law and this discipline is not yet available at Howard College in Durban. Luitpold has set his heart on becoming a diplomat (strongly encouraged by all of us!) and we already know that law is a prerequisite for entering the Department of Foreign affairs in Berlin. There would be options for him to read law at Stellenbosch, but then it would have to be in Afrikaans and we realise that studying in the English language would be to his long-term advantage.

Frieda continues to teach braille to a few elderly Afrikaners who are suffering from sight loss, but finds it impossible to find common ground with the *Untermenschen* – thrust upon her from the local German mission. She has tried visiting the mission, but this has not been a success. She is in correspondence with your friend, Prue, by the name of Danielle, who also teaches braille, and I know that she would like to meet her in person during our visit.

Another purpose of the visit is to attend the popular classical concert in the Durban City Hall on Friday week. As you know, we love the great composers and any opportunity to listen to a real-life symphony orchestra must be snatched at. I gather the programme will include the Overture to the Flying Dutchman (very appropriate, since that the captain of the ship is doomed to sail for ever around the Cape of Storms!), and Beethoven's Seventh Symphony. We gather that some kind of surprise performance will be given of volkspele, and some kind of pre-programme exhibition to commemorate the presentation of the Bible by the administrator of the Cape Colony to the trekkers about to set forth. Apparently advance copies will be displayed of the Afrikaans Bible being printed in Britain, which are due to arrive in the country in March; I hear about 10,000 copies are expected eventually. I suppose this is a kind of symbolism demonstrating the unity of two great nations, nevertheless going their separate ways. I heard the word 'apartheid' coined to describe this separateness.

We look forward to hearing from you – and, if possible, visiting you.

With best wishes and RSVP,

Hubie

PS: Frieda's sister Anna will of course be with us. We will be railing the car down.

"Prue?"

"Well, there's nothing else we can do," said Prue. "We will be obliged to welcome them with open arms. I have to let Doctor Scobie know, and both you and I know what his answer will be – just that – welcome them with open arms. Do you think he has some kind of hidden agenda, or is he just being naive? Last time we encountered Luitpold he was a brat – remember that live moth he showed us in a matchbox? Coming to think of it, was he not a butterfly collector? Yes, I think he was. Perhaps we can build a little bridge of our own by introducing him to Scobie's sister, Annette. Admittedly there will be a huge age gap, but there is a common interest."

"You may have something there. I won't trust the mail; I'll send him a telegram extending a welcome. A Friday, is it? I'll have to level with Cane Growers and take the Friday afternoon off… Nothing much happens in the office at that time of the week, and you will not be working on the Friday anyway, so perhaps we can welcome them for lunch? We had better keep your mother at bay – but better let your parents know."

Scobie's sister Annette arrived for morning tea at eleven on the day she was asked, and she and Prue found much to talk about. She had not visited Chelmsford before, so was intrigued by the fact that the property bordered virgin bush, where the flora and fauna had not been recorded, even though it was so close to town. The summerhouse perched on the edge of the cliff fascinated her, as did the bell pushes throughout the house. She was not privy to her brother Scobie's clandestine activities, but Prue did warn her that the von Weldenburgs were very German-Swiss in behaviour and outlook – and to be prepared to cope with Hubie's manner and possible outbursts. She asked Annette Scobie to take Luitpold under her lepidoptarian wing, if at all possible.

The huge Horch, freshly washed by hotel staff, twinkled in

the sun beneath the Chelmsford fig trees, preceding Donald's arrival, outshining the Morris Cowley – a company car that came with the job. The Horch was a monster, by comparison. Donald had collected the children en route.

"Aha! I recognise the windpump from Ntambanana!" exclaimed Hubie as Frieda, chic as ever, her sister Anna, and Luitpold climbed out of the car. "Was für ein schöne Zuhause … und diese riesigen alten Feigenbäume – eh, Luitpold? [What a beautiful home amongst these big old fig trees.] Ach – how the children have grown – how strange to see them in school uniform! You of course remember my sister-in-law, Anna? Donald – what a pleasure to meet you again – we are all growing a little older, except for you, Prue, who has managed to keep time standing still – as pretty as ever."

After the usual tour, which the children insisted had to include a visit to the summerhouse, lunch was served, with conversation drifting to farming matters, until Donald led the subject away by asking Luitpold about his plans for the future, and congratulating him on his matriculation results. "We will miss him now that he will be studying in Sleepy Hollow. How is your butterfly collection going? Have you managed to snare a white-barred Emperor? Our friend here is Annette Scobie. She is a lepidopterist of note, aren't you?" Donald said, turning to her, to draw her into the conversation, upon which Luitpold engaged her in a discussion about the territorial imperative of certain butterflies in the coastal belt, towards the end of which she said that her collection, upon which she was still working, was housed behind the scenes for the moment in the Durban Museum, and if he had any interest, she would be delighted to show him what she had netted recently in the Port Shepstone area, with fellow scientist, Trevor Pennington.

After lunch Prue drew the women away on a tour of the

house and garden, leaving the three men on one of the front verandas.

"I believe your intention is to go into the German Diplomatic Corps in due course," remarked Donald. "Things seem to be changing rapidly in Germany at the moment and the reports coming out of that country are, to my mind, rather disturbing. You probably have far more information than I do – so what is your opinion on the takeover?"

Before Luitpold could answer, Hubie interjected with, "The Weimar Republic was doomed from the beginning, run along the lines of 'anything goes', with the Bolshevik Slavs and their running dogs threatening to bring down the country once again. I believe the new regime is long overdue. The Nordic races (yours and mine) are the rightful Ubermenschen. The Jews and the Slavs have been allowed to operate for too long. I tell you, the Jews have a plot for world domination and they are our greatest enemies. Greatest, because they are very, very clever."

"You have obviously studied this topic at some length, but we must agree to disagree – from what little I know, I believe this whole notion of racial superiority arose in France in the seventeenth century, and later filtered through to the plantation owners in the United States and was used to justify the whole system of slavery and the treatment of slaves as expendable Untermenschen. From what little I have read, I seem to remember the name of Gorgoneau driving this idea along – and in the nineteenth century it being perpetuated by such people as Hugh Chamberlain."

"Ach, ja! And he was English, like H G Wells and a whole lot of deep thinkers, including your George Bernard Shaw."

"I remind you that I am Scottish, more than English, and George Bernard Shaw is Irish; but I get your drift that you kindly include the English-speaking races as being the

Nordic-cum-Aryan and all part of the jolly old master race. What about the Mediterranean races such as the Greeks, Portuguese, Spanish and Italian?"

"They could be considered second-level Aryans. The Japanese are considered honorary Aryans by the new German regime, also."

"That is quite convenient – to bend the rules when politically expedient. And the rest?"

"They are Untermenschen – expendable – up to the point where a quantity of them is needed as menial labourers; all come from the same sewer and the sooner the new regime, based on the superior Aryan principles, gets rid of them completely, the better. The same applies to this country... You English people are far too soft, even though you are mostly of Aryan extraction. All these Indians swanning around the town, spitting, bringing disease... We should send the whole lot back to India."

"Well, you know that won't happen, Hubie. I have always had some good workers."

"Not the ones on my farm!"

The conversation was interrupted by the return of the women and Frieda saying, "Hubie, they have a piano and the children are taking piano lessons... Maybe I can go and see it?"

"I will always remember that evening on your farm when Frieda sang to your accompaniment – it was such a pleasure to hear that beautiful music in the wilderness. It was Schumann, wasn't it? My knowledge is very limited when it comes to classical music, and I remember that you sang beautifully, Frieda." The group reached the piano by this time, and Hubie immediately sat down before it – after sweeping the dust cover off it, embroidered in gold letters on green felt with 'Ivan Cohen Pianos', and Hubie muttering, "You see...Jewish... They're creeping everywhere," launched into the first bars of the Appassionata. He played well, but soon broke off and said, "The A minor and the C need tuning.... You like music, of course! Frieda, let us invite Donald and Prue to the concert tonight! We have two spare tickets because Anna, although loving music, is feeling tired and prefers to go to bed early this evening – and Luitpold has made an arrangement to meet up with some undergraduate friends this evening."

Looking at Donald, who sighed imperceptibly, Prue said, "That's very kind of you, but we would prefer not to leave the children alone in the house."

"But you must bring them with you... After an early supper at the hotel we can tuck them into our bedroom while we go to the concert across the road!"

After they had left, Donald said, "How on earth did we get into this? I have been listening to Hubie's Ubermenschen twaddle for far too long as it is. How can an intelligent man, who runs a highly profitable sugar estate, get caught up in all this rubbish? Perhaps it's in the Teutonic genes – anyway, we will just have to put up with it, for the sake of the cause."

The City Hall, across the road from the Royal Hotel, was an enormous neo-Baroque structure built in the early 1900s, that thundered 'British Empire'! It closely resembled the Belfast City Hall in Northern Ireland and had an unsettling resemblance to the main civic buildings of Melbourne, created at around the same time. The Durban structure, topped by an imposing dome and four smaller domes, housed three libraries, a museum, the municipal Art Gallery, a cluster of municipal offices and a grand Concert Hall which could be reached from Farewell Square through a fanfare of elderly palm trees.

On their way over to it from the hotel, the party encountered an oxwagon of the type used by the Boers in the Great Trek to the interior, manned by Afrikaans men and women dressed in the attire of the time. The wagon must have been towed in by tractor. Pausing to talk to them, Donald said, "Ek sien jy't die osse agtergelaa!" smiling, to which one man replied, "Nie die plek vir 'n span van sestien osse nie!" which led to the man leading him to the oxwagon and showing him a replica of the original great Bible presented by the governor of the Cape to the trekkers. Prue also showed an interest, and in her best rooinek Afrikaans enquired about its significance, to which the man replied, in structured English, that it demonstrated the friendly separateness of the two great nations of the Dutch and English settlers; mentioning that as another demonstration of how close this was, ten thousand copies of the Afrikaans Bible had been printed in England and presented by the British Bible Society – the shipment being expected in the near future.

Hubie studied Donald and Prue with what seemed to be approval, grunted, and moved to a table outside the entrance manned by several Greyshirts offering copies of a pamphlet expounding their cause. It seemed that Frieda pointedly ignored them and started to move up the steps of City Hall, although Prue politely took a copy. The leaflet was titled 'South African Gentile National Socialist Movement'. When Prue asked what it was all about, one of the men explained it was a movement aimed to enlist as many English and Afrikaans whites as possible, but to resist the incursion of Jews, who were flooding into the country from Germany by chartered vessels. He said that it was linked to an organisation in Germany, 'Die Nichtjüdische Nationalsozialistische Bewegung.'

"Thank you", said Prue, "we will read it later. If we have

any interest, how do we contact you – ah, I see there is an address and phone number at the foot of the page," and smiling she handed it to Donald to pocket. Hubie lingered at the table while the rest moved up the steps until Frieda called him briskly to join them.

The Kirkwoods discovered they had the best seats in the house, in the front row of the Circle, and had enough time to study fellow concert-goers, as the orchestra were tuning their instruments to 'A' before the lights began to dip. Prue spotted quite a few friends and discreetly waved, noticing that the von Weldenburgs did not seem to know anyone in the upstairs audience.

The programme notes featured biographies of the visiting German conductor, Rudolph Alberts, and other performers, though the first part of the programme for the evening performance included a 'To be Announced' after the first piece – the *Overture to the Flying Dutchman* by Richard Wagner. Some members of the audience started with surprise when Wagner's overture began with a crash of strings, brass and tympani. It was a popular piece.

After the applause died down, the conductor turned to the audience and said, "And now we have the first of two surprises. Ladies and gentlemen, the *Volkspele*!", and started clapping as a group of men and girls, dressed in stylised Voortrekker costume, emerged from the wings and the orchestra struck up a medley of songs, while the group broke into simple set dances. It was claimed that the songs were composed during their journeys north, though the final song, led by a young tenor, was a song composed during the armed struggle against British rule – the Anglo Boer war – 'Sarie Marais.' It was a song of longing for a girl he'd met before the war had begun. The group joined in with the chorus – 'O bring my terug na die Ou Transvaal' – and many members of the audience joined in. After the applause died down, the conductor turned to the audience and said, "Would you like to hear that again?" The audience applauded and many of them shouted, "Yes, yes!" And so the song was sung again.

When Frieda disappeared during the interval to 'powder her nose', as she said, and Hubie had drifted to the bar, Donald said, "When we get home I would like to read that leaflet. We seem to have been welcomed into the herrenvolk all right, the intention of our being here in the first place. Either Von Weldenburg has a plot of his own, involving us, or he is just being naive. It will be interesting to know what Pickering Street thinks about our being in amongst the 'Angels'."

The second half was devoted, mainly, to Beethoven's Seventh Symphony. Donald and Hubie nodded off during it, until the full-throttle tympani jerked them awake during the slow Allegro movement. After the triumphal end and applause, Rudolph Alberts turned to the audience again and said, "Well, it's almost time to go home, but not just yet... Not before we hear the beautiful voice of Mariana von Hesseler, direct from the Bayreuth Festival, to close the evening with Senta's song of undying love before plunging into the sea, when Erik reveals himself as the Flying Dutchman, swooping out of the clouds, rescuing her from the sea and sweeping her into the heavens."

As he spoke, the flaxen-haired Mariana came in from the back of the concert hall and took her place beside the conductor, facing the audience, as the auditorium lights dipped and twin spotlights shone on her. A scrim curtain on the stage was backlit with the film of a roiling sea. The finale brought the house down, with most of the audience standing and applauding, before the lights came up and the orchestra played 'God save the King'.

"Well, thank heavens that's over!" exclaimed Donald, as they drove home.

"I'm afraid it's not quite," said Prue. "The von Weldenburgs invited the children – and of course accompanied by us – to visit the Oceanic Hotel, on the ocean side of the Bluff tomorrow, to ride the funicular down to the beach and swim in the private tidal pool. The children got so excited about the prospect – as described by Frieda – that I felt obliged to accept."

"Oh Dodo! I was looking forward to a quiet Sunday with the children at Chelmsford. That explains why I heard Hubie shout to us as our car departed. Isn't the hotel owned by two German brothers, the Mullers?"

"Frieda said that the Mullers were distant relations of hers, from Munich. Apparently the hotel is more like a resort and quite swanky. She said there is a freshwater pool beside the hotel terrace, squash courts and tennis courts – peacocks too."

"That means a drive around the head of the bay and a bumpy ride to the far side of the Bluff – what a place to put an hotel."

"We will be special visitors and go there by launch across the Bay, after parking our car near the yacht club. From what I gather, it's sort-of 'swanky-German', and that's why we have never been. Apparently, it enjoys a contract with the Deutsch Oost-Afrika Lijn, offering an exclusive stopover for first-class steamship passengers travelling up and down the east coast of Africa. I don't need to tell you that there is a residue of German business left over from the times when Tanganyika was part of German East Africa, and I suppose a residue of postwar Germans who like to revisit the place. There's a ghost of the old German Empire hiding in the wings."

"Of course, I have heard of it – I believe they even have

a nightclub there called 'The Firefly' where it is rumoured that all sorts of shenanigans go on. Is it the kind of place to take the children, I wonder?"

"Oh, I daresay that would be tucked away somewhere, behind the scenes. What excited the children was the chance of riding the cable rail down to the private beach. I believe that there is a tidal pool there and even a private jetty for the hotel launch to shuttle guests into the harbour to moor on a jetty close to the yacht club."

In fact, the Mullers' Hotel Oceanic even boasted shuttle buses to whisk guests from the hotel to a jetty inside the harbour on the Bluff side, to cope with inclement weather. Small shuttle buses were likewise parked in readiness, to transfer guests to and from the German liners, the railway station and carry them to Greenacres, Ansteys, Stuttaford and other smart shops. Scenic and game reserve tours were also on offer.

The Mullers' father had owned a fashionable hotel in Munich before the war, and the two brothers had grown up in an atmosphere of upper-class hostelry. They immigrated to Durban many years after the war, after being attracted to the benign climate and bustling economy – compared with the depressed circumstances in their homeland at that time. The older Muller walked with a slight stoop and had no children, made up for by the three children of the younger who attended a private school on the Berea, so that shuttling to and from across the Bay every school day became routine, though not so to their visiting schoolfriends.

The architect of the Oceanic designed the low-lying buildings in a blend of Jugendstil and Art Nouveau – not always a comfortable one, but enhanced by a gallery of art works that decorated the entertainment and dining rooms. All the guestrooms overlooked views of the Indian Ocean from an elevation of 120 feet or so, offering magnificent views from an attractive height, and the sight of all manner of liners and freighters passing by on their way into and out of the harbour. The hotel nestled among venerable flamboyant (as distinct from flame trees, which are native to South America) and wild fig trees, flower beds of strelitzia regina and other subtropical species. A family of peacocks would occasionally awaken light sleepers with their early morning screeches, and fascinated the children whenever the peacock chose to display his tail.

The extensive grounds were surrounded by high natural stone walls, softened by extensive outcrops of ferns. Huge iron gates wrought in Jugendstil style were manned by turbaned and uniformed Sikhs, who also operated the cable railway serving the private beach and jetty.

(Of course, the Oceanic is no more, although the collapsed ruins can be picked out by a diligent explorer not deterred by the threat of encountering snakes. The hotel burned down in mysterious circumstances in 1942. The private beach is no more and nowadays swarms with bathers, who – a few of them – are tempted to trace the rail lines, now mostly covered by beach sand, as is the wooden stepway of 239 steps, relieved here and there by landing stages. The tidal pool is still there, and the concrete moulding, all overgrown by barnacles and seaweed.)

"Ah! Der aristokratische Engländer und seine charmante familie," said Hubie, rising, as did the two Muller brothers, when the Kirkwoods walked from their car to the terrace.

"Hello," said Donald, "but I am neither aristocratic nor English: but I will accept that my family is charming." (Donald was reminded of an occasion when, as a young representative of his father's lace factory, he had been sent on an educational mission to meet the factory agent in Hamburg. This was well before the First World War. He had been invited to the agent's home where the maid who opened the door announced his arrival to the agent's wife as 'Der aristokratische Engländer!' as it was assumed in Hamburg, at that time, that rare British travellers of means must be aristocratic and English, with far less familiarity of the other nations which populate the British Isles.) "Prue is half English and half Scottish, so our children are a mixture. I am Scottish."

"Aha, you see! I talked to Donald in German, he understands, and answers me in English. Welcome... Please meet the Muller families." They were seated on the terrace, awaiting their arrival. After the usual introductions, Alfred Muller, the elder brother, said that they planned to have a picnic lunch on the beach, if that suited the guests – and invited them to change into swimming costumes in preparation to swimming in the tidal pool. Hubie and Frieda were already in swimming costumes, as were the Muller families. The Kirkwoods were shown to the changing rooms at the side of the terrace near the funicular railway engine house, and when they emerged, Alfred said that the picnic would go down first, followed by the children with one adult – and then the rest of the adults. Turbaned Indians in hotel uniform were waiting at the small railway carriage, and at a signal from Alfred they loaded up the picnic and then disappeared downwards, out of sight in the little carriage. The last sight was of the turbans seemingly sinking underground.

"I see you have brought your Vöigtlander, Donald. A fine camera. I hope you will take some pictures of this pleasant location? Please – let me take a photograph of you and your daughter... there – on those rocks over there. So, she can sit on your knee, ja? May we have a family picture now, sitting behind the picnic, before we start eating and making a little mess? Good!"

"Why is the meat so thin?" asked Ewan, which made the Muller children chuckle. "Because the people in the kitchen hit the meat with big hammers until it gets quite flat – so when it is baked it is much nicer because all the juices have gone right through," answered Alfred Muller. Turning to Prue, he asked, "How did you enjoy the concert last night?"

"We enjoyed it very much indeed, but my personal view was that the *Volkspele* was rather out of place in a concert devoted to serious music. Beethoven has always been a great favourite, and the Wagner 'snippets' – that is, only the overture and Senta's song – before the main work was a little inadequate, but it is understandable that they would have had to sacrifice the Beethoven; but Wagner liked to make full use of the brass!"

Donald said, "It was very kind of Hubie and Frieda to invite us to a thrilling evening."

"We have just returned from the Bayreuth Festival," said Alfred.

"Oh really! That must have been wonderful – describe this to us, please!"

"Well, there was a certain amount of controversy about the stage setting which broke away from the original Wagner creations – thought by many, including members of the Wagner family, as spoiling the composer's concepts. However, the new Chancellor, Herr Hitler, sanctioned the changes so they just had to shut up. I was surprised to see that some of the main performers were Jewish, such as Max Lorenz who was married to a prominent Jewish woman, but I was told that his continued presence was at the behest of Hitler himself… And the Italian, Arturo Toscanini, was committed to continue conducting there, despite his public pronouncements against fascism. We did not attend the entire festival but did watch *The Flying Dutchman* in this new setting, sanctioned by Hitler, which was very good."

"I don't understand this obsession about Jews in Germany," said Donald. "Could you explain? As far as I am concerned, they are good business people and have helped to bring a lot of prosperity to this country…"

"The German state was almost overrun by that Russian Bolshevist, the Jew Trotsky and his lot, determined to spread the poison of international communism in Europe. In fact, it reached as far as Britain, and only the determined stand of the National Socialists in Germany helped to push it back. Subversive influences were permitting it to spread, as part of a plot to take over the world – or so we have been led to believe. The National Socialists are cleaning out the stables, not only of Jews but of perverts, cripples and mentally backward people, to build a master race, employing the principles of eugenics," said Hubie. His wife Frieda caught Prue's eye and raised hers as if to heaven – implying "Here we go again!"

"I see," said Donald. "I realise that George Bernard Shaw, along with H G Wells and many others, followed the theories of Hugh Chamberlain and Gorgoneau, but I'm sure they are merely talking speculatively – even when Shaw suggested gassing painlessly to death cripples and backward people, I'm quite sure he was writing ironically as he was prone to do about many subjects. Here in this country, I think you will agree, we have more moderate views and pursue an attitude of 'live and let live'."

"Then how does that apply to your Indians and natives?"

"We have a responsibility of caring for them and helping them, in due course, to rise. Prue, I think we had better gather up the children and prepare to head for home – it's quite a long way across to the other side of town and we have quite a heavy day tomorrow."

After the Kirkwoods had said their thanks and left, and the other wives had shooed the remaining children into the hotel for baths and an early supper, von Weldenburg and the two brothers wandered to the terrace railing overlooking a restless ocean, when Hubie said, "You realise that the Kirkwood woman is the daughter of Jardine, the harbourmaster. It is he who makes important staff appointments, and although the position of a lighthouse mechanic is not all that important, it's a key role in our future scheme of things. It so happens that the present lighthouse mechanic is about to retire and it is important that we manoeuvre one of our men into the position. You, Alfred, must contact the Ossewa Brandwag headquarters in Bloemfontein to locate a suitable well-qualified electro-mechanical engineer to get the post. There should be someone suitable in this area…And you are to put forward his name to the harbourmaster with the assistance of his daughter Prue – so do keep in friendly contact and do not let this opportunity slip. Once you know the name of the suitable candidate you are to meet him, and establish a suitable story – something like you are remote cousins several times removed, and that you would appreciate Jardine giving him a good hearing.

"The job comes with a good salary and rent-free accommodation. It would be best, however, if he was helped to buy a house near the lighthouse, rather than his living on the lighthouse premises – so making it more difficult for his comings and goings to be monitored. You will be seen to be sufficiently prosperous to act as surety for his buying a house – and we will see to it that your financial position is never jeopardised.

"As for your relationship with the Durban business and social community you must go out of the way to continue and maintain excellent and friendly contact… And that means even with Jews. Your true position must remain in deep cover until that time comes… and it will."

It had become less than a halcyon late afternoon, so the hotel shuttle-bus took them down to the harbour jetty. The Kirkwood family were the only passengers. On the way, the children begged their parents to stop at the lighthouse, where they all climbed out and went to the edge to look at the view of the harbour entrance. The 85-foot white painted structure was poised close to the extremity of the Bluff, and they could peer down at the rocky caves which formed the end of the promontory. It was dusk, and they were on time to watch a Deutsche Afrika-Lijn liner, deck lights twinkling, rise and fall gently as it passed out of the entrance of the harbour to meet the rolling Indian Ocean. It was followed, at a safe distance, by the pilot boat into which the harbour pilot would clamber after the liner was well over the bar. To the left and below, the harbour was going about its work; only Salisbury Island remained in darkness.

On the way home, Donald said, "I think we must talk to Jean-Pierre's friends, the Cohens, about all this. Probably the Jewish community knows all about this peril, but Germany being so far away, they may not gather the import of getting their relations out of that country as quickly as possible. Mind you, I suppose they are pretty alert – bearing in mind the widely known chartering of ships to extricate Jewish families for their transfer to South Africa and other parts. It might be an idea – and give us access to better knowledge – to plant an Indian employee at the Oceanic."

"I think that Frieda, while she tolerates these outbursts, is not party to such sentiments – and the Mullers remained silent during Hubie's rant. They seem to be quite benign and doing pretty well where they are."

"Mmmm... perhaps... not sure!" Prue said. "Lovely place, but I don't think I would like to go there again. There was something unhappy about it – couldn't put my finger on it. The way those children had to change back into lederhosen after their swim – and the arrogance with which the Indian servants were treated."

"Oh, you're just a mushy left-winger, like your mother," Donald teased her.

"Have you looked at the propaganda leaflet I handed to you at the City Hall steps?"

"Yes, I have – an extraordinary load of twaddle to be ignored, if it were not for the dangerous sentiments expressed concerning Aryanism, the building of a master race and the disparaging observations about the Jews and most eastern nations. I'll read it to you after supper tonight. No point in keeping it otherwise as I'm sure your Pickering Street Irregular no doubt got copies of it, perhaps even as it came off the press! I saw something about a mass meeting on the Grand Parade in Cape Town. I think there is a protest planned, timed for the arrival of the ship of Jewish evacuees."

Sunday supper was a homely affair, without servants cooking and hovering. The children were expected to prepare scrambled eggs on toast, an omelette or toasted cheese, followed up by milky coffee and a few mint chocolates. Emilia would do the cooking and Ewan the washing up. After the food it became a habit to listen to the Nine O'clock News on the BBC Empire service shortwave radio – that is when it remained possible to listen between the crackles of interference. The time was accompanied by Donald or Prue taking turns to read to them. *Alice in Wonderland* remained a firm favourite for both of them – Emilia was wanting to branch out to *Lorna Doone* while Ewan would want to stray from time to time into an adventure story, of which there were many on the tiers of bookshelves, such as *Kulu the Hare* (based on the adventures of the hare the Zulus saw in the dark shapes on the moon).

With the children off to sleep, Donald said, "I'm glad the children were not within earshot when Hubie delivered his worst ranting. We have enough prejudice in this country as it is without his contributing all this herrenvolk rubbish. Here's the leaflet – I will read a few bits to you before I throw it away…"

"Aryans of South Africa, unite! The world of Jewish Bolshevism threatens to take over the world, spread by the Jewish plague which is insinuating itself from Eastern Europe.

The protocols of the Elders of Zion prove that there is a Jewish plot to take over the world and gentile property, step by step; you will find copies of the protocol in most South African libraries.

We Aryans are western Europeans (who consist of Germans, Swedes, Icelanders, Norwegians, Danes, British, Irish, Dutch, Belgian and Northern French); olive-skinned white southern Europeans (who consist of southern French, Portuguese, Spaniards, Italians, Romanians, and Greeks), are called the Mediterranean race.

"It goes on with similar muck which I won't insult you by continuing to reading… On the reverse there is more twaddle with pictures illustrating the ideal Aryan man and ideal Aryan woman – with measurements saying 'ideal space between the eyes, forehead – chest dimensions, leg length and even hair colouring'.

"Astonishingly, there's not a single mention of the

indigenous races and indentured Indians – suggesting to me that the pamphlet was even printed in Germany... Quite a few spelling and grammatical mistakes, too. Perhaps the leaflet was developed in Germany for distribution in Britain by Oswald Mosley's Blackshirts, although Mosley was such a brilliant parliamentary orator, I am sure he would have corrected the grammar and spelling if he had ever seen it; possibly for use by one of his more thuggish underlings."

Prue put down for a moment Ewan's school shirt which she was repairing, (playing 'Cops and Robbers' during school breaks had a punishing effect on his clothes) and said, "I think the Greyshirts and their propaganda will only appeal to the almost illiterate far right – even Hertzog has rejected their request to join his party – but certainly the anti-Jewish sentiments expressed will have a wider impact on the Afrikaner. The dictum of the Broederbond, after all, is to sweep the British and Jewish influence 'into the sea', and to declare a republic free of British rule."

"Such sentiments will inevitably permeate sections of the English-speaking community here. In fact, they have already... I pick up murmurings about Jewish influence and exploitation of Gentiles, whether they be true or false – there is a growing groundswell of mutterings.

"It's always been thus...The throwing out of the Temple of the money-lenders, the folklore tales from the Middle Ages of the taunting of Jesus by a JEW, on the way to Golgotha, condemning the race to wander the earth. The Alhambra Decree of 1492, leading to the eviction of Jews from Spain except for those who converted to Catholicism, the many pogroms in Russia, inspired by the orthodox Christian church, Shakespeare's portrayal of Shylock as a characteristically greedy moneylender outside the norms of Christian society; the Russian pogroms. – centuries of prejudice deliberately spread by the Christian churches to anchor Christianity as the One True Faith."

"I must remember to wind the grandfather clock before we go to bed, but one passing comment about Jews is that they have always been so integrated with Russian, European and American society that it is easy to classify them as pariahs, for those readers wishing to do so. Easy to wipe out, because they are just a small segment of society, whereas getting rid of a whole subcontinent of Hindus and Mohammedans would be so much more difficult. All we can do is to actively oppose prejudice and implant in our children a resistance to prejudice, in the same manner... Come on, we are sounding so jolly high-minded I am getting very tired. The one thing I am prejudiced against is that damned rat I'm sure I heard in the servants' kitchen ceiling. Its days are numbered, before he eats through the electric wire insulation. Mind you, he might electrocute himself in the process."

Chapter Six

From several floors up, low tide in Durban Bay revealed hidden sandbanks. Keswick watched as a dingy lurched on to one of them, and a couple of inexperienced sailors climbed out of their boat in ankle-deep water and proceeded to push their boat off the sand bar.

The windows in Keswick's vast office provided a sweeping view of the harbour. He was always first to arrive in the mornings, allowing him time to study the bay, with all its movements. The whaling station on the Bluff side was dormant, with flensing completed several days before. The tumbling sound of coal barges being loaded further up the bay was as sharp as the voices of the stevedore hands arriving for work. The Old Groaner, the less than popular dredger, had started up its racket near the Salisbury Island mangroves, while seagulls squabbled over bait left on the docks by a departing fisherman.

As any sailor will tell you, all harbours have their own distinct smell – and one old salt swore that he could identify, blindfold, the harbour where they had docked, by that distinct smell. Over centuries Durban had acquired a smell of flotsam and jetsum, marine oil, rusting chains, barnacles, bunker coal smoke and mud, all combined with molasses and other bulk cargo smells wafting from the Congella docks serving quayside processing plants.

Picking up a pair of binoculars from his desk, he stepped out onto his balcony to sweep the far stretches of his beloved harbour, past Cato Creek, to the Umbilo River where it discharged into the bay; then turned his glasses to watch the steamer activity at Congella. He was startled by Miss Wainwright's tapping on a window and pointing to the tray of coffee and a few biscuits she had left on his desk. Inside again, she reminded him of the first interview for the post of lighthouse man, and pointed to a file which lay on the table.

"Good morning – thank you for the coffee, Miss Wainwright. Well, it's going to be difficult to replace old Fred. How long has he been with us now? Must have been close on forty-five years! One wonders what his wife thinks about it."

"She told me that they had bought a small property in the Drakensberg close to a river, which is regularly well stocked with trout fingerlings. That area is very popular with fly fishers and I believe she is a good cook and he is a keen fly fisherman, so between them they intend to set up a small business in fishing tackle, including camping kit. That will be coupled to a modest bed and breakfast."

"That sounds idyllic… We will have to arrange a presentation of some kind and a good send-off. Let me have your thoughts about a suitable presentation piece… I wonder if a good electricity generator might not be a good idea? They will be rather stuck in the bundu, won't they?"

"I must remind you that you have to interview another candidate for lighthouse-man this morning – in fact he's due in half an hour. His name is Jannie van Niekerk and comes with a recommendation of good standing from a fairly remote relation of his, the senior Muller, who, with his brother, owns that rather swanky Germanish hotel on the Bluff. Apparently, the Kirkwood family were guests of the hotel owners a few weeks ago. The older brother contacted Prue about this chap you are about to interview, asking how he could pass on a recommendation; so Prue suggested his writing a letter to you, you'll find it in the file. You can expect Fred to be here ahead of the candidate. I've also included proof of his certification from the Natal Technical College and the chief engineer at the Umbilo power station. He seems to have done well and has a clean credit record."

"Why does he want to move?"

"His young wife is expecting their first child, and the Oceanic cousins have helped him to buy a modest cottage on the Bluff close to the lighthouse. It would make sense if he had a job closer to home, rather than having to come across by launch every day."

"I wonder if he plays rugby. Ah, here's Fred – do come in. Would you like some coffee? I believe the Drakensberg is going to snatch you away from us. Wonderful retirement idea, but we will all miss you, Fred."

"And I'm going to miss the lighthouse, but my wife and I love those mountains. Funny thing, isn't it – when we decided to go on holiday we'd head for the Drakensberg and all the Free Staters would come down and clutter up our beaches. We fell in love with the little Mooi River in the Kamberg area. Nowadays, no re-stocking with rainbow fingerlings is required – the fish life is self-sustaining, and the brown trout too... The yellowfish are real fighters and becoming quite popular. We like isolation and would feel trapped in a little town bungalow called 'Mon Repos', with me spending my life clipping a garden hedge. After all that time up and down inside the lighthouse, I'll be quite comfortable climbing up the chain ladder at Njasouti every now and then."

"What about your assistant lighthouse keeper? Is he good for promotion?"

"Yes – that much would depend on how he got on with the new engineer we are interviewing today – the others that we have seen were not up to much."

"Well, this new chap looks quite good on paper. If this interview goes well, I presume you'll be taking him across to the Bluff and introducing him to it all today. Here's his file… Better go through it quickly before he arrives."

The candidate was a pleasant man who was quite willing to explain the background. He said that his father had been a rock mechanic on one of the mines, but he died of pthisis some years ago in Benoni, whereupon his mother and the children migrated to Northdene, outside Durban, to share the house of his aunt. The mother always felt herself to be a 'vreemdeling'. Her mother tongue was Afrikaans and she felt an outsider in a predominantly English-speaking part of the country. She returned to Benoni with the rest of the children, leaving him to complete his apprenticeship at the Umbilo power station in Durban. His wife, he explained, was Northdene born and bred, but from an Afrikaans family. She was now expecting their first child and his distant but wealthy cousins, the Mullers, had helped them to buy a small cottage on the Bluff very near the lighthouse.

"Were you working at the power station when they had that flood?" asked Fred.

"Yes, that was in my first year! Wat 'n gemors! Water flooded into the intake chamber with many, many, small jellyfish, and clogged up the works. Durban was threatened to be without power for weeks, but I had the idea of borrowing three fire engines, linked together to produce enough power until we could clean up the mess."

"Won't you miss work in the power station?"

"Because my father died of dust inhalation underground, I found the power station very smoky, and fear the long-term effect on my lungs – so I would be happier to escape to a cleaner atmosphere."

"Well, you certainly will get a cleaner atmosphere on the bluff headland! You'll get enough clean air to blow you off the edge every now and then! You will understand that this vacancy has attracted quite a lot of applications – principally because the pay and job security in these troubled times has created quite a lot of interest; but you stand a good chance of getting the job, much depending upon what Fred and his assistant think about it. Perhaps, Fred, you should take Mr van Niekerk across and show him in detail what his duties will be – not least in cleaning the lighthouse windows from the outside, hanging on to the catwalk! The lighting is independent of the municipal power supply and depends on two mighty diesel generators – the second being a backup."

After they left Keswick called in Miss Wainwright. "Well, what do you think of this candidate? I don't mean concerning his qualifications – they seem pretty good, but his general character... You know, woman's instinct and all that."

"I get the impression that he's stable, and qualification-wise, with their buying a little cottage near the lighthouse, he's an almost perfect fit for the job... Almost as if he had learnt it off pat."

"Well, I suppose I would prepare a piece in much the same way. A fine howdy-do if you were stuck on a cold, dark, windy, rainy day without being prepared... Depending on what Fred thinks, I would be inclined to appoint him."

"By the way, you haven't forgotten your Turf Club meeting, have you?"

"Oh, golly," he said. "Between you and me and the dredger we can see, I find these kinds of meetings tiresome, followed by a questionable lunch. It means I have to drive all the way into Greyville, and sit through an irritating hour discussing the merits and demerits of allowing the use of aluminium horseshoes. I wouldn't be sitting on the Board of Governors if it were not for Cordelia – who enjoys the social occasions in the Member's Pavilion where she can cajole businessmen out of their money for some honourable cause… And she has so many under her wing."

"Well, you had better start thinking about leaving your office, to get there in time!"

Other than the view of his harbour just before dawn, or the view from his front veranda at twilight, sipping a sundowner with his wife, one of his great pleasures was to walk along the Esplanade from the Dick King statue, passing the Magistrates Court, the Durban Club and the Royal Natal Yacht Club, ending up at Albert Park. However, on this occasion he had to indulge in the view from his car, taking the long way round to the Greyville Turf Club buildings and yet another boring Governors' meeting, which was all about the legality of alumites.

He had no particular interest in horseracing, but served on the Board of Governors in the performance of what he saw as a civic duty. He had been irritated by a telephone call from one of the members remarking that there were only five or six important horses running in the upcoming July Handicap, the top race held in Durban in the year. "The rest are just cockroaches to fill out the field." The man had explained that the alumites, aluminium alloy horse-shoes, were expensive and wore out quickly, so that it was likely that only the important horses would be shod in this way, possibly providing an extra turn of speed but reducing unfairly the chances of an outsider winning. While such a situation would be a bonanza for bookies, the gullible punters would be misled. Words sprung to mind such as 'shoddy', and 'shoddy' he decided to use in making his opinion clear. He felt that all horses should be aluminium-shod or that the practice should be forbidden completely, and inspections should be made immediately before the race to prevent last-minute switching.

The ruling went against him at the meeting, and it was decided that the wearing of aluminium horseshoes would be permitted if the owner so wished. A picture sprung to Keswick's mind of the cognoscenti among the punters viewing with care not only the horses' mouths but also their hooves. At least the curry after the meeting was excellent, but he resolved to resign from the Turf Club after the next July. The members of the board were mainly 'captains of industry' and umbrella members of the Breeders Association. Keswick sighed inwardly with relief that he was seated among several shipping-line people, one of whom was Oreste Merino of the giant Italian Line. He was a prominent supporter of various local Roman Catholic charities. Opposite sat Donald Harvey, a man of few words, but who gave the impression of listening intently.

"I see that Mussolini is at it again... Forming an alliance with the Vatican and making Catholicism the state religion. Do you think that's a good thing?"

"Well, you know I'm a Catholic, but I don't believe in ramming it down people's throats; and making it the state religion will tend to oblige anyone climbing the ladder of officialdom to follow suit. At least Mussolini has some prominent Jews in the administration and is rejecting any calls by that maniac in Germany. I read somewhere that the Vatican, rather pointedly, employed a Jew prominently.... But the storm clouds are gathering, aren't they?"

"Extraordinary that Mussolini managed to reconcile a dictatorship with the Catholic Church. I ponder how he's going is to confront sanctions from the League of Nations...

the Ethiopian war and all that. Now there are rumblings of his invading Albania. If Italy gets sucked into a Germano-war against the West, fighting on several fronts, I foresee disaster; but in the meantime one must admit, through dictatorship he has managed to force through modernisation of Italy – just look at Fiat and all our racing cars.

"You have greater insights than I, but I do also pick up strange rumblings, with a sudden naval interest in Tristan da Cunha – that remote little lump in the Atlantic Ocean... That's according to someone I know, who told me. Now why should the British be doing that, I wonder? Perhaps just a routine precaution against the worst eventuality?

"Going back to what we were talking about before and that you are interested in sponsoring charities, it would be a great idea if you met up with my wife over dinner at our house, if you'd like that. She's a great protagonist for better educational access by the downtrodden and unwashed – particularly the Indians, though I must say that they seem to be doing a better job of pulling themselves up by their own bootstraps... Establishing quite a few schools up to secondary level, despite an extremely sluggish Natal administration, which seems to tinker with the illusion that they will all go back to India."

"Thank you; we would like that, and I look forward to hearing from you – this is my card with our home telephone number."

"Right! Cordelia will be in touch. We're not Catholic, you know."

Oreste smiled and said, "Well, nobody's perfect. I am more of a 'collapsenik' myself. Besides, genuflection and my rheumatism are bad bedfellows! My wife however is far more Gregorian – goes to services where such chants are sung... Beautiful mumbo-jumbo."

The Union Castle man and Keswick left the lunch at the same time and walked to their respective cars. The former, who Keswick knew well, said, "None of my business, but it might be wise to proceed cautiously in your contacts with the Italian... When I was in Lourenco Marques recently (the Rochester Castle calls in there) I had been invited to one of the usual rounds of consular cocktail parties – this one was to celebrate Portugal's national day in June, and I was introduced to the new Italian consul who had just arrived, called Umberto Campini... Quite a young fellow for such a position. I learned that he is one of the new Italian order – an ardent fascist, throwing out dark remarks about Jews and a new world order. He likes to emulate El Duce and wears a similar cloak which he flings about in the same manner.... Has a strong penchant for coloured bar girls at the Penguin Bar near the Polana Hotel too, I am told. Our Italian Lines member was there at the same reception, and he seemed to be getting on very well indeed with Campini and a group from the German Consulate; the Japanese consul from Cape Town was also there – all almost strangely 'matey' – the Jap's tiny wife is very beautiful but never says a word... Comes up to your knees."

"Well, your lunch friend is Italian, after all, so one can't see any real reason why they should not be friendly; but I get your point about the Germans and the Japanese. Thanks for the tip."

He was glad to be back in his office. "Any tips on the July?" asked Miss Wainwright.

"Pamela," (she knew that he only called her Pamela after he had a glass of wine at a club luncheon), "you know how little I know about horses. And if I did have an inside tip, I wouldn't be able to let you know. I did hear of a horse, a thoroughbred filly, being mentioned...Her name is something like Campanejo, but I absolutely forbid you to put any money on it... Look again at the horses and find out which of them are shod with 'alumites' – I think I have the name correctly. Actually, it really is anybody's guess."

Pamela Wainwright was a brisk and pleasant person who had adopted the children of her brother and wife, who had died in a road accident while holidaying in Reunion. She shared a house in the Berea with her one remaining brother and valued her job and employer. She yearned for marriage – "But what man is there who is willing to take on two children from unknown parents?"

"Have you heard from Fred?"

"Yes, he said the man was obviously very well qualified, and as he has set up home so close to the lighthouse it seemed to be almost a perfect choice. The only flaw is that he is Afrikaans, Fred said, but you know how he is somewhat prejudiced against Afrikaners in general. The saving grace is that he plays rugby at the Railways and Harbours Rugby Club... Something about 'wing', but I know nothing about the game."

"Ah... Rugby. If he plays wing he must have quick reactions and be fleet of foot. So Fred approves, I take it?"

"Yes."

"That being the case, would you go through the rigmarole of letters, employment agreements and sort out any possible muddle between the power station pension fund and medical benefits scheme, please; but first get Fred on the line again and, just as a double precaution tell him we are going ahead. Would you also find out when he intends to depart and make arrangements for a farewell 'do'. Could you establish with him whom he would like to attend and add to that as many harbour bigwigs as possible. Also find out if a generator as a presentation would be acceptable, and also see what to give his wife. Talk to the accountant and establish how much we can provide as a 'golden handshake'. Lastly…Your thoughts on this one…How say you to a plinth at the entrance to the harbour, inscribed with his name and his service in lighting the way to safe harbour for mariners? For the July, please invite Fred and his wife to sit at our table.

Chapter Seven

One of the relics of the old farm which Donald clung on to was the original Huntley and Palmer biscuit box which he used as a post box, nailed to a wooden stump. It had been dressed up a bit, but relics of the original paper advertisement remained. The box was now secured to one of Chelmsford's huge eucalyptus trees at the entrance to the property. It was into this box that the sweating postman delivered three envelopes: a weather-worn letter with an Ayrshire, Scotland franking. It was a letter from his sister Winnie: the second letter was postmarked Balgowan, the post office for Michaelhouse school in the Midlands of Natal; and the third was postmarked Empangeni in Zululand. He immediately opened the letter from Scotland as he walked back down the drive:

Dear Donald,

I have some very sad news. Last week, old McAlpine's son David discovered his father crushed to death by his tractor while he was piling up silage. During the season he had been experimenting with various crops for converting into silage, including the options of maize, oats and one other of which I can't remember the name immediately. Apparently he was piling up oats in the silage channel when the accident happened.

Little sister Jean was away on an archaeological dig in Santorini and could not be reached, but Jim and I rushed up from Richmond, immediately we heard the news, and stayed at the farm. His wife, Susan, was beside herself, though their son, David, and daughter Sue and her husband were a great and steadying influence. The sad and smallish funeral service was held at the Presbytery of Ayr, and attended by the farmer families from the district.

Angus McAlpine was a quiet man, always willing to come to the assistance of local farmers, and was highly regarded. He was getting on in years and was beginning to develop arthritis, so his son had taken over much of the day-to-day running of the farm; however, they were very close. You will recall that David had graduated quite well at his agricultural College and was eager to introduce new ways of doing things – so there was the occasional clash, both being rugged and determined that their way of doing things was best.

Sue married the man who owns that long strip of a farm, a lada, and the marriage has turned out really well. He argues that poultry is a far more cost-effective way of producing protein and of better land use than requiring thousands of acres to support our 'four-legged behemoths'. He has a point and a healthy bank account to prove it. For years he 'inspanned' (I learned that work from you) a couple of his horses to a dray and trotted eggs and poultry into market at Kilmarnock. We were told that the horses knew the route so well that all he had to do was to sit on the dray and hold the reins lightly. On rainy days he covered the dray with canvas over a framework. On one occasion, he had fallen asleep under the canvas, creating the impression that there was no human on board – leading to a visitor clambering up to rein in out-of-control horses! Nowadays, of course he has to drive in supplies by truck as it is too dangerous to go on using horses in the traffic.

We stayed in the farmhouse for the days we were there and wandered through the stone-walled bedrooms we knew so well as children – changed of course to the McAlpine tastes (not quite ours). I remember so well the days we spent before your leaving for Africa... The night by the fire during the lambing season when Papa talked to you about the significance of the Scots pine as an emblem of the MacGregor clan, and our giving you those Walter Scott books as keepsakes. From the bedrooms, as the snow began to fall, we could hear the sound of sheep and newborn lambs coming up from the sheds.

Kim has become enchanted by our ancient woodlands, rich in Scots pines and other indigenous species, the bark and lower branches covered in lichen and green moss. Of course, most of the oak was felled at the beginning of the war, but the new growth is doing well. There is another word you taught me in Zululand – 'wandelpaaitjies [small wandering paths] and there are several in the close-by woodland – mostly started by deer and hare, which we children used to trace... Remember? I took Kim's hand the day after the funeral and ran into the forest, like we did as children.

A few pines have swollen so large that they have dislodged one of the dry stone walls, so Kim is being taught by David how to repair it – gradual tapering, the anchoring by flat cross stones, and the parts in between with assorted pebbles. I can see that it is going to be difficult to wrench him out to come back to London!

I'm confident that the farm is in good hands being managed by David McAlpine, so our investment is well taken care of. This means that we can proceed with our original plans to visit, and this will include a protracted stay in Lourenço Marques, in Mozambique, at the Polana Hotel. As you know Kim is a consultant geologist. I am very hazy about the details, but he has been charged by the diamond industry's central selling organisation to investigate the illicit diamond buying activity working out of Lourenço Marques, which is costing the legitimate diamond mines a fortune in lost revenue. There is talk of an Italian consul being involved (all this is hush-hush please!). Kim's cover story exploits his outstanding knowledge of how foliage and soil type reveal minute particles of precious and semi-precious metals. Apparently, trees with deep roots suck up quantities of minerals in liquid form, which permeate the growth of an entire tree – trunk and foliage. In the search for minerals and oil, using these exploratory techniques, he has the enthusiastic support of the Portuguese authorities... There seems to be a heightened interest in investigating sources of uranium as well, though no new explorations are forthcoming... So Kim will be actively encouraged to wander the landscape (and at the same time, clandestinely, to pick up tell-tale signs of smuggling routes).

As I will get bored with staying in the Polana hotel for a long period of time, and Kim is reluctant to take me on his ventures into the interior because he says it could be dangerous, would you ask Prue if she would *mind very much my staying at Chelmsford for part of the time? I guarantee to pay my way and try not to spoil the children rotten.*

RSVP and all that. I can't wait to go swimming at the Country Club beach!

Love you all muchly,
            Winnie

PS: I should have mentioned that little Jean did very well at Cambridge. While not exactly graduating with a First it was a good Second, which has inspired her into doing her Masters. The letter we received from Greece was full of seeking Minoan and, different era, Egyptian relics near the Sacred Way…as clear as mud to us… In my innocence, I would have thought all relics would be Greek. She raves about Minoan pottery decoration – so there is much for us to learn!"

After Prue had read the letter she said, "Well, thank heavens that we get on so well. She takes a keen interest in everything, is an educated bookworm and reads wildly, loves the garden, and Durban in general. Can she drive, I wonder – do you remember?

"I'll reply to her – will make them feel most welcome from the outset. And my parents like them too – and Daddy being so dyed-in-the-wool Scottish is automatically akin. Perhaps Mummy might come across as politically overbearing – but we can sort that out."

"Besides, Winnie – and Kim, when he is around – would add a good presence at Chelmsford whenever I have to go to Zululand," added Donald. And these comings and goings seem imminent, from what I have gathered."

"By the way," said Prue, "do you know who I stumbled into today? Masheila Reddy! She was coming out of Pimm's pharmacy, just as I was walking in. We practically bumped into each other... You remember Sonya Broccardo (sister of poor old Zeno, who lost his life in that shark attack at Richards' Bay)?"

"Well, I could hardly forget Sonya who is married to Toby Strafford, and he is one of my best friends! Sonya and I got on very well – sorry, I interrupted...", Donald responded.

Prue continued, "Sonya employed Masheila in her little accounting office at Ntambanana when things were going so well, but had to close down when all the farms collapsed and she had to let Masheila go; but Fred and Edna supported her education, she achieved a matric, and since then she has been employed by the Natal Indian Congress in its offices at Grey Street. I have her contact details and thought that your mother would be interested in meeting her?"

"Certainly she would. How should we all meet up, I wonder? She being Indian, we might put the noses of Jeeves and his wife out of kilter if Mummy invited her up to the house – and the same will apply here – we could hardly invite her to sit down at a table to be served by Chinnamama. She can't be invited to a restaurant for the same reason – all these bloody segregation laws! I'll talk to Mummy and have a think – perhaps there's a cafe somewhere in Grey Street; it's an Indian area anyway, where the management could be persuaded to look the other way...one of Mummy's contacts. I seem to remember there was a place in Greyville called 'The Bombay Parrot' which is patronised by people from the Indian Congress.

"Can you imagine what it's like to be an Indian in Natal – as Gandhi said, 'We are in the middle of a sandwich, neither white nor black.'

"That, of course, applies to Zulus just as well... Expected

by the Europeans to 'know their place' – being described as 'nie-blanke' [non-white] and expected to sit on tram-stop benches labelled as such, and a suitable distance away from 'European' benches, so they don't contaminate. You remember that Gandhi was a racist as well, in a manner of speaking – he objected to Indians being labelled with the umbrella term of 'non-whites' like the Zulus, who he described as fit only to acquire some cattle, then spend the rest of their days in idleness.

"Over to you, then. Let me know what your mother thinks."

"On an entirely different subject... I received a letter from Frieda von Weldenburg, the other day which I intended to hand you to read it but didn't. I quite like her, despite the general aura of efficiency she radiates. It seems that our occasional hospitality extended to young Luitpold has gone down rather well. The letter is just full of general chit-chat – clothes and things which I'm sure will create the MEGO effect if you set to and read it [this was a secret term used between them, and short for 'my eyes glaze over']; but she did drop a snippet or two in which both of us and the Pickering Street Irregular would be interested. Apparently, Luitpold is a promising legal student and it looks as if he will graduate with a Cum Laude, and following up the plans they announced earlier he will be entering the diplomatic service, firstly in the training ground of Berlin, but later leading to a possible appointment at the German embassy in Pretoria. With his knowledge of South Africa, this would make good sense. Then there was a passage in the letter in which she let slip some news that she received from Germany. It seems that, behind the scenes, the new Chancellor of Germany is authorising rearmament, trebling the size of the army from the League of Nations' limit of 100,000 men, creating a secret air force, strictly against these limitations, and there are plans afoot to build over fifty submarines. She also said that she hated war more than ever after witnessing the effect of mustard gas in the last war, and hence her involvement in teaching braille in a Swiss hospital open to the worst cases of men from both sides. She remarked that any preparation for reopening old wounds was revolting and her friend in Germany (didn't indicate who he or she was) had the same views.

"Well, I haven't heard anything like it in the news – it is rather a curious topic for her to touch on. She could possibly be dropping a red herring, designed for us to pass on (although I am sure she hears nothing about our links, so I would say this is pretty impossible) or she is deliberately sounding a warning. I'm sure London must have picked up these kinds of reports from all over the place, so do think we should actually bother to pass it on?"

"I think we should pass on the letter, with the caveat that might just be a load of old codswallop, and leave it to them to sort out. This is far past what we were charged to do – just monitoring the von Weldenburgs and the brandy salesman, du Quesne, or Captain Whatsizname who keeps on changing his name – Pickering Street or Dick White in London is used to developing sources who play cat and mouse. After discussion, I am sure they will suggest you just reply in the usual chatty way and, while indicating all sympathy for her concern, indicate that there's nothing you could do about it – and if there is any fire beneath the smoke, you have no doubt the appropriate authorities would have already spotted what was going on behind the scenes. I have reason to believe…"

Smiling, Donald interrupted with, "What do you mean, 'reason to believe'…? I know damn well you've been talking to Pickering Street again!"

"I won't answer that accusation, but just to say that our

brandy man has changed his name to du Buisson and has suddenly begun to show a keen interest in professional boxing from his agency office in Bloemfontein. Apparently there is a rising star in professional boxing circles called Robie Leibrandt. The belief is that he'll do well at next year's Empire Games, so could be heading for the Olympics in Berlin in 1936 as a light heavyweight. Unusual fellow is Leibrandt – a strange mixture for a light heavyweight boxer to be interested in gliding at the Bloemfontein Gliding Club... you'd think he'd be too heavy to get into those fragile machines. He's is mixture, a German father and an Irish mother – a good combination for not liking the English very much – like Padraig O'Grady and his Afrikaans wife Marie."

"Oh yes... Anyway, Frieda mentioned that they are planning to come down again and hoped to see us. They will be staying at the Royal and want to go and see the Marlene Dietrich film, *The Blue Angel*. Let's read Ewan's letter in bed – you're better at understanding his handwriting than me."

"So that's what you are going to do in bed tonight!?"

"I never said exclusively. You will remember to wind the clock in the dining room. It wakes me up if it doesn't chime during the night."

"I will, curious girl..."

Balgowan, as postmarked, remains little more than a small railway station and a trading store, inevitably run by Mr and Mrs Moosa, surrounded by wealthy timber estates; the area being so dubbed by an early Aberdeenshire settler in the district: it reminded him of home. It was also the site of a private boarding school, called Michaelhouse, where many wealthy sugar farmers sent their sons. Donald was appalled at the cost, but was slightly mollified by Ewan being awarded a scholarship to attend it. Prue disliked the idea of sending a child to a boys-only boarding school, but gave in to the idea after her father said, "It'll give him a bit of polish, and toughen him up a bit – after all, Donald went to Dulwich." An introduction to the principle of toughening the boys was given shortly after his arrival, when Ewan, accompanied by the rest of Form One, was instructed to run a five-mile scramble in bare feet through marsh, uphill and down along ponding muddy slopes to a finishing line where several masters stood.

Years passed, and he became accustomed to the routine of the dawn school bell being rung in the tower by an unfortunate First Year, then huddling in the boiler room, slurping something warm that vaguely resembled coffee, accompanied, if one was lucky, by what the Michaelhouse chef regarded as a rusk; the serving of early morning communion wine, after he had been Confirmed, and the discovery of an aardvark subterranean hideaway when the boys were obliged to go on Free Bounds in the surrounding countryside. He was a duffer at trigonometry, perhaps because he could never find any use for it, but the same Rector (headmaster) who taught it also taught him how to play a decent game of squash. He was fascinated, however, by physics, and managed to stumble along in the other subjects.

His first girlfriend was one of the Rector's daughters who attended Roedean and was often on holiday during Ewan's termtime – an attraction which did not meet her father's approval, but he let things be. Ewan was now halfway through his secondary education, had had his ears painfully rubbed playing lock in many a rugby game, his mind expanded by Shakespearean plays performed at the open-air theatre, and was now allowed to walk in the quad, with his hands in his pockets and his blazer unbuttoned. He was even allowed to wear the special white scarf given to boys in their final years, discreetly embroidered by his girlfriend with his initials.

It was still the days of G-nibs fuelled from ink wells, and trying to ensure that one grabbed a desk as close as possible to the small fire during night-time study. The fire had to be encouraged to burn strongly by narrowing the gap in front with a sheet of newspaper held up by a poker (or equivalent), until it began to roar from the draft thereby created. On Sundays pupils were expected to write home and then attend a selection of societies, not least an appreciation of chess or music. Ewan also discovered that masters could be human – well, at least some of them – like Mr Barnard, the Afrikaans teacher, who took part in *Arsenic and Old Lace*, staged by an all-teacher cast. Barnard played the part of the daft brother who imagines he is Teddy Roosevelt, whose main job is to bury the poisoned older men in the cellar, under the impression they had died in the construction of the Panama Canal.

The subject of history was a puzzle to Ewan, taught at length on European history – not least the string of English monarchs. It seemed that South African history only commenced when Jan van Riebeek dropped anchor in Table Bay in 1652, the indigenous people, the San bushmen and the Khoi agriculturalists from the north who followed and settled mainly on the fertile lands along the coast getting pushed into oblivion, as they were in reality; while the Great Trek in the 1830s, when the Afrikaners pushed north to escape the British domination, was returned to over and over again with mind-numbing regularity. The relevance of the indigenous people and even the indentured Indians was brushed aside with little mention. However, in *Practical English Writing* he was taught how to write not only business letters but the correct way to write and answer social invitations. During holidays, towards the end of his school days, he was not surprised to receive invitations decorously couched as, 'Miss

Jane Reunert takes pleasure in inviting Ewan Kirkwood to a dinner and dance at her parents' house, 21 Essenwood Road, Berea, on Saturday, 14th of July, 1933. RSVP.' Invitations to a morning tennis party at the Durban Country Club were couched in a similar manner. Simply put, such children of ODFs [Old Durban Families] were brought up in a neo-colonial Eurocentric bubble.

Dear Dad and Mum, thank you very much for the seed- and fruit-cakes you made, and thank you for the one guinea which will be spent very carefully at the tuckshop; my Primus stove we take on Free Bounds was running very low on paraffin. There will be lots of money left to buy sausage rolls until the end of term. We like to fry the rolls in butter. I can also buy another tin of marmalade for the breakfast table.

It's getting very cold here now and ice is beginning to form around the edges of the house plunge. Nevertheless it's the done thing to break the ice and plunge in the water very quickly. Never were hot coffee and rusks afterwards so welcome!

Nothing much more to report except I had a bit of an accident in the chem lab with some nitric acid, making the fingers of my left hand turn bright yellow before Tas Strickland, our stinks teacher, managed to bring things under control.

Unlike me, but I got involved in a punch-up with Rory Campbell in the dorm. For several months I noticed that pairs of my socks were going missing, until I caught him nicking them. I got my socks back and we shook hands afterwards.

It will be exciting to come home again, and the school train is an adventure in itself – especially when and after the St Anne's stop and the girls boarding the train at Hilton and Pietermaritzburg! It will be interesting to meet Bruce Holden, when he gets on the train at Hilton. I've never met anyone from Kenya, and seeing he's going to spend the holidays with us at Chelmsford, I hope we get along!

Only 19 days left to go!

With lots of love,

Ewan

PS: almost forgotten to mention that over last weekend, many of the sixth-form boys including me are going on a trudge to the top of Isituba mountain, accompanied by our maths teacher, so that the sleeping bag you gave me for my birthday is going to be jolly useful because it's going to be jolly, jolly cold! Isituba is a smallish cone-like mountain. It gets its Zulu name from the description 'Breast of a virgin'. We are camping under an overhang near the top.

"It seems he is being toughened up satisfactorily – although it is a bit too much being 'toughened up in style'", Donald said. "I'm glad he's landed up on the right side of the fence, so to speak – a healthy interest in girls and all that, as long as he doesn't go girl-crazy. Can happen, after being cooped up in a predominantly masculine society. Emilia's so different, isn't she – pretty but studious, with a small selection of very nice girl friends."

"Don't be deluded by our young maiden, Emilia! I came across a few photographs of several boys that we have never met and that Afrikaans one I have met. They hired horses one day while you were away, and the first thing I knew about it was when I saw them riding down our drive. Decent fellow

– Neil van der Bijl. I learned he is studying architecture at Howard College."

"This is the first I have heard of it."

"They only arrived the other day. Good sign, I think. She took him down to the summerhouse... They are local 'Anglicised Afrikaners' and have a house in Overport, close to Howard College. I believe his father has a post in the town planning department of the municipality."

"The mother?"

"Housewife; drives a car, keen gardener and a great cake-maker, according to Niel. He has two older sisters, one at Howard College – studying literature, and the other studying pharmacy at the Natal Technical College. Interesting. Let's watch this space!

"Just before you turn out the light, I was having a chat with our 'usually reliable source' the other day, and we got on to the perennial subject of events in Germany. Now that Hitler has managed to sack (or murder) his main opposition in all key departments, he has done a deal with the Vatican that minions of the Catholic Churches in Germany and Austria will be left untouched. The Catholic Church is regarded as an implacable enemy of communism, so the Nazis leave them alone.

"That man Heinrich Himmler seems to be making quite a name for himself. Apparently his family is devoutly Catholic, as was he until about the age of nineteen. His father, upper middle class, has links with Prince Heinrich of Bavaria, and Heinrich Himmler's godfather. It seems that Himmler is very good at compiling lists of his enemies and it was he who called the bumping off of Hitler's roughnecks, the storm troopers – along with their head and long-term friend of Hitler's, Rohm, who was as queer as a nine-mark note. Himmler has replaced them with an internal force called the

Gestapo backed by the Scutzstaffel, which is set to control just about everything in the new Nazi state, including the way the people were allowed to think."

"Disturbing stuff. And that's enough for tonight. Right now, I'm far more interested in kissing your neck… In the dark, and yes, all the clocks in the house have been wound!"

July in mid-winter dawns late, and the days are cooler. Prue awoke first as the dawn breeze creaked the old fig trees, and realised that she and Donald still remained entwined. A distant dog heralded the early milkman who established his presence by the faint sound of their dogs stirring and the clink of milk bottles which lived in the usual place on the back veranda. Jesse gave token barks, as she knew the milkman well. Prue, listening to the remains of the dawn chorus, realised that it was Wednesday when Basessa was likely to arrive early, so she disentangled herself gently and set about washing herself and getting dressed. Emilia was beginning to stir when she walked through Ewan's bedroom, where she paused, thinking of these post-child days, to find Chinnamama and Layani already in the kitchen preparing the breakfast and laying the table. Prue took the prepared tea tray through to the bedroom. Far below the summerhouse she heard the clanking and whistling of the early Zululand train crossing the Umgeni River on its way to the main station, as late diners gulped their coffees while staring out of steamy windows.

Basessa was an Indian with a wide-set face, grey hair and grey moustache who lived at Sea Cow Lake, which he pronounced as 'seekollik'. He would tether his mule and cart at the foot of Buttery Road, which rose steeply between the two quarries. He had already travelled to the main fruit and vegetable market, then returned across the Umgeni River bridge. From the quarries, he would load two baskets with a selection of produce and suspend them on either side of a split bamboo cane positioned over his shoulders. There was a rhythm to his laborious, squeaking ascent, turning left at quarryman Clarkson's grounds and up and along Mount Argus Road, servicing the few large estates on the way. He always wore a rather dirty waistcoat over a clean white shirt, with braces supporting a pair of creaseless trousers. Scuffed black shoes and a tired brown hat with a hatband completed his unchanging assemblage.

He was always offered a large enamelled tin mug of sweetened, milky tea, attended by 'doorstep' slices of white bread and jam. These he ate sitting on a large stone under one of the fig trees near the swing. This was the only occasion when he would remove his hat, which he would place on another stone. His selection of vegetables and fruit was splendidly subtropical, not least the shiny brinjals, ladyfingers, mangoes, guavas and passionfruit. He was also 'gossip-central' for Chinnamama, who regarded herself as way above him in rank, but listened to him eagerly as they chatted away. After his departure, Prue would plunge all the produce into a strong dilation of Condy's crystals to eliminate the risk of amoebic dysentery.

The comfortable week-day routine Donald, Prue and their daughter had established was to breakfast on maltabella porridge, made from sorghum grain, a slice of lightly sugared pawpaw with a squeeze of lemon, followed by toast and marmalade and coffee. Then father and daughter went off in the car to Durban where Emilia would catch the tram to varsity. On library days, the ride into town was accompanied by Prue.

Chapter Eight

In July, 1934, Bush Telegraph was tipped to win the Big Race of the Year in Durban, the July Handicap, with also-runners, Jamaican Rumba, and Dynasty hot contenders. Guided by Keswick's wife, Cordelia, his table of ten was rounded out by leading businessmen and their wives, plus important colleagues of Keswick's. 'The children' – Donald and Prue, and their good friends positioned in the table adjacent – Toby and Sonya Strafford, Jean-Pierre and Caroline Meyer, Dr James Scobie and his sister Annette and, at Keswick's particular request, Ivan and Joelle Cohen, the musical instrument dealer and his wife.

To his surprise, Donald spotted an ageing Kim Logan accompanied by a slender silver-haired woman who he assumed was Logan's wife, sitting at the same table as Howard Creighton, with a pretty young girl with a floppy hat, half his age, who turned out to be his daughter; both sitting at the same table as his erstwhile bank manager, now close to retirement. When Donald realised that Annette and Dr Scobie knew them well and their eyes met, Annette murmured, "Just recognise them, if necessary, and wave – we do know them commercially, after all." Scobie ignored them, however.

On the surface, this highlight in the social calendar in the Members' Pavilion at Greyville Racecourse represented a scene of pleasant engagement and social intercourse: enough good wine and spirits to precipitate noisy conversation, the titillation of betting generally modest amounts on a series of races, winding up with the main race, the July Handicap; and a cheerful exchange between Durban's people of consequence.

Donald, never speaking much, was reminded of the experience of swimming in the estuary at Port St Johns, where, on the surface, all seemed tranquil enough, but beneath the surface, it was turbulent with swirls of warm and cold eddies sheltering sharks.

The luncheon was a buffet and followed the acceptable Durban standard of the time, with cold hors d'oevres, soup or avocado ritz, a carvery of beef or mutton, with a barracuda option – these, for which guests had to queue, followed by trifle with sherry, and ending all with water biscuits and a cheese platter. During one of these queues, Keswick found himself standing in front of Howard Creighton whom he did not know; Creighton greeted Donald, who then introduced him to Keswick. After the usual pleasantries, Creighton said to Keswick, "This is not the time nor place, but I wonder if I could visit you in your office? There is some information I would like to pass on…not of a commercial nature."

"Well, yes, I suppose so. I am really quite a busy man, but I'm sure I could fit you in. Here's my card. Call my secretary, Miss Wainwright. Where are your offices?"

"I am in and out of the office, and it's a bit in the country. It's in Pickering Street, near the docks. My manager is a fella called Kim Logan. It's an export agency for sugar and cotton."

"Pickering Street! Not exactly the best address in town."

"It's convenient to be near the docks, as you will understand."

After Creighton had walked away to his table, Keswick turned to Donald, with a puzzled expression, and said, "I wonder what all that is about," to which Donald reacted with a puzzled shrug.

At the table, Keswick played the accomplished host to his wife's well-phrased appeals to the munificence and generosity of some of the leaders of commerce who could influence her causes. She did this so gracefully that she never acquired the reputation of being a 'do-gooder', and restricted the length of her discussions by exchanges with the womenfolk about department stores, fashions and changing hairstyles. The raising of nutrition, health and living standards among the Zulus and Indians were touched on lightly but aptly, and intended to lead to further action. Her latest interest, knowing that the subject would trigger female response, was the creation of a municipal nursery school or kindergarten for children of unmarried women in the notorious dock area of Point Road. Prostitution there was rife.

When one of the stewards came across to the table, on the principle that he and his fellows should circulate and chat to the guests, Donald asked provocatively, "So what should we put our money on for the Big Race?" The man replied, "Haven't a clue, old chap, but they say that it is always best to spread your bets on second, third and fourth places, as well as plonking it on some other horse whose pedigree you fancy. Take a look at fillies bred in the calcium-rich fields of the Free State, as well as those horses from well-known stud farms in the Mooi River area. Lots of good pedigrees for the big race! And really…I haven't a clue as to which will come out on top." Then, clearing his throat, he said, "Perhaps you should train your binoculars in the pre-race enclosure at those horses that are guarded by security men. Good luck!" he said, before wandering off.

Prue nudged Donald, and said, "There are the M-m-mullers with what must be a group off one of those German boats; sooner or later they all see us – and yes, the younger brother has and is coming across... Better be pleasant – perhaps introduce them formally to Daddy and M-m-mummy." Donald noticed the return of her stammer.

"Hello, hello! It is so good to see you again. I see you continue to move in the best circles!" said Muller, gesturing to the influential people sitting at the two tables.

"I think Kepler would have preferred to call them ellipses," said Donald, smiling and rising to his feet and shaking his hand, resisting the attention to mockingly click his heels, and introduced him to the Jardines, leading to Keswick introducing the friends sitting on both tables, making a point of introducing the Cohens first, as if the most senior in standard. It was, perhaps, only Keswick Jardine who spotted the humorous reference to Kepler, aware of his massive contribution to navigation.

"Ah yes, the music man. I recall you specialise in very good German pianos like the Carl Ecke Hoffman. They make beautiful German music..."

Cohen said, smiling, "Musical instruments make beautiful music from all nations. The music is, fortunately, not nationalistic, with a few exceptions, perhaps, including Wagner. I think it is a pity that he has become associated with a regime with which he might be tarnished."

There was a perceptible freezing of Muller's expression and Prue interjected, by saying, "Mr Muller, you have not, I think, been introduced to Dr Scobie. His sister is a great lepidopterist and shares a common interest with the nephew of Frieda, the wife of your friend Hubie von Weldenburg." Keswick spotted Prue's diversion and winked at her. The conversation rambled on with more introductions, after which Muller declared he had better proceed, but before departing turned to Ivan Cohen, and said, "If you do not like the regime Wagner is comfortable with, it would be best if you stayed here, Herr Cohen." Then he really did click his heels, bowed stiffly to Keswick, and, nodding to the rest of the party, drifted away.

Keswick said, "It's a pity that such a great nation of composers, philosophers and everything else cannot resist following some lunatic into the abyss, as it seems to be doing. With all this talk, Prue, I read somewhere recently about 'Moral Re-armament'?"

"I know very little – only the odd newspaper article. I think the movement was started in America and then came to a head in Oxford where I think it is called the Oxford Group. Full of fine ideals, and the implementation is being applauded by a lot of influential academics."

"I think that the movement is a bit – er, flabby, and is somehow tied up with the move to appease Hitler (I might be wrong about this, it could be the other way round), and at a time when rumours abound that Germany is re-arming while the rest of the Western world seems to be sitting around twiddling their thumbs," said Toby. "It could lead to 'ignorant armies clashing by night' with the creation of untold misery, unless the rest of us do something about it."

"Why 'by night'?"

"Oh, I was merely quoting the last line of 'Dover Beach' by Matthew Arnold, referring indirectly to an earlier disruption. I think he ended with 'by night' to rhyme with the words above – 'flight'. Regretting the ebb of the sea of faith, or at least as he saw it."

"That's very erudite!" said Caroline.

"Not really, it's the only poem I learnt at school, which stuck in my head. After a term or two at Winchester I went off and joined the Navy, relieved with the idea that I would never have to learn another poem again; but it stuck, because I thought it was very good."

"So how did you wind up going farming?"

"After the war, the Navy just said, 'Thank you very much, now please go away.' I was in Durban at the time, rather bitter with my treatment, had no job but a little money; so I decided to go farming in Natal, which seemed a land of opportunity where I could be my own master."

Towards the end of the luncheon, before the main race, several men circulated selling tickets for a raffle, with the main prize being a first-class return trip for two from Durban to Lourenço Marques, with a stopover at the fashionable Polana Hotel. The collection was organised by members of the Berea Masonic Lodge in aid of St Mungo's Children's Home, with ticket prices high enough to raise the eyebrows, but by this time, alcohol had loosened the wallets.

Punters, not least the Jardine guests, were beginning to drift over to the pre-race horse enclosure. Jean-Pierre, Donald's sailing friend, mentioned that he and his family were considering relocating to Madagascar because his parents were getting on and finding the management of their estate too much to handle. Looking steadily at Donald, as they stood slightly separately from the rest, he continued, "There is another reason which your acquaintance, Howard Creighton, knows about, but I won't discuss further – except to say that I will continue to trade from Durban and additionally from higher up – between Beira and the North of the island – near the French naval base."

"I will be immensely sorry to lose my old sailing friend! Now I will have to crew for my father-in-law on his Flying 15 – not exactly the same sailing experience at all."

As with all events of this nature, guests began to gamble

increasingly large amounts. Donald handed over the car keys to Prue, saying, "I've had enough to drink; here, you drive, you're as sober as a judge."

That night, Donald's dreams were a macabre mixture of horses within devastated buildings, half collapsed and full of masonry dust and his dying porters in the East African jungle of wartime.

At one time, when his wartime leg was hurting from the sudden drop in temperature, due to snow falling on the Drakensberg and sweeping frozen air down towards Durban, crying out with a wartime pain, he had woken with a start and a shout, which woke Prue. She was familiar with these cries, and pulled the bedclothes over them and put her arms about him in comfort. He had complained that the cold made his war-wound ache from the thigh to his foot, again.

The next day, Prue said that he should seek some comfort from his doctor, which Donald had said was not much use, and that all these 'quacks' would prescribe would be a variety of painkillers, and that he would prefer just to cope with what he had inherited: his inborn strength.

A week later, Creighton was ushered into Keswick's office by Miss Wainwright, who after she had offered tea and ginger nut biscuits and withdrawn, Keswick said, "Now, what is all this about?" Far away at the yacht club, the metal stays of cradled sailing boats were slapping and playing in the wind, while the new lighthouse mechanic, high up on the catwalk, struggled to wash the outside panes in the face of strong gusts, while the wind whinnered and wuthered against the large windows of Keswick's Harbour-Master windows.

"I have a confidential message for you from the British Admiralty."

"From the Admiralty! But I thought that you were an import/export agent."

"That is Kim Logan's job, with the rest of his small staff. Ostensibly, I am the overseas agent and do perform regular tasks for him."

"I'm sorry, old fellow, I need some serious proof of all that," whereupon Creighton produced convincing evidence and credentials. He said, "I am not going to ask you to sign a secrecy act or anything, but may I have your word that, as harbourmaster, you keep what I have to tell you as confidential, and take into your confidence only those technical staff and contractors necessary on a 'need-to-know' basis?"

"You have my word."

"I have been asked to do this early, with the realisation that construction and preparations take a long time to complete. I'm sure that you are only too aware of the threat of Germany's expansionism. This may not come to anything, of course, but from reliable information received, it seems that Germany will invade Belgium and France and the low countries in years to come – suggesting that Britain will be the next target. The prospect is not made less disturbing by Mussolini's fascistic developments of his army and navy. If the worst came to the worst, the Suez Canal would cease to be a safe passage, meaning that Western allies would have to traipse all shipping down the west coast of Africa, and round the Cape to get to Singapore and possible battlefields in North Africa. Thus Durban harbour will become highly strategic. If France falls, so will its possessions, including Madagascar, introducing a new threat."

"This is all very speculative, but do go on."

"As there is an agreement that the Royal Navy shall patrol the South Atlantic and Indian Ocean, with full access to South African ports, quartering at Simon's Town, it's logical that Durban harbour, with its important facilities and strategic importance, would attract the interest of Germany. Accordingly, there is a request to develop submarine nets at the entrance of the harbour, to increase naval facilities at Salisbury Island in the harbour, and to plan ahead for the expansion of the dry dock and a floating dock adequate to repair damaged naval vessels – and other craft. Durban would also benefit from the expansion of small ship construction. All this can be done under the cloak of harbour improvements."

"I think this calls for another cup of tea," said Keswick, reaching for a ginger nut. "And who's going to pay for all this?"

"The British Admiralty proposes to pay its part, as it does for Simon's Town. Of course, all this is subject to detailed negotiation, and our conversation is merely to alert you to correspondence you will be receiving. While explaining developments on harbour facilities, in the shape of drydock and floating docks, land developments on Salisbury island might be a little bit more difficult to justify. However, I understand that there is a move afoot to provide reasonable access to university facilities for selected Indian students. The land facilities could be developed for this purpose, with the understanding that facilities will be adaptable and taken over by the Navy if there were cause. The Admiralty will be in touch about all that with the appropriate authorities. More difficult to cloak will be the antisubmarine nets installation at the entrance to the harbour, but as the whaling station attracts a pestilence of shark and barracuda, you might think it appropriate, when the time comes, to put out the story about experimental shark nets being installed, if anyone asks, co-opting the Durban Marine biology unit to play along."

"You do realise that I am approaching retirement age? I

was already tinkering with the idea of buying a reasonable sized yacht to explore the reaches of the Mozambique channel. However, all this seems to be intriguing and challenging and I hope my masters will consider keeping me in tow for the next four or five years. My wife Cordelia would be relieved, as I tend to get under her feet with protracted stays at home! So what next?"

"You will be receiving correspondence from the Admiralty through the usual post. Construction plans concerning the submarine nets will be couriered in either by me or the British High Commissioner's offices. If you have need to contact us, you can reach us through the Consulate's Chief Passport Officer (it's a notional title for the person concerned with covert operations). Don't make a mistake by asking for anyone else. A last word... I know that you will understand that we did, as the Americans would say, check you out, and Miss Wainwright, and you both came through with flying colours! The reason being obvious that quite a lot of confidential information will be flowing through your hands in the years to come. By the way, were you able to get over to the British Empire Games last year?"

"Alas, no. They tied me the desk; I was inundated with work right here."

"A pity that they shifted the Games from Johannesburg to Britain. I believe the reason was the fear that African athletes would not have been treated fairly. I was quite impressed with that swimmer, Victor Shore, in the relays, and I was able to watch Robie Leibrandt win a bronze medal boxing at Wembley. I believe he has been tipped to fight for South Africa at next year's Games in Berlin."

And he was gone.

Chapter Nine

In July 1936, the ladies of Durban were gripped by patchwork quilt fever. It all started by Angela Knight, the women's editor of the *Natal Mercury*, inviting readers to support the Durban community chest by entering the metropolitan competition for the best patchwork quilt. The leading sewing machine manufacturer was offering attractive prizes, with all entry subscriptions going to the good cause, to which would be added a substantial donation from the manufacturer. Not to be outdone, Coates' Needle, Thread and Yarn company were supporting the contest with other prizes, and a substantial donation to the charity chest. This portion of the contest was supported by the *Natal Daily News*, in the form of Angela Day, the women's editor.

The leading stores were encouraged to participate, with displays of patchwork quilts and associated items in their windows. In one of John Orr's very large street windows, there was a splendid display of a patchwork eiderdown lent to them by Lady Beatrix van Iddekinge (she possessed a Nederlander aristocratic title inherited from the great-grandmother, Countess van Iddekinge). This set the tone and proved hard to match by the other stores. The bedspread decorated an enormous brass double bed, and was accompanied by other accoutrements on sale in the store.

As patchwork eiderdowns were padded with down of the

eider duck, Dr James Scobie was persuaded to research and provide an article about the origin of this noble bird, leading to the main entrance to the library and museum carrying a display of the taxidermist's art and a collection of important books containing articles about the duck, and the earliest origins of the patchwork quilt.

Not to be outdone, Turber's Pet Emporium displayed live eider ducks in its window; the Bombay Bazaar advertised "the greatest ever variety of patchwork off-cuts"; and Moosa's, in Grey Street, famed in the Indian community for its imported six and nine-yard saris, likewise advertised a huge variety of offcuts, sewing materials, scissors, sewing boxes and so on 'for the delight of all ladies' and re-advertised in the *Daily News*, which ran a special supplement directed at the Indian community, titled 'The 1860'.

The fever spread to Natal Sheets and Sheeting, which offered to mass-produce stuffed simulated patchwork quilts for distribution, at cost, to black families living in tin shacks at Cato Manor.

Swept up in the enthusiasm was Prue's good and long-term friend Sonya Strafford (erstwhile Broccardo). They decided to meet up at Chelmsford, with children at school and husbands at work; Sonya arrived with a basketful of colourful offcuts to which were added Prue's more modest collection, and they set to with needle and thread, scissors and sewing machines well employed between bursts of tea, scones and buttery anchovy toast. The winter sun waned and a thick mist crept up from the valley while they worked away. Sonya had arrived just after lunch and was surprised when, as they settled down to work, they heard a series of large explosions coming from the region of the summerhouse. Prue managed to calm her alarm when she explained that the explosions were merely the blasting in the quarry every two o'clock during the week.

"It's quite safe and we are very used to it – except for the occasion when a lump of dislodged bluestone landed on the front lawns. We were out at the time and were rather surprised to find the stone at the front door with a yellow ribbon tied around it – this was Layani's idea of a joke. Donald complained to the blasting master, and I gather that suitable precautions have been taken ever since. We've never had any more trouble."

The children arrived with Donald, who had collected them by car from points in town. It was customary for Donald and Prue to enjoy a sundowner on the front verandah, joined on this occasion by Sonya, after which she said, "I must fly, otherwise you will be getting telephone calls from Toby!"

It was misty and almost dark when Sonya turned from Mount Argus Road into Buttery Road, which descended to the Riverside between the two quarries, so she did not see the huge rock lying in the road, as she descended at some speed. The right front wheel struck with such force that the car rose up and rolled over before plunging over the side into the quarry. She died instantly, and her body lay entangled in the wreckage until an alarmed Toby and Donald found the car, late that night in the heavy fog, aided by the cadmium yellow sodium street light.

"Oh, my God! Oh, my God! My poor girl," cried Toby, as he went towards the wreckage, with the intention of setting her free from her entrapment. Toby stopped him, with the admonition that inexpert moving of her might do even more damage to her fractured body. He ran to Riverside Road when he saw car lights moving slowly towards them in the fog from the junction of North Coast and Riverside roads. It transpired that the driver was the owner of the pharmacy on the corner of the North Coast Road. Arthur Tedder had practised there for a long time and had dealt with many emergencies, including broken limbs and snakebite. He was quick to assess the situation, and instructed Toby to accompany him back to the chemist shop, leaving Donald to protect the site. It was Tedder who made the calls for the ambulance and the fire engine after pouring Toby a shot of brandy, which he kept for such emergencies. He also phoned Prue, before returning to the crash site.

In 1936, long-distance telephone calls to party lines in Zululand were almost unheard of late at night – the Empangeni switchboard operator leaving at ten pm; but fortunately the Indian girl on duty had taken her time to switch off for the night and Prue managed to get through to Joy Broccardo, Sonya's younger sister. She also phoned her mother, Cordelia Jardine, with the shocking tidings and she immediately volunteered to drive to the Strafford house, near the Durban Botanic Gardens, to prepare the Strafford children for the terrible news.

Before Toby and the chemist arrived back, Donald sat on a rock, beside the car, flashing his torchlight and shouting at stray dogs. It seemed an age before the distant ringing of the fire engine and ambulance were heard racing past the Britannica hotel and turning onto Queen's Bridge, then again into Riverside Road.

It was a miserable convoy of ambulance, fire engine and cars that eventually wound its way back over the bridge for their various destinations, the yellow fog swirling about them.

Joy, Sonya's sister, and her parents, Bianca and Paolo Broccardo, were to take the early train from Empangeni, accompanied by Reverend Short, the Zululand minister who had married Toby and Sonya. The parents said practically nothing at dinner on the way down, with only Robin Short and Joy exchanging a few words between courses. It was the same at the railway breakfast next day, while they all stared gloomily out of the dining car window, watching the disappointing scenery drift by. They were met by Toby, Donald and Prue. It had been arranged that the Zululand family would stay in the Strafford house, which was well endowed with spare bedrooms, and that the minister would stay in his counterpart's rectory.

The three Strafford children were waiting for them at the house, along with Keswick and Cordelia; inevitably there was a long sad conversation about the accident, with Toby's almost expressionless face describing what happened. Such a death was so unexpected, in the same way as that of the Broccardo son, Sonya's twin brother Zeno, dying in the shark attack at Richards Bay, that it left a gnawing emptiness, leaving him and the children wondering what the rest of life would be without Sonya, whose touch was everywhere.

Paolo's grandfather had married a Russian woman by the name of Olga Belyakova who had handed down many items of Russian jewellery, and these had been passed on to Sonya upon her marriage to Toby. There were hints that Olga enjoyed some connection with the Royal Court, supported by her impeccable aristocratic French. This had led Sonya into attempting to trace her background in Russia, and Toby led the parents to Sonya's open escritoire, with its collection of correspondence with Russian addresses and a letter half written on the blotting paper. The shelves displayed the Russian silver frames holding family pictures and other treasured items, such as a magnificent silver ink well stamped in Cyrillic and zolotnik numbers.

Prominent in her collection was the group photograph of her parents, holding the hands of her brother Zeno and their two daughters, Sonya and Joy, in a large Russian frame. Her mother broke down, and her father was also in tears.

The house was near the Botanic Gardens, and Toby

suggested that they might walk the paths to seek some solace; and this they did while Donald and Keswick slipped away to make funeral arrangements on behalf of Toby who felt he should remain with the Broccardo family.

During their stroll, Prue said that she was very fond of the old gardens, partially because they originated in the small botanic garden established at the bottom of the cliff below her Chelmsford summerhouse. She said that Sonya grew particularly attached to Russian writers' works of the late nineteenth and early twentieth centuries – and whenever she had visited Prue in the library she would make a beeline for the Russian literature section. As part of her interest, she had assembled a little group of expat Russians and those particularly drawn to Russian literature, one of whom had brought his Chinese wife to Durban via a circuitous route, including Singapore. His name was Andrei Pugachev and he had painted endless portraits of her in exotic colours. Prue warned them that he and his wife would no doubt be at the funeral. She went on to say that she had considered Sonya as her best friend, and it could also be said that Toby and Donald were likewise, as the four of them had shared many stressful as well as happy times over many years; thus Sonya's loss was an inconceivable wrench.

She led them to one of the oldest trees in these venerable, ancient gardens, the African Flame Tree. On frequent visits, Sonya and Prue had wandered in the gardens and would often find themselves sitting beneath its branches on an old bench donated by a certain Mr Currie, after whom Currie's Fountain was named. She told them that the fountain was reliably steady in its flow and was the source of Durban's early water supply.

"Sonya and I took particular delight in sitting beneath its branches when it was in full flower, during late October.

At that time of year, the blossom attracts bees in their thousands, and sunbirds, the only bird that can reach deep into the nectar well." Her eyes were full of tears. "I walk here often, sometimes just to seek the peace of it, and occasionally when I am rather cross with the children or my husband! I will always think of Sonya when I sit here. The tearoom here offers legendary pancakes and honey, topped with cream. We used to go there often and make complete pigs of ourselves. Would you like to come along there now?"

Toby and Sonya's children – Olga and the twins, Luke and Michael – had come in quick succession. Olga disliked her name with the intensity of a teenager and insisted on being called Elge. She was pretty, but was tinkering with the idea of cutting her beautiful long hair – much to the horror of her parents. The boys were robust, and were entering that stage when they found heroes surprisingly interesting. They adored her father, who had frequently regaled them with stories of life on the farm and also of his naval experiences. Both their bedroom walls were decorated with pictures of grain clippers, dreadnoughts and tractors – with a new departure, the building of a large model of a Gloster Gladiator biplane – the latest thing.

By this time, the original church organ had been transferred from the chapel where the funeral was being held to the newer and larger church on Musgrave Road, and the original St Thomas Chapel had to make do with a small Hammond organ; but played very well by Ethel Kerkin, a well-known piano teacher, who lived nearby. The chapel filled quickly with well-wishers, to the point that the balance had to stand down the sides and back.

Reverend Short had not overcome his stammering but had devised all sorts of tricks to avoid certain words and passages;

however, conducting the service in unfamiliar territory exacerbated the stammering before a congregation that was not familiar with the supporting shouts to aid him from his Empangeni congregation. Fortunately, Toby, Donald and Prue came to his rescue, by saying out loudly difficult words whenever Short encountered them. This struck members of the Durban congregation as rather odd – and then sufficiently funny to generate many a suppressed giggle. Prue, with her own stammer, which still emerged from time to time, was the quickest to come to Short's aid.

After struggling through his address, readings and recall of things in Sonya's childhood by Paolo Broccardo, with other early memories, and including a weeping address by Prue, Short said, "We are about to go outside and lay our beloved wife, mother and friend to eternal rest in our churchyard; but before we do, I invite Andrei Pugachev and members of the Russian society to lead us in singing 'God the Omnipotent', first in English and then in Russian. The melody used to be the Russian National Anthem, 'God save the Czar'."

The result was a thunderous egress for Sonya's coffin leaving the church, carried by Toby, Keswick, Donald and a close friend of Keswick's, deputising for Sonya's godfather who was too frail for the task. This was the second family burial endured by Sonya's younger sister, Joy, who was asked to cast the first handful of soil after the coffin had been lowered into the grave. (The first burial was that of Sonya's twin brother, Zeno, who had died from a shark attack at Richard's Bay.) Despite the closeness to her parents, she was overwhelmed by an irreversible sense of aloneness, and turned to cling to her mother. Both her parents suddenly seemed very old; but she was then distracted by the sight of the Indian girl Masheila Reddy, the only person of colour present, who was sitting gravely alone and weeping openly.

Sonya and her parents had helped her finish her education and find a good living.

Ewan caught sight of her, moved across, and put an arm around her compulsively to comfort her. Soon afterwards she took his arm away, thanked him, and prepared to slip away; but not before Prue said quietly, "Thank you so very much for coming. Donald mentioned that he had bumped into you and it was agreed to invite you up to the house, whenever convenient. I know my mother is very interested in local Indian affairs, and when I told her that you worked for the Natal Indian Congress she expressed great interest in meeting you. You may not know that she has been championing Indian interests for many years – even before she and her husband settled here from Singapore."

Masheila said, "Thank you; I should like to visit, though it might take a little arranging as non-European trams are few and far between – and in fact if I don't leave immediately, I will be stranded. The Bells and Sonya have been very kind and supportive since my mother and father died – helping me to complete my education up to the Matriculation. We will see each other soon," she said, before walking off. She was wearing a yellow sari – the appropriate colour worn by unmarried girls at funerals. Prue noticed Ewan's gaze followed her as she got to the graveyard gate.

Walking back to the cars, Donald said to Toby, "I suppose Sonya's desire to correspond with Russian sources explains the pronounced presence of the Russian circle."

"Yes, although they also shared an interest in their literature. She couldn't speak Russian, so she used a friend in the circle to translate her letters into Cyrillic. When it came to corresponding with a Russian woman now living in France, she resorted to utilising someone from the French Consulate in the same manner. I don't know where the correspondence was leading to, and all I know is that the French correspondence flowed currently from a place that sounds like Ekatinaburg. Now of course we will never know what lies behind it. For example… Look at this." He gestured to an envelope marked HMS *Marlborough*, containing an ageing photograph of a little old lady, seemingly dressed all in black, standing on the deck of a naval vessel. Scrawled on the back was the legend "Вдовствующая императрица Маруа на корабле в Ялте – с добрыми пожеланиями – Вера…". When Pugachev, the most flamboyant of her Russian friends, saw it, he got very excited and said it was a picture of the dowager Empress of all Russia, suggesting that it was taken on board the British battleship as the Russian royal household saw the last of Yalta. He suggested that Vera was the Christian name of the Dowager Empress's personal assistant.

Alcohol loosened tongues back at the house where refreshments were served, and led to more convivial topics being discussed by friends. The children were kept distracted by asking them to circulate with sandwiches, and Toby and Donald, in a similar manner, with sherry and other spirits.

"I think it was very good of that Indian girl – what was her name? – to attend," said Cordelia to a group of friends. "She was the only Indian there and must have felt very out of place. Shows determination to 'do the right thing'. It's unfortunate that we Whites still think of them as undesirable robots – just there to do our bidding."

"Yes, but quite unlike the robots in RUR, the play by Karel Capek, who can reproduce only when the old ones wear out, the Indians here can breed. The robots in RUR rose up and took over the world, after killing off the humans, didn't they? The fear of the Indians is there in this country now, not so? Demonstrated by ever harsher acts of Parliament to keep them in their place and prevent them from getting out of control…"

"I say, on a more cheerful note, there's talk of a party to visit the Empire exhibition in Johannesburg. Or have you been there already? That £10,000 prize for flying a plane from Portsmouth to Germiston Airfield turned out to be a bit of a disaster – I believe nine out of ten either crashed or ran out of fuel or bumped into each other! It will be many days before they will be able to establish a reliable aeroplane service. Far safer by zeppelin, or good old Union Castle."

Changing the subject, Clinton Nelson, Sonya's godfather, an arthritis sufferer, who had to rely heavily on his walking stick to remain mobile, said, "I was delighted to read that American Negro sprinter – what was his name? Jesse something…Jesse Owens! – has won four gold medals at the Berlin Olympics. I heard a radio broadcast from the stadium where the crowd chanted O-Ven, O-Ven, over and over again – clearly the darling of the German spectators, but much, allegedly, to the fury of Hitler – that's one up his nose to counter all that Aryan balderdash. Mind you, watching the Pathé newsreel in the bioscope last Saturday, I had to admit that it was a magnificent coup for Nazi propaganda – it was very moving watching the Olympic torch arriving after a 2000-mile journey from Greece – the first time it was ever done, despite that obscene and overwhelming display of Nazi swastikas everywhere. Ah… Thank you, my dear, sandwiches, whisky and a walking stick! Donald, excuse me."

Donald's sister Winnie and her husband Kim had arrived back from Mozambique once again, and were staying with the Kirkwoods. Spotting Clinton Nelson sitting alone, they pulled up a couple of chairs. "Hello," Clinton said, introducing himself. "I was Sonya's godfather. Terrible business, eh? What the children really need now is a godmother rather than a godfather, but I'll have to do my best. Ghastly – especially seeing that the Broccardo parents had lost their son, Sonya's twin. I suppose Joy will have to take over the reins, as best she can. Difficult, she couldn't exactly move into Toby's house. At least the family is very tightly-knit with the Broccardo parents. Are you related?"

"Not at all," Winnie said, "I'm Donald's sister...and I have just arrived back from Mozambique. Kim has been wandering around the African veld looking for likely bits of metal, occasionally accompanied by me; but the rest of the time I was 'obliged' to suffer the Polana Hotel's cuisine and wading my way through *War & Peace*. Fortunately, I made friends with another woman in the same predicament. Anyway, the job is done and I have managed to pick up a bit of Portuguese. Sounds a bit like Russian on a sunny day, and the Portuguese administration seem to be very pleased with his discoveries... He's a geologist – and, you know, he has managed to find some useful deposits for the Portuguese."

"What kind of metals did you discover?"

"Well, knowledge of their actual location remains the secret of the Portuguese government, of course, but I won't be letting the cat out of the bag if I tell you that one of them is a huge deposit of bauxite and the other is a useful deposit of titanium. Alumina is extracted from the first, which can then be smelted into pure aluminium, and the second, which has a high melting point, is excellent for the developing technology of radio circuitry. Both materials are of strategic importance – especially in the light of those idiots, Hitler and Mussolini, determined to march us into war. Aluminium alloys are reasonably lightweight yet tough, and are likely to be useful in aeroplane construction. You get the drift... Although one can extract aluminium from clay, it's an expensive alternative – and South Africa might need aluminium rather badly in the near future. Anyway, I'm finished with all that so I have been employed by a local mining company rather keen on extracting titanium from beaches towards Zululand. Sorry, ladies, you must find all that rather dull!"

"Weird how many odd people one comes across in Africa! I once bumped into a geologist, on secondment from the German embassy in Pretoria to look around for uranium deposits. Fascinating fellow with long whiskers who consistently wore an 'African explorer' type of solar topi. I bumped into him in Manicaland when he had just returned from Mavusi in the Tete province, near to the Zambezi River. At one fireside chat, after he had satisfied himself that your man was Irish, and thus 'against the British' policy (or so he assumed!), he hauled out a silvery piece of rock and said he had discovered a deposit of uranium. This is not my sphere of study so I asked him what use it might have, and how did he know it was uranium; he showed me a photographic plate on which he had tested the rock for some time, then developed the plate to demonstrate that the rock was radioactive.

"The discussion, aided by a few whiskies, went on to using this sort of stuff to divide the atom. When I reminded him that the atom was, by the very nature of the name given to it by Lucretius 2000 years earlier, the smallest of indivisible objects, he said, 'No, no, no: it can be done!' He said that German scientists were working on such a project."

Prue was listening to him intently, and said, "Fascinating story! But what was the name of the metal again? Uranium?" to which Kim nodded.

"At the moment, Winnie and I are a bit betwixt and between... Obviously, she has no desire to give up her Richmond Hill house outside London, and of course, she still has her share in the Scottish farm to consider; whereas the only piece of property I can call my own is in Ireland, not necessarily the safest place to be in at the moment. We are tinkering with the idea of finding a property not too far from Durban, to which we can go in the northern hemisphere winter months – 'flying south for the winter' as it were. At the moment, we are boarding with Donald and Prue – and of course that has to end.

"By the way – entire change of subject, but the Hotel Polana prides itself in offering the latest available leading newspapers from around the world – including American and French; usually only about a fortnight out of date. Winnie and I noticed that although there was no mention of the fact in British papers, King Edward's high jinks with an American woman called Mrs Simpson are all over the American and other foreign papers... It's pretty clear that they are closer than friends, during a royal yacht tour of the Mediterranean. There are pictures of them whooping it up on foreign shores. The British press appear to be keeping mum, but the news must surely trickle through. When he was here in 1927 I believe he broke up a formal banquet by throwing breadcrumbs at other guests. Being Scottish and Irish, Winnie and I are not particularly starchy, but his general behaviour might not seem to be entirely appropriate for the head of the Church of England, who don't 'do' divorce."

"And it is rumoured that they are well received in Nazi circles," said Winnie. "What do you think of it all, Donald?"

"He who sups with the devil will need a very long soup handle," he replied. "I suppose it could be said that Edward has stepped off the unpopular pedestal of his father King George V and got closer to the people, but I can't see Stanley Baldwin standing for it once the news hits the British press. I read somewhere in the *Natal Mercury* that the new massive hospital for natives being built in Umbilo Road is going to be called King Edward VIII Hospital… Perhaps the authorities should review that decision."

The laterite in the driveway was glowing a rich gold, as it does just after sunset in Durban, when they, the Kirkwood family with Kim and Winnie, arrived back at Chelmsford tired out by the emotionally exhausting funeral; and all agreed to make it an early night.

In bed, Prue said to Donald, "What an awfully sad day it has been. Interesting story about meeting that German geologist in Mozambique. We had better invite Dr Scobie to dinner with his sister soon, so the subject can be casually leaked to Pickering Street."

Both dreamt disturbing dreams that night. Donald dreamt of his father, who with the mad logic of dreams was sitting opposite him at a table in the Clyde Bank in Threadneedle Street, London, before it was taken over by Lloyds, where they were sorting out, not money, but different kinds of rock…when his father was met by wraith-like Askaris who were threatening to shoot them… making Donald awake with a start. Prue, on the other hand, was dreaming of her children when they were very young, but now grown. Sonya was weeping, her face deeply scarred. Beside her was a glass cage of exotic iridescent butterflies, by which her toddlers were fascinated, completely ignoring Sonya.

Next day was Saturday, which always started off with a convivial family breakfast, and the conversation among the adults turned to Kim and his strange wanderings about Mozambique – not least the meeting up with that German geologist and all the talk about atoms. When Ewan challenged him and asked his father exactly what an atom was, Donald advised him to go and look it up in the

Children's Encyclopaedia. More accommodating, Winnie said that the very word derives from the tiniest thing, invisible to the eye and which could not be divided. Prue chimed in and said she thought the word was invented by a Roman poet called Lucretius, who wrote in the chaos of those times, in the long poem called *The Nature of Things*; and was later utilised by another man called Epicurus to accompany the theory that the ancient gods had no influence over humans and all disturbances were caused by natural things, such as when a collection of atoms did not behave predictably and swerved.

"It's rather like looking at a flock of goats from afar. From far away they all look the same when going through a field gate – but occasionally a goat will break away and do something different, by cutting off from the others," Donald said. "It is thought that the universe, atoms and everything else, are subject to four forces – gravity, electro-magnetic, strong nuclear and weak nuclear. Sometimes, an atom or groups of atoms break away from the pack, like an errant goat, and behave inexplicably according to the known laws. It is speculated that there is a fifth force which might introduce these anomalies, but so far, not identifiable. You could call it (if it exists) the Umami force – and name it after the fifth taste detected by the Japanese – the kind of taste they discovered in mushrooms, some cheeses and certain types of seaweed. A Japanese company has been marketing this as Umami for over a hundred years, under the name of monosodium glutamate. Before that time, there was no recognition that a fifth taste existed. Nowadays, the Japanese sprinkle it on food to enhance the taste – a bit like we do with salt."

"That's the best and simplest explanation I have encountered about anything for a very long time, Donald. I think you have lost your vocation – you should have been a lecturer or teacher," said Kim.

"Thank you for the compliment, but I am just a simple ex-soldier, equipped by experience with a certain degree of agricultural knowledge. My wife is the one with the brains! Although I must confess that I'm greedy for knowledge and devour many of the scientific books that she brings home from the library from time to time."

Chapter Ten

It was the tenth day of Muharram, and Chinnamama was away visiting relatives, as part of her annual holiday which was always spent with cousins in nearby Phoenix, just north of Durban. A centre focusing on Indian concerns was established there by Mahatma Gandhi. Muharram is the most important Muslim festival of the Mohammedan year, and a period of cleansing and renewal. Before the era of India's partition, Hindus joined in the celebrations.

It was on this day that Prue and Cordelia had decided to meet up at Chelmsford, inviting Masheila to join them in their work of completing the large patchwork quilt started by Sonya and Prue which, indirectly, led to Sonya's fatal accident. Cordelia had arranged to pick up Masheila from her Grey Street offices. Being Saturday, when the offices closed at noon, Masheila was free to visit.

As their car reached the end of Umgeni Road, it was caught up and surrounded by Indian men, with faces and bodies painted to resemble tigers and wearing little more than loin-cloths, and their way was slowed by tajiyas – intricate, three-tiered bamboo 25-foot high constructions, resembling mausoleums and covered in silver, gold and crimson tinsel – blocking their progress along the road to Chelmsford. Ahead of the tiger-men were young boys engaging in fighting with sticks.

"The procession commemorates the death in battle of Imam Hussein, the grandson of the Prophet. We will just have to the follow until the procession branches off to continue celebrations on the riverbank. There will be much competitive wrestling until the senior celebrants announce the winner of the ultimate wrestling match."

"I don't think we will be out of the woods when we get to the bridge. Just look at the crowds hanging over the barriers, to get a view!" said Cordelia. "I think that when we do get to Chelmsford, we should go down to the summerhouse to watch the celebrations, don't you?"

"Yes, I think we will be just in time to watch them throwing the tajiyas into the river and watch them float away. The throwing of the mausoleums into the water implies the cooling of fiery emotions. In India, these mausoleums would probably float away to the sea where they would be broken up by the surf, but here the mouth of the river is blocked by a sandbar which is only washed away during times of flood. The forlorn remnants gradually disintegrate there until a particularly high tide takes care of the rest."

Thus, on arrival at Chelmsford, the three women hurried down to the summerhouse with small binoculars, in time to watch the heaving of the tajiyas into the river.

Later, during a tea break from the patchwork labours, Cordelia turned to Masheila and said, "Why aren't you down there with them?"

"I am Christian, but nevertheless am drawn closely to such events; but it is not my place to take part. Mmmm, these toast and anchovy sandwiches are delicious! We don't get anything like that in the Congress offices – anchovies on toast was one of many discoveries when I first moved to Durban – those and the discovery of the infinite variety of curry spice at the Indian market."

"You may not know that I have taken an interest in Indian affairs ever since we moved to Durban from Singapore, and I was appalled to discover their unjust treatment – which has not improved much. Tell me about the role of the Natal Indian Congress and what you do there."

"Yes, we have heard of you and your fruitful work in improving conditions for the Indians employed by the Durban municipality – and we are very grateful. My job isn't important – in the sense that all I do is to type reports, answer and make phone calls...you know, that sort of thing. But I find the work fascinating – especially now that Dr Monty Naicker is in control. Unlike me, who has never been out of the country, Monty qualified as a doctor at Edinburgh University, where attitudes towards people of colour are very different – to the extent that he never felt marginalised because of his skin colour. Returning to Natal, he experienced the same culture shock as Mahatma Gandhi being thrown off the train because of his ethnicity.

"Despite endless petitions to the authorities, the lot of the Indian population – as in 'second-class citizens' – remains practically the same, and beginning to deteriorate as recent proposed acts of Parliament go through the house, whittling away rights such as property ownership, and so on. The objective of the Natal Indian Congress (we call it 'NIC' for short) is to achieve equal rights for all. Oh, look! They are about to put the tajiyas into the river!" At which point the women rapidly passed the binoculars between them.

"Marvellous things, binoculars are," exclaimed Cordelia.

"Yes, they are – when I look through them I could almost reach out and touch the tiger-men; although I think the Afrikaans word for binoculars – verkykers ('farlookers') is far better than 'two eyed'. Even though the Afrikaans language is limited, compared with English, it does hit on better descriptions now and then. Well, should we take to our knitting – or rather our patchworking? Let's go up, and I'll put the kettle on."

And thus the work on the quilt continued, until Donald's working day at the office ended and he returned home, accompanied by Ewan from University, in his first year of his five-year architecture degree; With their arrival the talk swung to other interests; Donald had recently returned from visiting a country sugar estate and staying with their friends and fellow cane-growers, the Cundels. It had poured with rain much of the time, turning the un-shod country roads into a quagmire, making tyre-chains a necessity; even with them the risk of slithering off the road was an ever-present danger. Ewan, on the other hand, was full of his flying lessons given as a reward for his good matriculation results. He waxed lyrical about the Tiger Moth dual-control trainer, sitting on his parachute and the scariness of blind-flying with a hood over the compartment to block out daylight. The ladies were politely interested in the ultimate achievement of a three-point landing.

He was equally enthusiastic about the history of architecture, but mystified by Hitler choosing to close down the Weimar Bauhaus. Masheila, gathering her things, said, "I really have to go," but realised that she had lost one of her earrings.

"It must have dropped off when we were down at the summerhouse."

"Ewan, be a dear, do go down to the summerhouse with Masheila – take a torch and see if you can find it," Prue said.

On the way down to the viewing point, Ewan found his hand caught hers, and so they walked until they reached the railing. Without a word they swept together and

Ewan pulled her soft body and pressed it to his. With no indication of any desire to break away, she rather entwined her arms around him and kissed him longingly and gently. Before Ewan's gestures might indicate an urgent desire to take things further, she pushed him gently away and said, "I cannot explain why I am so drawn to you, and I know that you are feeling the same; but this is not the time or the place. See, shine your torch at my hand: I found I had my other earring in my pocket, all the time. We must go back quickly, and if you want to see me again, phone me at my offices and say your name is Sammy calling – to put them off the scent. I have a friend who works at the Blue Lagoon hotel on the beachfront. She is part of the team preparing for an international Marine Biology Conference to be held at the hotel next week. During the time, the hotel will have 'International Status', which means that scientists of all races can stay at the hotel for the duration of the conference. I will ask her to provide you with a label identifying you as one of the organisers attached to the hotel – then we can trip away upstairs…If you like?"

They unclasped hands and disentwined arms, well ahead of reaching the house. Kim and Winnie arranged to drive Masheila, with the latter sitting in the back seat of their car, to give the impression that they were taking a servant home. Kim drove, with Winnie beside him in the front passenger seat. Ewan had been keen to go with them but a frown and a quick shaking of the head, when no-one else was looking, persuaded him to resist the temptation which was raging inside him.

Masheila lived in a quiet little courtyard off Grey Street. A small flat overlooked by a palm tree in a bed marked by large seashells. One of the children was backward, and had a harelip; but he adored her, rushing to her and hugging her tightly. He had been given a toy pistol which used caps, which he fired off excitedly, bringing his mother out to call him inside. The family were very friendly with Masheila and it had become customary for them to eat their supper together, much of the time.

At the entrance to the hotel, a sign read 'International Conference on Marine Biology / Conférence Internationale sur la Biologie Marine', above which fluttered the flags of many nations. On the facade of the hotel itself the reconstructed skeleton of a young whale had been erected – all of which was floodlit at night. It was windy, and beach sand was skimming across the car park when Ewan entered through the staff entrance. It was Friday, and conference newcomers were continuing to arrive, so this entrance was unlikely to be noticed. The plenary conference was planned for the Saturday. There was a mild disturbance when a unwieldy sculpture of hugely enlarged interpretations of plankton was manhandled out of a van, and taken into the hotel entrance foyer, with other people carrying last-minute displays also straggling in. One of the workmen dropped a packet of sandwiches accidentally in the car park, which almost immediately attracted three vervet monkeys from the beach across the road. Two of them managed to dismantle the packet, and jumped on top of a car to devour their prize.

True to her word, Masheila's friend spotted Ewan immediately as he came through the door. She was dressed in hotel uniform, and said loudly, "It is Ewan, isn't it...? You're here as a Conference observer. Let me pin on your Conference identity badge." While saying this, she did so and whispered, "Tenth floor, room 101. Just knock. Masheila has already ordered dinner in the room."

Waiting for the lift was a rather impatient American who

said, when Ewan joined him, "This darned establishment is distinctly under-elevatorised. I've had to wait at least ten minutes... Mind you, this is Africa, I suppose. I see you're here for the conference. Going to speak?" to which Ewan replied, "No, no, I'm just a student observer. I am a student of architecture, but am interested in all things marine."

"Yeah? Well, a lot happens to concrete underwater – crystalline corrosion and all that. I'm the slimes man," as the lift arrived. "Any ship's hull acquires the beginnings of slime as soon as it goes into the water. Barnacles come next to eat the slime – and that's the problem – worldwide, a ten billion dollar problem.

"So what's the solution?"

"Dunno. That's why I'm here. Copper paint is a solution but fouls up everything else, so we have to look elsewhere. Here's my floor – see you at the conference."

She was in a simple red cotton dress, was bare-footed, and her hair was up in a chignon. "I hope you like curry," she said. "There's milk, beer and wine in the fridge. Come to the window," she said, holding out her hands. Ewan's self-confidence had begun to dwindle as he rode the tram to the hotel. It was at a low ebb by the time he knocked at the door, but Masheila's arms-outstretched gesture and the subsequent twining of arms as they looked out at the crashing ocean, far below, restored his equilibrium. Bar a few matriculation dance fumblings, however, and the embrace at the summerhouse, he remained a very inexperienced young man.

"In case you were wondering if I'm used to this kind of thing... I'm not. It just so happens that I had a week off from the office which coincided with this conference and I offered to help my best friend, Daksha, with some of the associated secretarial work – you know, meeting and greeting, labelling and directing delegates where to go, putting together conference papers, and all that sort of thing. So this is my official secretarial bedroom, my official meal, which also means you and I can have breakfast with the delegates tomorrow morning. I have never done this before, but I am pretty used to organising and assisting. My work is over for the day – so, as the English phrase goes, I am all yours. Let's drag this little table to the window. You haven't answered my question yet – is curry okay? This hotel does it rather well, with all these yummy sambals. Bread-and-butter? Would you like some wine – although beer goes better...?" Masheila realised she was chattering to cover up her nervousness.

After Ewan had poured the beer, Masheila said, "A friend of mine who got out of South Africa wound up studying medicine at Lissom's on Long Island. She became fascinated by the modern art at the Guggenheim and a particular picture titled *You and Me*, so much so that she sent me several postcards of the picture – see, I brought one along. The original is a portrait of the girl artist, to the right of which is a mirror, the same size as the portrait; the couple was cradled in a larger frame. This means that anyone gazing at the mirror inevitably catches sight of themselves staring at the picture."

Assisted by the beer and the relaxing effect of the food, Ewan was carefully drawn out by her to talk about the childhood memories, of growing up at Yonder which blended with her completely different memories of growing up with her parents, who were indentured labour, and the kindness of the Bell family.

"Strange to think we grew up so close, but almost in parallel universes," she said. "You do realise that what we are doing and possibly may do is almost illegal – and I hear there is talk of the state making it absolutely illegal with yet another draft being prepared for Parliament called The Immorality Act. If the authorities get to know we will be watched and duly branded as Communists or immoral, neither of which we are… Just two simple souls dangerously attracted to each other."

Ewan reached over and kissed her, noticing how slender her limbs were and the small mole on her lower left cheek.

"Despite the very altruistic attitudes of your grandmother, Cordelia, do you realise you have just kissed an 'undesirable'? I wonder what she would think of that. Fine-sounding thoughts are one thing, but complete non-segregation and integration could be quite another." And then she, in turn, leaned over and whispered in his ear, "Make love to me," which swept them under the bedclothes and much impatient fumbling of bothersome and unnecessary clothes by Ewan's unfamiliar fingers.

"Wait! Let me help you. You did bring some 'Friends of Malthus'?" Upon Ewan's obvious puzzlement, she whispered, "French Letters."

"Of course," he said, confidently, only partially masking the embarrassment of whispering his request to the chemist, after waiting and dawdling for what seemed hours until other customers had left the shop, the chemist discreetly popping them into a little brown paper packet for him. Mr Pimm, the chemist, was a kind man with a harelip.

"Wait, I'm older than you. This may teach you how to make love…slowly and gently," while slowly helping to undress him and her. It was almost dark and the crash, thump and roar of Indian ocean breakers reached up and cloaked all other sounds. Out at sea, the beam from the Bluff Lighthouse picked out the north coast breakers, then swept out to sea, encountering a distant fishing boat, glimpsing a liner, and then going behind their building, until it emerged to gambol with the northern shore again.

Masheila was the first to wake, with a full moon shining upon them. Ewan grunted and turned in his sleep, disturbed by the rustling of a paper packet, as Masheila drew out a book of etchings illustrating the Sun Pyramid at the Sun Temple sculptures at Gudjara in Modhera, India. The Sun Pyramid writhed with human bodies engaged in every possible positioning of copulation. The main text was in Sanskrit but the book carried an introduction in English. The rest of the book was devoted to illustrations and descriptions of the steps surrounding a large pool, populated by turtles to this day, and the micro-temples devoted to gods and goddesses – not least the goddess of smallpox. The author pointed out that the temple structures straddled the Tropic of Cancer and were so designed to withstand earthquakes by means of skilful interlocking pieces. It was said that the architect Frank Lloyd Wright had studied this method of earthquake-proofing when it came to his designing the earthquake proof structure of the Imperial hotel in Tokyo.

In the flyleaf, Masheila had pasted one of the 'Me and You' Guggenheim postcards, leaving the card blank. When Ewan stirred and awakened she turned on the bedside lamp and said to the still befuddled Ewan, "I brought this along for you – seeing you are a student of architecture, knowledge of these Indian structures might stimulate thought. They are over a thousand years old." The next hour or so they spent in more erotic engagements, simulating several of positions adopted by the sculptured figures, to much giggling, breathing and gasping, until they fell asleep again.

Ewan awoke again to the sound of teeth being brushed, and raising his head from the pillows saw Masheila, wearing only his shirt. "You have to get up and go and I must get ready to assist the delegates."

As they showered together, Masheila said, "I am too old for you and too brown. You must find a pretty young white student. What we did last night was wonderful and will live with me for ever. Tomorrow, when the world is free of prejudice, there'll come the time for such couples as us; but now it's too dangerous. Already, the Indian Congress is being watched by the security police – I know it is because the friendly Indian police constable warned us. The security police cannot get out of their heads that we are not communists. This suspicion we predict will force us into an alliance with the African National Congress, with much trouble to come.

"For you, it is too dangerous, and I would not be surprised if the security police will find out about us."

"How on earth will I ever be able to do without sight of your pretty nose. No, this will be impossible. I have fallen in love with you and all you stand for."

"And my body?"

"That too I cannot do without – it's so beautiful."

"No, no, no. This cannot be. Here, you start getting dressed. Here's your shirt."

When he drew it on he realised it was faintly perfumed by the Arpège she had been wearing. It was very expensive, and worn with anticipation of the night that might follow.

He was joined at the lift by a woman delegate, who asked, "I see you're an observer – I hope you'll be there to listen to my plankton presentation?"

"Plankton?" he asked, innocently. She too was American or Canadian.

"Yeah, I've been studying phyto-plankton for the last twenty-six years or so. Microscopic organisms that basking sharks live on and which produce seventy percent of the world's oxygen since whenever. Pollution run-off is beginning to kill off plankton in certain parts of shallow oceans, and if we let this continue mankind is doomed. Okay, not this week but in the foreseeable future. When we die off and all our structures have collapsed into dust, mankind will merely be a layer in the Earth's future crust… The Anthropocene."

The slimes man from the day before stopped the lift at the floor below and said, "Well, let's see what they do for breakfast," and then retired into his thoughts, as they rode the rest of the way in silence. Ewan had made up his mind to escape from the hotel. On looking up, he saw Masheila leaning over the balcony, and waved.

It was a wiser man who left the Blue Lagoon Hotel that morning than the one who had entered the hotel the previous evening. His shirt still whiffed faintly of Arpège when he got home from university that evening. When Chinnamama came to do the family washing, she smelt his shirt with a knowing interest. "This young man is growing up a little. I wonder who she was." He had slotted in the Indian temple book among the rest of his architectural books in his bedroom-cum-study, behind the slanted drawing-board, which took up most of his desk at the window. He was an untidy student and his book shelves were never in apple-pie order, despite Prue's regular encouragements, with her librarian's mind, to make them tidy. This would never be easy, exacerbated by the migratory swarm of books borrowed between the family, and never returned to their rightful places, even including his father's battered old copy of *The Thirty-Nine Steps* by John Buchan. Ewan's taste in reading, from Buchan's 'shocker' (or so it seemed) to British authors of some prominence, included Greek tragedies and everything else between, not least the fascinating range of books that Prue borrowed from the library. In fact, all four of them were inveterate bookworms, which extended to haunting the Durban bookshops of T W Griggs and Adams. Thus, it was not surprising that Emilia came across Ewan's book on the Sun Temple during one of her book-raids.

The book vanished from Ewan's shelves and its extraordinary contents were secretly shared with a university girlfriend who came to visit, study and giggle over the contents when no one else was about.

Despite numerous attempts by Ewan to maintain contact with Masheila, she was as good as her word and avoided all his efforts to get in touch. Up until their first encounter, Ewan, like the rest of the whites, had automatically treated Indian (and African) girls as taboo. After that encounter he secretly looked at Indian girls in a different and disturbing perspective, although he never shared such thoughts with anyone else, yet hinting as much to his closest friend and ally, Emilia. He became far more conscious of the inequity of the political system, and this led to many heated debates during family meals.

Chapter Eleven

Kim and Winnie, accompanied by Prue and Donald with their late-teenaged children, were sharing sundowners on the stoep in the Jardine garden towards sunset on a Friday. The conversation had turned to 'skebengas', the common word for African scoundrels; the remark had been prompted by a Jardine neighbour reporting a break-in, almost unheard-of in pre-war Durban.

They were watching a ragged formation of hadeda ibis finding their way home, with their prehistoric cries. In the garden, nodding-headed blue agama lizards called off for the night their raiding of birds' nests high up in the golden oaks; and a sudden shivery gust of wind encouraged the guests to move inside, as Keswick turned the ship's wheel to close the French windows. Just before that, Prue and Donald had shown Ewan and Emilia the 'Mind the coconuts!' notice, now much faded, below the coconut tree on the path leading up to the veranda. Donald said that he'd first noticed it "the winter I was courting your mother, and I arrived at the Jardine house for the first time in the Model-T Ford I called Kelpie. I took her off to a Saturday afternoon briefing on the League of Nations in 1919; Jan Smuts shocked the audience by suggesting the appeasement of the Germans, to reduce long-term burning resentment and a flare-up in years to come. Perhaps we should have listened to him. There will always be revolt brought about by the long-term suppression of peoples."

"Well, we are suppressing the natives and Indians," Emilia said.

Glancing at Prue, he said, "Exactly."

Keswick had brought home the first issue of *Picture Post*, offered to him by a ship's captain the previous day. It was filled with pictures of the handover of naval facilities in Ireland to the Irish Free State, as part of the signing of the Anglo-Irish trade agreement. Other photos were of the new American ambassador's children, John, Robert, and Edward Kennedy, opening the new children's section of the London Zoo; soldiers goose-stepping into the Sudetenland; and a photo of the PM. Neville Chamberlain, stepping from a plane on his return from Munich, waving a piece of paper and uttering 'Peace in our time!' And another of Chamberlain appearing on the Buckingham Palace balcony with King George VI and the Queen. On the same page spread, and alongside the balcony pictures, was one of British adults being issued with gas masks. Among the many 'people-pictures' were shots of the launching of the *Ark Royal*, an aircraft carrier, later sunk, and the opening ceremony to mark the commissioning of the Singapore naval base.

Donald said, "As is her wont, Prue brought home another bundle of books for us to wade through, a couple of days ago – one titled *Rebecca*, which is more for her and Emilia than Ewan and me; but a book by a fellow called George Orwell (I think his real name is Blair) titled *Farewell to Catalonia*, which has proved riveting stuff. The politics of Spain remain bewildering, but what has become clear is that Stalin and Trotsky are at opposite ends of the Marxist spectrum, and seem to dislike each other very much, with Stalin's agents hellbent on bumping off the Trotskyites. I read a report of some of the latter being tortured to death in a summerhouse just outside Barcelona. It seems that Orwell got shot in the throat, but he survived and escaped with his wife and a few friends over the border to France. Although Orwell appears to be an exponent of working-class Marxism, he is full of hate against Stalin and all that he is doing in Russia… and through his NKVD agents in Spain."

"Of course, German fascists in Spain (in collaboration with the Catholic Church there) portray themselves as a bulwark against Russian Bolshevism…The saviours of the Western world, so to speak," said Keswick. "I guess we have all read between the lines and can see another war is coming against the Germans, with Britain being totally unprepared, despite repeated warnings by Churchill, at this point a senior member of parliament; due to the dithering of that silly appeasement-wallah, Neville Chamberlain. Look at this picture in the *Post*! Peace, my eye!" At which point, an ageing Jeeves could be heard sounding the dinner gong in the depths of the house. Jeeves, like his employer Keswick, was beginning to show signs of rheumatism, so his son had been recruited into the ceremony of serving at dinner. His father retained the careful institution of table-laying, with silver candlesticks and correct tableware and all. Donald was always amused that, despite the fact Prue had not been living as a child in the house for so many years, her starched napkin was put down rolled in her childhood silver napkin ring, in the same manner as Keswick's and Cordelia's, yet Donald's was placed napkin-ring free, like those of the rest of the family present. He thought back to an occasion when he had come across Jeeves and his son sitting at a table in the kitchen garden polishing the entire collection of silver; and remembering the remark of an American guest at the

Durban Club that he had more cutlery in front of him than in his entire household.

Keswick held fast to his marine and naval background, and all evening meals were preceded by the naval grace of "God bless our meat; God guide our ways; God give us grace our Lord to please. Bless, O Lord, this food to our use and us in your service; and keep us mindful of the needs of others. Amen." And after the soup bowls had been cleared away, he would, on these occasions, proudly turn to his grandson (after previously proposing the toast to the King); he had trained Ewan to rise to his feet, as if he were the most junior officer, and propose the toast for that day. It being Saturday, Ewan was obliged to utter, "To Wives and Sweethearts," with those who were familiar with the toast responding, "May they never meet," uttered laughingly by Cordelia, Prue, and Donald, who was now familiar with this rejoinder.

Cordelia said, "I was in two minds to invite Toby and his children, then realised that the Broccardo parents and Joy were still down from Zululand, so felt it best to let them settle down; but I have every intention of inviting Toby and his children to join us frequently when the parents go back to Empangeni. I have a feeling that Joy might well stay in Durban for a while to draw closer to her nephews. Ewan and Emilia, when you do meet up, please do go out of your way to make friends with them. Keswick and Donald, I know you are in touch with Toby, so that is all for now that we can do, in the circumstances."

"I happened to pass through the little settlement of Waterval Onder recently", Donald said, changing the subject, "very close to the Mozambique border, and came across President Paul Kruger's house in which he dwelt towards the end of the Boer War, before he left for Lourenço Marques and subsequently departed for Europe in an effort to raise funds for continuing the anti-British fighting; and found his modest house satisfyingly moving. Rabbie Burns's wee house in Dumfries, with a poem he scratched on a window-pane, still enshrined along with his modest furniture, I find moving in the same way as that small house Kruger lived in. I suspect I will be untouched by this new granite edifice about to be built in Pretoria to commemorate the Great Trek of the Boers.

"I have no basic argument about the creation of appropriate memorials, but it does seem to be in unseemly haste... almost as if those responsible were engaged in a nation-building exercise. The Boers-cum-Afrikaners are a brave and rugged people; but hastening to create a storyline does seem to have an affinity with all that rubbish about Aryanism going on in Germany, rather than allowing history to evolve slowly and in its own good time. I believe the architect of the Pretoria monument was sent to Germany to study those rather ponderous and ugly new creations of the Nazi state. It seems to be a year of fossils, ancient and new," Ewan continued; "For truthfully that seems to be the reason for laying the cornerstone of the Pretoria Monument, to fossilise and glorify supposed recent Afrikaner heroism."

Ewan continued, changing the subject, "When I was coming back on the tram from Stamford aerodrome" – at which Donald interjected saying "What were you doing there? Did you manage to fly?"

"No, and I did intend to mention this to you and Mum... but I had a strange sight from the top of the tram: the upper storey of the Lion match factory. I've always rather liked that building with all its white windows; but all I could see was line after line of what looked like something rather strange and disturbing: big machine gun shells, chugging along. Surprisingly they left the windows open, but I suppose in the circumstances it was done to reduce the effect of blasts if there were an explosion.

"No, Dad, I didn't go flying on this occasion; it was to attend a small informal gathering to meet Sir Pierre van Ryneveld. I didn't know much about him before, but I learnt that after flying for the Royal Flying Corps in the First World War and for the White Russians, he was captured by the Reds and only released in 1920.

"It seems that Smuts has invited him to form a South African Air Force. He was full of the threat of war and invited suitable candidates to be put on a waiting list. I was one, as I didn't see any harm for the moment."

"Are we close to war?" Prue asked in agitation.

"God forbid! Not again, after the ghastly First World War and all those poor young men being shunted to the front as cannon fodder!" Cordelia said.

"Well, you know what I think about war," Donald said, "and I agree with your mother; but it looks as if Britain and perhaps the Commonwealth will be sucked into it unless there is some kind of Deus ex Machina who might descend from the clouds to stop that German idiot in his tracks. The West seems so weak…fancy allowing an aggressor like Germany to just march into Czechoslovakia as a bargaining chip for peace – and look what has happened in the region of Bohemia. Hitler is now threatening Poland. Mind you, the West is equally hard-hearted about Jews – Britain and the United States have refused to accept any more refugees, followed by Sweden and Switzerland. Can you imagine the ghastly predicament of those poor souls?

"Your father, Prue, attended a Durban Business Chamber lunch the other day, and the talk was of the looming crisis –

what preparations should be made. If the worst happens, we could run short of oil, and we heard that the Coronation Brick & Tile Company has put in an order to Leyland for a fleet of steam-powered trucks... and Bakers Bread is expanding its fleet of dray horses to cope with bread deliveries."

Donald said to Ewan, after glancing at Prue who was showing distress, "You are going to finish your degree first before indulging in any heroics!"

"Hear, hear!" Keswick thundered – an imperative which surprised the dinner table, as Keswick was always such an even-tempered man – causing Jeeves to falter as he entered with the trifle, richly laced with sherry.

"We'll talk about this later," said Donald. Inscrutably, Cordelia was studying Ewan's expression when Donald was saying this.

After the cheese and biscuits, the dinner ended in the time-honoured Jardine ceremony of the younger generation blowing out the candles while pronouncing words like 'Who!' 'What!' and 'When!' in which Prue joined with gusto, and at which Jeeves could be heard fondly chuckling.

Chapter Twelve

It was Sunday, 3rd September, 1939. Chelmsford was a gathering place on Sundays for the extended family and close friends, and this day was no different from the informal tradition, which had gathered force. It was customary to go to church early so that the family could be ready for the visitors and Sunday afternoon tennis. To that end, Donald rose in good time to a sultry morning. Leaving Prue to her dreams of a childhood Singapore, he stole out to release the ponies from the stable, seeing with pleasure that Layani's son, at present on holiday from Adam's Mission, had already watered the tennis court lightly, and was putting the finishing touches of freshness to the white lines with the heavy court roller. Layani was already laying the pavilion table – more a shelter from the wind, provided by creepers climbing a trellis, than anything grander – when Donald said, "Sabona, Layani," to which he gave the customary greeting, "Ngilapha ukuze," and Layani replied, "Ngibonwe." ['I see you', and the customary polite reply, 'I am here to be seen.'] Then continued a pleasant exchange between two men who shared a strong bond. Donald had gone to great lengths to learn to speak, in a stumbling way, "Nizwe inyoni yemvula ekuseni kakhulu. Ucabanga ukuthi lizokuna namhlanje?" ["I heard the rainbird very early this morning. Do you think it's going to rain?" to which Layani, gesturing to the sky, and wobbling his right hand to suggest an improbability and replying in his own brand of patois Portuguese, "..em chuva – luna no céu durante o di" ['Moon in sky. No rain'] – and it was true that if all of the moon could be seen during daylight hours it was unlikely to rain.

Donald wandered away, past the far corner of the house, with the wind pump turning gently in the early morning breeze, looked into the underground wells and saw a brindled-headed middle-aged man looking back at him; and reminded himself to turn on the fountain, then strolled past the mango-grove, past the big-veranda trellis, now beginning to be covered again with early grenadillas, rounded the front of the house past huge decorative boulders, and examined the lichen that was extending its blue-grey grip; stared, for a while, at the pale brown river-boulders that the garden boy continued to dig up, wondering how on earth they found their way to the hilltop as it was today, and then drifted inside as Prue was waking; and found Chinnamama and one of her daughters clanking about in the kitchen, preparing sorghum porridge, frizzling brinjals, sugared tomatoes, bacon, eggs, and coffee. Chinnamama took great pride in grinding the coffee beans freshly each morning; and now the aroma was wafting through the house.

"Thank you, God. I am content," Donald thought.

As the extended family started to arrive in dribs and drabs just before noon, in between greetings, he turned on the wireless to catch the BBC news on the shortwave Empire service, and was surprised to hear the sound of Bow Bells, which ran on for several minutes. This was most unusual. It faded away to be replaced by the voice of Stuart Hibberd announcing a special broadcast by HM King George VI. "Something serious has happened, it seems," he said, calling the visitors and immediate family who drifted in and perched here and there, as if posing for a Manet picnic tableau. Donald noticed that Emilia, sitting on the pouffe and leaning against her mother, was twiddling her thumbs; Prue was doing the same. Catching sight of Cordelia who was similarly occupied, Donald reflected that he had married into a long line of thumb-twiddlers.

The monarch's drawn-out voice announced that his country was at war with Germany – for the moment, as no confirmation had been received from the German Chancellor that he would withdraw his invading forces, which had entered the Gdańsk Corridor in Polish territory; and the King reminded listeners that Britain and France had a written agreement to come to Poland's defence, if it were attacked. He described the coming fight as one for justice and peace against bondage and fear, and called for all the citizens of Britain and the Commonwealth to stand firm in the dark days ahead. The King mentioned that this was the second war most of his subjects would have to live through. The long pauses between his words added to the sense of gravity, giving the impression of his struggling to find the right words, in this manner concealing his lifelong stammer.

The broadcast ended with the British national anthem. Only Kim and Keswick got up for the anthem, leading Donald to say "We're at home, not at a bioscope." (It was customary at that time to stand for the anthem which sounded at the end of all cinema performances.)

There was a long silence. Even the children had to understand the implications for the Anglo-Irish, when Toby said, "Well, in the words of Yeats, 'All is changed, changed utterly and a terrible beauty is born.' Children, don't be surprised that we just may have to move to the Cape as a result of all this. It may not happen, but someone from the

Royal Navy made contact some time ago and asked, if war did break out, would I consider rejoining the Navy, stationed as Commander of the Royal Navy dockyard at Simon's Town."

"But Daddy, that's so far away... And all our friends are here. What about school?" Olga said.

"It may well not happen – and nobody knows exactly what will take place yet. We'll all sit down and talk it through at home once we know what's happening. Probably nothing will happen for many months – and even then we might just find ourselves in exactly the same place as we are now."

Prue said, "The servants take the rest of Sunday off, so let's go out to the tennis pavilion and have lunch," although it was said with a heavy heart, thinking of Ewan's enthusiasm for flying, the inevitable progress of the coming conflict and the possibility of enlistment being introduced. Donald's limp had deteriorated over the years, so he was no longer able to play adult tennis; nevertheless he did do his best to give the children a run for their money. Among the adults, Toby and Kim were the acknowledged terrors of the court among the men, though Winnie and Prue made a formidable mixed-double opponent, with Prue, being left-handed, able to catch many an opposite number off-guard.

By sundowners, the children had drifted off to lead the shetlands back to the stables, with little sense of foreboding; but for the adults it was different.

"Well, I suppose we will all be roped into doing good works by the Victoria League," Cordelia said. "I've already had a call even ahead of the news this week from Margaret Maytom, full of talk of providing tea and sandwiches for the troops in Wesley Hall – as if swarms of them are going to appear overnight, marching down Soldier's Way."

After they had all left, the traditional Sunday supper of

scrambled eggs on toast had been cleared away, the wireless switched off, and the children were engrossed in interests of their own, Donald said, "I think we should go along and chat to James Scobie and Pickering Street, to see how we can help – what say you?"

"I think just go to bed. They will be in contact with us soon enough. I kept on meaning to tell you that I had a call from Jim Bell, by way of routine sugar business last Friday. He did mention that the von Weldenburg's farm is up for sale and von Weldenburg and Frieda had left. Bell said that one of his sons, Andrew, had been invited to manage the farm until the sale goes through, and that Hubie had a Post Restante address, care of the Swiss Consulate in Lourenco Marques. He seems to have made provision for his farming staff on a fair scale, and also that Andrew has unearthed some inconsistencies in trading and other matters. I would love to have asked him if Andrew had stumbled across evidence of aerials and transmitters, but I have no doubt those have disappeared too."

"I'll get hold of Deepika through her cousin who works at the Masonic hotel in Empangeni and try to repost her somewhere else. She has been doubly useful to Pickering Street, as you know. Things could happen here... but we are so very far away from the fighting in Europe."

"Well, you know really far more about what to expect, and I think we will just trundle on as before, until the Axis drops a bomb on the Suez Canal, or blocks the Gibraltar Strait – or both, forcing all naval, military, and commercial stuff to flow around the Cape of Good Hope and dock at Durban. Then it will be blackouts, black market and whale meat. I don't think enlistment will take place, though there will be much pressure to join up, and much opposition from the bulk of the Afrikaner population – not all of the bulk, but those stirred up by the Ossewa Brandwag and the rest of that gang. The 'Angels' will be busy, and while some voluntary joining up by loyal Indians and Africans will occur, the latter, in the main – those who will not be employed in the war effort – will regard it as a white man's war and just carry on. I expect the Germans to be rounded up. Sadly, many of them have been here for generations and are more loyal to the British Crown than the over twenty thousand Afrikaners who, most certainly, are not – but you know all this far better than I. I suppose the Muller families will be arrested and imprisoned for the duration, like the thousands of German-descent Germans in South West Africa. If Italy declares war against the Allies it will be the same old charade... Poor old Paolo, I hope they leave him alone. I'll call the servants together after breakfast tomorrow and let them know – but I expect they'll know all about it already."

"One wonders what all those internally banished Germans will do. Perhaps, like Ovid in Tomis, some of them might write poetry. I think I will investigate whether we could operate the library service for local internees. Could be useful to Pickering Street," Prue said, yawning deeply.

"To bed, Dodo-sleepy-head, and no lending of Mein Kampf if your internee idea gets off the ground," he said teasingly. "I certainly won't 'kamph' to get to sleep tonight!" he said, rising to make his familiar round of locking up for the night.

Their sleep was disturbed by cries coming from Emilia's bedroom. On rushing through they discovered that she had been having a nightmare of monstrous invading machines trampling underfoot the shetland ponies and her favourite cat, and it took a long time to convince her otherwise. The day before, Donald had taken the family to see *The Good Earth* starring Paul Muni. Before the interval was a Pathé Gazette documentary reporting the invasion of Czechoslovakia – with much footage of tanks and goose-stepping soldiers. Donald and Prue surmised that all that long-distance view of the awfulness of war had worried the girl far more than they had realised. From early childhood, Emilia was often seen sucking her thumb as she went to sleep, and despite her age, Donald saw her doing the same thing. He remembered Sonya Broccardo doing this after her brother, Zeno, was fatally attacked by that Zambi shark at Richards Bay, and her being cradled by Toby in the back of the car on that dreadful car journey back to her parents.

Emilia was comforted when Bunty, her favourite cat, leapt onto the bed and purred loudly. The battered Dodo ragdoll of childhood lay on her pillow beside her head as she went off to sleep. Years later, she recalled the comforting sense of hands lifting pillows and tucking in the blanket about her body. "It was just the comforting sense of loving hands... Just hands."

The next morning early mist from the valley curled about the trees in the lower garden and rendered the summerhouse as a pale ghost. The bushbuck had again taken advantage of concealment provided by the vegetation to emerge and nibble away at the youngest-looking of the autumnal leaves.

Ewan had managed to acquire a car, a DKW, predominantly wood and canvas, for a song from a fellow student who was now moving on to grander things: the Der Kleine Wunder was unpopular not only because it was German, but primarily because the sound it emitted from its exhaust was very loud and sounded like a high-pitched bumblebee caught in a small jam jar. Even the sound of Christmas beetles was far more tolerable. He and Emilia had left in it for university a few minutes earlier, followed by Donald and Prue to their respective offices half an hour later.

The ponies had been taken out of their stables and tethered on the lawns, and the last sight of the morning was of Layani raking up autumnal eucalyptus leaves into a pile, which he had later set fire to and left to smoulder.

Prue loved her job at the library, especially now that the cataloguing had been left to more junior hands. Donald's occupation at the Cane Growers was challenging and interesting enough, though battling with Equalisation Fund figures was the least attractive task.

They parked the car on the Esplanade near the level crossing at the yacht club, and with time to spare they agreed to saunter to the end of the mole, where they sat for a while, looking out at the Bay. The concrete bench upon which they sat was beginning to crumble with age; it was the self-same bench upon which Donald had sat with Emily Bell, in 1919, during the Spanish Flu pandemic, and a few days before she sailed away to Cape Town, never to return. As Emily and he had sat on the bench, Donald had unwrapped a clumsy escalope sandwich given to him by the cook at the Durban Club, with an exasperated remark of "Thatzalligot". It had been high tide, and every time the swell sank, the water trickling out of the barnacles encrusting the edges of the mole giving off bubbling sounds as the water dribbled away.

Donald and Prue leant together with affection and in silence, until Prue said, "Daddy loves the Bay, and so do I... All those smells and sounds, the ships coming and going. Over there, they've almost completed building the second half of the floating dock. Daddy said that old Fred Paterson would be heartbroken to see them dispensing with his dear old lighthouse simply because it's deemed too much of a landmark for the enemy ships. He says they're going to blow up the caves at the point because they obstruct our artillery What's going to happen to us all, I wonder. I wish you hadn't given Ewan flying instructions! He'll be pressured to volunteer."

"Well, at least it would be in the Air Force – and the immediate priority will be to patrol our waters, simply because we have no naval vessels to do the job."

As if on cue, a three-engined Junkers flew over the harbour from the south-west towards the Stamford Hill aerodrome, almost within sight from Chelmsford, across the Umgeni River. Ironically, the entire fleet was of German origin – indeed, there was a photograph of the German chancellor Hitler alighting from one of them somewhere in Berlin.

"I'll never forgive you if something happens to our son. Gosh! Look at the time. We must dash."

He and Prue, now rather late, hurried across the railway tracks, jay-walked the road, then dashed up Gardiner Street, passing a tobacconist shop-window displaying a large map of Europe, decorated with little flags pinned to show the advances and retreats of the opposing armies. At the corner of Smith Street a newspaper boy was clipping new billboards in place – one reading 'FRANCE FALLS' and another 'ITALY DECLARES WAR'. The Indian paper-boy looked emaciated, and Donald wondered how on earth he had managed to carry that weight of newspapers at his feet, from where he had collected them as they came off the huge Hoe printing press in Pine Street. Donald had often watched in fascination how the brindled Indian dispatcher would bundle piles of papers with twine, and, deftly snapping the knot with his fingers, throw the bundle to the next newspaper boy waiting in line.

"Never kiss your husband or boyfriend in the street! Not done!" Cordelia had taught her daughter, and Donald complied with the same mode of manners, inherited from his reserved father; but their eyes meeting when they said goodbye implied their private intimacy, when he took her a copy of the *Mercury*.

"We are in for it now, it seems," said Donald, his face full of sadness. "Bloody Krauts."

The Cane Growers' boardroom was hazy with pipe and cigarette smoke when he entered, to find his chairman, Sholto Douglas, reading out passages to the other board members. "Ah – late, Mr Kirkwood! Not like you to be late... Punctuality is the courtesy of kings, you know. Never mind, the news has disrupted everybody. The purpose of this informal meeting is to discuss what impact this new development will have on the sugar industry and to review our contingency plans to be developed for just this situation. With France gone Vichy, and considering Italian possible supremacy in the Mediterranean, it will be inevitable as we expected that most shipping from Europe will have to take the Cape route and wind up in Durban, with much shipping having to ply from here to Singapore, et cetera..."

The meeting ground on, reconfirming contingency plans, well past the usual lunch break. When Donald emerged he found three messages, one – unusually, as he had not spoken to the man for years – from Creighton, the Admiralty Room 40 man, whom he had first met in Logan's commodity export offices in Pickering Street, so many years ago. The most pressing was from Prue, to phone her very urgently indeed. The last message was from Kim.

"Do you realise what Ewan has done? He's joined the Air Force and he is sitting here in his uniform, sketching as usual!" Donald could almost see Prue wringing her hands in distress. "You talk to him and tell him how foolish he is being – breaking with his studies and just following the sound of the first tin drum, like some of his friends! Darling, you must talk to him immediately – if you can pry him away from my girls."

"Hello, Biggles. I know you're fond of flying but you know that I have been through the last war – watching my friends being blown to pieces and all that, and flying in wartime conditions is very similar. It would be a pity to throw away your studies and all that acquisition of knowledge, to land up in a mangled wreck of a plane. I know you will find it difficult to talk about it over the phone – especially in front of all those girls – so let's have a serious chat tonight. Meanwhile, think about what I said and hang fire on any immediate plans please, not only for your mother's sake, but also for mine. You must know that we love you dearly and think only of your interests. Let me speak to your mother again…Prue, we will talk to him again tonight. Meanwhile, I will try and get hold of the recruiting officer; failing which, I will ask your father to give van Ryneveld a blast – he carries more weight than I do. By the way, I have a message from Pickering Street, to call them… There'll be lots in the wind, I have no doubt. More about that later… Oh, I nearly forgot, I have another message to phone Kim. I'll get home as soon as I can."

When Donald called Creighton, the conversation was brief and limited to his being asked to attend an informal meeting in Scobie's office the following day, and to ask Prue to attend. "We have an infestation of butterflies, and I think you will be able to help," leaving Donald baffled.

After that, Donald called Kim, who said, "I need your help. Now that the Italians have thrown their lot in with dear old Adolf, they expect trouble on the north Kenya border. I have been press-ganged into going north to advise on terrain mapping and possible landing strip location. I'm too old to fight, but Winnie doesn't like my knocking about there, imagining the Eyeties will be taking pot-shots at me. Could you give her a call to settle nerves, a bit, old fellow – you're her brother, after all?"

Dinner at Chelmsford that night was troubled. By the time Donald got home, Prue had again berated Ewan for not discussing his intentions with them. It had resulted in Ewan retreating into his study-cum-bedroom with an appropriate door-slamming, reminiscent of Emilia's rages at the start of her going through puberty. Even the servants were drawn into it, insofar as that they could not help overhearing this unusual full-blooded family row – with Chinnamama shaking her head and clicking with disapproval. Donald knocked on Ewan's door and entered without waiting for an acknowledgement, and found him sitting on his bed beside Emilia. They had always been very close and were holding hands. Ewan was still in uniform.

"Hello, the two of you. Biggles, old fellow, you did take us all by surprise, but I don't think shouting at your mother is the way to go about it. I can tell she's very, very upset, because she has started to stammer again – and that's not a good sign. I found her weeping alone in her study. May I suggest you go through, apologise and comfort her? Emilia and I will follow through in about ten minutes, then we'll sit down to dinner – it's unfair to keep Layani waiting: he works long hours, as it is."

Donald left the door open, following the family principle of always leaving bedroom doors ajar, except when Emilia practised the piano in her bedroom or Ewan played 'As Time Goes By' on the Parlophone – the favourite of him and Beulah (a cuddly blonde with whom he was smitten), a song to which they danced at a student get-together. Emilia's playing was moderately fair, but the repeated practising of *Solfeggiotto* by Cornelius Bach, with phrases repeated over and over again, was irritating. The table candles had been lit by the time they went through, and they found Ewan and Prue in their places, with Layani hovering in the doorway that led to the main kitchen.

Next day Donald and Prue arrived at Dr Scobie's office in the museum, separately – as per their instructions, which both of them observed. Prue said, "Inevitably, it's a new development concerning wartime work; but wonder what on earth all this stuff about butterflies is…"

Creighton was helping himself to a ginger-nut when Donald arrived. He realised Creighton had never been in Scobie's office before, by the way the former was looking around and studying the many framed images and stray objects lying on the sister's desk. Prue was the last to arrive, causing all three men to spring to their feet, until she was settled in a chair. "Now, what on earth is this about all these butterflies?" asked Prue.

"Sorry about that – it was just to mislead anyone listening. It's a cock-and-bull story I invented about the threat of worms getting into our bulk storage, and the need to discuss with the nearest authority on moths, worms and butterflies."

("My God," thought Donald, "we are all looking so old – except for Prue, who seems to have inherited the gift of everlasting youth. I love this woman.")

"Thank you for coming. This is just to alert you that we have bought the old farm and farmhouse on the hilltop next to Chelmsford. The owners were delighted to get rid of it to the Service – or, at least, that's who we posed as. No harm done. We explained that we had to fence off the property as the authorities had developed a new-fangled weather forecasting system… Something to do with radio interference patterns – you know, the kind of crackles you get on shortwave. In secret, however, it's one of quite a few Y-stations the Admiralty is setting up all over the place, including the African East Coast. Their purpose is to eavesdrop on any radio transmissions, including what we ironically call 'The Angel Orchestra', in other words the enemy underground stations, including undetected weakish transmitters here. We suspect one down near Isipingo, another on the Bluff and yet another somewhere in the cane fields near Mount Edgecombe... No doubt there are others, and more will spring up. The farm next to you is beautifully positioned as it has good elevation and the masts will not be noticed from ground level. The Admiralty is also tinkering with some sort of marine movement detection system which I know nothing more about, and I must ask you to keep anything I might have told you strictly under your hat for the duration.

"The reason why I'm obliged to tell you all this is that I have to ask your permission to dig a part of your garden to lay our cables down to Riverside Road by the shortest route. That's a bit of an exaggeration, but we will have to cut across a corner of your tennis court then burrow through your mango grove and then down the edge of the quarry where they will never blast. We promise to repair damage to the tennis court and replace any flowerbeds that we might have to disturb. Also, the staff will come and go at odd hours and will be in mufti as, ostensibly, they are merely employees of a government office. You may wish to invite the few members of staff for tea, occasionally, as some sort of relief from them being glued to their earphones and instruments.

Chapter Thirteen

Despite his parents' attempts to persuade him otherwise, Ewan did join up and was swallowed up, for a time, by the Air Force, first on training somewhere in Rhodesia. After a short leave, his parents began to receive censored letters through the armed services postal system. Some references to his whereabouts were hinted at and escaped the Censor, particularly one where he had enclosed several snapshots of his fellow aviators in a dry and dusty landscape, with just the hint of what seemed to be a distant pyramid. What had actually transpired was that his now-operational new squadron had been assigned to collect a new batch of Gloster Gladiator biplanes and fly them to northern Kenya, where serious incursions by the Italians were taking place. During the defence from Italian attack at Manzini, his plane was struck by random fire, rupturing the undercarriage, so that when he came in to land, the remaining supports collapsed.

Conflict throws people together in circumstances where they would have been unlikely to meet at another time. So it was for Ewan, when he hobbled into the Officers' Mess tent of the Springbok Ninth Recce Armoured Division in Addis Ababa, a hot, dry and dusty place swarming with uniformed South Africans in a landscape beset by very tall date palms and the exotic sight of a camel corps.

"Crikey!" said Kim. "Rough night? What happened to you?" he said, after spying Ewan's bandaged and walking-sticked figure. "Here, come and sit down."

"Hello, uncle, what a surprise! What are you doing here?"

"I got involved in terrain mapping, as a geologist, so they threw a uniform at me, and I have been helping to map the terrain with the kind assistance of you blokes – flying sorties over terrain that was very badly mapped by the Italians. Whatever happened to your plane?"

"The undercart was shot away so when I came in to land the Glad dug its nose in and turned turtle; I finished my landing hanging from the safety harness, while some of the wing struts were collapsing and began to 'attack' me. I'm being sent back to recuperate and retrain on some new aircraft we're getting."

"How are you getting back – although I suppose I shouldn't be asking?"

"Apparently, I have to join a train transferring some Italian POWs from Addis Ababa to Djibouti, day after tomorrow. Conveniently, the Eyeties developed quite a good line to the French port which we have been able to use."

"Jeez! All that way in this stinking heat with a bunch of Eyeties – better you than me! But, let me introduce you to these blokes… That's Harry Schwartz over there, whom we call Blackie, for obvious reasons; that's Joe Slovo over there, sitting next to another Harry who is rather good at joined-up writing so they sent him to Oxford and now he is in intelligence. His dad owns a few diamond mines down south. You've met your boss, I presume, Pierre van Ryneveld…"

"At ease, airman," van Ryneveld said, as he saw Ewan struggle to salute him. "Yes, we last met at Stamford Hill aerodrome in Durban, when I recruited him. Your parents were not keen on the idea at all, as I gathered from a telephone call I received from your grandfather, Keswick Jardine. He's quite a crusty old chap and I had to hold the receiver away from my ear as he bellowed at me."

"Let's drop formalities," said Kim. "Are you aware that Pierre flew for the White Russians before he was shot down and imprisoned by the Reds until 1920?"

"That experience of a one-party state I never want to live under again. Which brings us to what we were about to discuss – so you have arrived just at the right time. I had better explain that strong elements in South Africa are not only against this war with the Italians and the Germans, but are determined to develop a one-party state of suppression. Something must be done and we are discussing the formation of a movement which is open to all servicemen, regardless of race and creed, as the first step to countering such interference... And believe me, the snake of fascism is beginning to entwine itself like a python around South African politics."

"To start with," said the other Harry, "we have to call it a catchy name. Any ideas?"

"Well, we are all springboks here, so how about something like the Springbok Movement?" suggested Ewan, after spying a familiar packet of Springbok cigarettes lying on the table.

"Springbok! Good idea, but I think 'movement' is a bit wishy-washy. How about 'Legion'? It suggests many people marching together, and it snatches a good idea out of the awful Nazi habit of torchlight parades."

After glancing around the table and meeting lots of approval, the other Harry said, "Agreed! Ewan, isn't it? We have another secret weapon – an Indian cook from Durban. Knows how to make a really hot Natal curry – his father came from Madras." No sooner had he spoken than tureens of rice and curry arrived, with a clatter of plates and cutlery.

In manoeuvring army terms, this was high living indeed, with orderly service at the table.

"A torch commando – that will be a good idea too," Joe said. "We'll put it on the shelf until the Springbok Legion gets off the ground. Harry, with all your high-falutin' joined-up writing skills, perhaps you could draft something, and then the rest of us could tear it to pieces and add bits of our own?"

The conversation drifted on between mouthfuls of curry, when Kim said, "Ewan, could I hand you a letter for Winnie? You'll be able to post it from Durban. As you have experienced, our postal service is hardly fleet of foot."

Ewan had taken a small full sketchbook from one of his pockets and laid it on the table beside him when he sat down. Kim, noticing this, said, "I forgot your passion for sketching as a child. I can see you are still at it…"

"Yes, whenever I have an idle moment. The world is full of fascinating stuff and creatures. You may remember that I broke out of my architectural studies when I joined up, but my desire to record things goes on unabated, even more so. I've always been fascinated by vernacular architecture and my present wanderings have alerted me to the differences in these homespun structures. I'm fascinated by the regional and tribal differences in the hut structures and overall appearance – for example, the striking difference between the beautiful beehive huts of the Zulu and the rondavel-like huts on the local indigenous here… see, something I spotted… A series of 'rondavels' where the beams of the circular roof protrude, all the way round, by at least a foot and half."

"But surely, as a student of architecture, you should be more engrossed with the architecture-designed stuff created by the Italians before we kick them out?"

"Plenty of time for that after the war, when I go back to my studies; but all the books of architecture concentrate on the history of architect-design structures, compiled and written by academics with eyes wide shut to the 95 per cent of world structures not created by the combined efforts of architects and engineers. I think that Le Corbusier was one of the first architects to wake up to this. Simply put, architecture is a skill able to produce a fabric around an activity – but with architectural professionalism can come an arrogant dismissal of all structures – from a simple cowshed upwards. Toby once showed me a collection of drawings he had made of the stone walls in the Burren and the Aran Islands off Ireland – all assembled without mortar, yet withstanding the weather of centuries… And it got me thinking. Here, and in so many other parts of the world, there was indigenous work to respect and study."

The train for Djibouti, which was crammed with Italian prisoners and some South African guards and a few private passengers, had been parked in the sun for many hours, and was hot, and stank. Now freed of Mussolini's stranglehold it was also spectacularly late in departing. Ewan found himself locked in to a coupé with an Italian priest and Italian doctor, it being assumed that neither would attack him. Despite receiving charges not to fraternise, it was self-evident that they had to get along somehow – eased by Ewan offering them Springbok cigarettes and a swig or two of Opsaal brandy from a small hip flask he carried, which oiled their tongues sufficiently to discover that both of them spoke English. The priest, Father Oreste, short, dark and already beginning to lose his hair, had spent a year in an Oxford seminary before the war as part of an exchange programme. The languid medic turned out to have studied a postgraduate degree at the School of Medicine in Edinburgh. The doctor was long and bony and had eyes as sad as those of an Irish wolfhound.

The conversation drifted to questions about South Africa and what conditions were like in POW camps, of which Ewan expressed little knowledge but suggested that treatment would probably be strict but fair, South Africa and Italy being signatories to the Geneva Convention. The doctor said, "How long has your leg been in plaster?" to which Ewan replied that he had been treated a little over a fortnight before, and the doctor said, "Yes, too short. It must be very uncomfortable in this heat, but too early to remove it. If I am permitted on board ship, perhaps I will be able to remove it for you in a week's time."

Ewan thanked him and then, taking two envelopes out of a pocket, indicated that he wished to read his correspondence. Neither of his companions had any reading material, so the heat and rocking of the train soon sent them nodding off to sleep.

"Darling boy," he read.

> *I am writing to you from the escritoire in my special room, beside the sitting room. We have two new puppies that have adopted me, but I will tell you all about that later. We are constantly reminded not to 'talk about ships or shipping' and to keep whatever we write to things of a domestic nature – so I hope that the Censors will let this through without too many pencil marks! However, even the most stupid and uninformed spy will have told the enemy that we now have to endure evening lights behind heavy black-out curtains in Durban's hot and humid climate – although I'm sure you have to endure far hotter conditions up north. Believe it or not, the mosquitoes still manage to get through. I do know where they come from… your father pours paraffin into any natural reservoir they might be hidden in – like the bilbergia leaves and the old water wells.*

Dad and Emmy will be writing separately – and by separate post, so I won't steal their news, except to say that Emmy is still living with us, has joined the Navy and is engaged in work that I am not allowed to talk about – in fact don't understand; but she is working not too far away, meaning that she doesn't have to travel to work at all hours of the night, in some faraway town.

Your father's limp acquired in East Africa during the last war has become more pronounced, but, in addition to his normal duties and work, which become more numerous as most of the younger men in the office have gone off to war, has signed up as an air raid warden. We now have a notice in red, white and blue, headed 'ARP – air raid precautions' which is small enough to paste inside the door of the grandfather clock. He spends several evenings a week touring the hilltop with Bill Hirst, looking for chinks of light, but also, with his BSAP experience, acting as an auxiliary to ensure general law and order in our area.

With Kim away up north, Winnie found herself stuck in the house in Kloof with inadequate petrol, due to rationing, to travel in to town; so she has closed up the house for a few months and moved back with us. She and I tramp down the hill and across the bridge to catch the tram to Wesley Hall three days a week, where we cut sandwiches and serve tea to the troops for sixpence a generous serving. It's organised by the Victoria League.

With the assistance of the library and the book trade and the MOTHS (the Memorable Order of Tin Hats) – you may remember, it was started by Jock Leyden, the cartoonist, after the First World War – we have developed an organisation to distribute excellent *literature at low cost to any servicemen eager to read. A separate organisation has been developed to provide library services to prisoners of war and internees.*

Thanks to Father's important war work, we are at least able to utilise the car for essential journeys, although it is very difficult seeing where you're going with those ugly black tin pieces over the headlights allowing just a glimmer to escape – rather like driving with a couple of candles.

Rationing does bring some delights, however. For example, Bakers' Brothers have put up all their petrol-driven vans on bricks and now deliver bread in covered drays drawn by magnificent horse-teams with beautiful brass-decorated harnesses. The horses always seem to know when their day is done and they are turned homeward, with the driver allowing them to break into a brisk trot. Quite a noble sight.

When the humidity and heat become unbearable, we turn out all the lights and open the blackout curtains and listen to the wireless – especially the BBC overseas service, which, despite the crackles, comes through on shortwave. The Nazi English service from Zeesin is very powerful and positioned very often alongside the BBC broadcast, with that awful 'Lord Haw-haw' spewing out hateful rubbish, pretending to be the BBC service. But on the brighter side, we also receive the French service broadcasting to the underground, which always start with the 'V'-sign sounded on a full-throated drum – the 'dash' sound, a few notes higher than the three dots. It is always followed by the words, 'Ici Londre'. I believe General Charles de Gaulle broadcast on the service from London the other day.

Emmy takes great delight in listening to 'Lorna Doone' which is being serialised, while we tend to prefer 'The Forsyte Saga' from the same service. We also receive transmissions from the Radio Club of Mozambique which broadcasts 'Lyons Hits of the Week from Mozambique' which brings Emmy glued to the set. Very strange to hear advertising on radio programmes – we don't like it very much!

We had two Rhodesian ridgebacks on the farm, well before your time, but you will remember the lovely replacements with the same names, Jesse and Bess. Both of them were getting very old. I'm sad to tell you that Jesse, whom you loved so well, was attacked by a puffadder that was lurking in the night-flowering cereus in the drive opposite the postbox. Nothing we could do for her and she died very quickly, followed a few weeks later by Bess who, we think, died of a broken heart. We buried them, within weeks of each other, at the end of the mango grove, near the summerhouse. A thunderstorm was threatening with rumbles when we laid them to rest, placing a very large boulder over their grave to make sure no wild animals could get at them. It was the first time that Emmy saw her father weep. It's awful how such a beast can become so part of us. A few days ago, your Dad arrived home with two small dalmatian puppies who have received the same names as their predecessors.

Almost forgot to mention – Emmy, father and I and occasionally Winnie still go swimming at the Country Club beach next to the lifesavers' headquarters. In theory, all the beaches are now blocked off with barbed wire, but the lifesavers allow us through a zigzag path to get to the water, nevertheless. But gone are the days of the Indian peanut seller calling 'peanutzalted', although there is reasonable access at Main Beach where the rickshaw men with their staggering ornamental headdresses still hold sway.

And that's it for the moment, except to say that you are always in our hearts. Do keep up with your wonderful sketches. I remember so well how you always had a small sketchpad in your pocket with several 4B pencils and how you sketched even while waiting at the tram stop. I hope you don't mind that we have framed a collection of them which now hang above our bed, along with that oil painting of Joan of Arc kneeling before an altar holding a huge sword with the hilt in the shape of a cross – your father loves it, but I know both you and I feel it's rather sickly Pre-Raphaelite; but I'm content to keep it in place for the sake of peace in the home!

Keep safe and remember to wash behind your ears. It seems just yesterday when you were helping Chinnamama and her daughter to shell peas in the kitchen.

With love
Mother

Chapter Fourteen

Embarkation on the *Nova Scotia* was a torpid affair in such heat, but the ship finally sidled away, skirting several small islands before making the Red Sea proper and heading for Aden, then pointing southwards for Durban.

It was troubled times to ply these waters. Singapore had fallen to the Japanese early in 1942, thus throwing open the waters of the Indian Ocean to Japanese submarines and other naval craft, increasing the opportunity to harass shipping serving the Indian subcontinent, as well as more easily attacking troops and merchant ships plying between Australia, the East Coast of Africa and serving Great Britain around the Cape of Good Hope and the west African bulge.

With the fall of France, Madagascar came under Vichy control, enabling Japanese and German submarines to refuel and replenish at Madagascar ports. Thus Allied ships navigating the East Coast of Africa from the horn to Durban and the Cape had to pass through the Mozambique Channel, making them easy prey for underwater predators. The concept of convoy protection, with many merchant ships being protected by naval vessels and, to a certain extent, aerial surveillance, was principally being applied to protect ships making the perilous Atlantic crossing between the United States and Great Britain, but was not universally applied for shipping along the East Coast of Africa. Thus, the *Nova*

Scotia, like many other vessels, travelled alone with merely members of the crew serving on torpedo-watch. Steamers still used coal in those days and tunnels still belched grey smoke which was visible for miles. The ship carried a full complement of 765 Italian POWs, 134 British and South African guards, included soldiers on leave, a dozen sundry passengers like Ewan, and 118 crew members. Alta Ignisti Taylor, the widow of a British officer killed in action, and her young daughter, Valeria, were also amongst the 'sundries', along with an Anglicised Italian couple, the Piccionis, and their daughter of eighteen, Vera. Her father took pains to point out, at the breakfast table, that two of his sons were serving with the South African forces up north. Mrs Piccioni – Wendy – was a nervous woman, whose hands trembled slightly, and she was relieved to be extricated from a difficult situation and to be going home to South Africa.

The ship's Master, Alfred Hendler, sat with the 'sundry others', and arranged for Ewan's plaster cast to be removed by the ship's doctor, so there was no need to deal with the Italian prisoner-of-war doctors, who had been relegated below decks. Hendler, it was evident, was growing increasingly apprehensive about his troubled journeys; inwardly, he was relieved to pass through the Mozambique Channel without incident, the ship almost within sight of its destination, off the coast of Natal.

Unbeknownst to him, a German submarine was lurking in the waters the ship had to pass through. U-177 was equipped, unusually – as these were the early days for a new technology – with a direction-finding aerial, the forerunner of German radar. Its use helped to pick up the trail of the *Nova Scotia* on 28th November, 1942, now clearly visible through the morning sea-mist, emitting grey smoke. The submarine submerged without being detected and was positioned to aim its torpedoes with a broadside attack. It was a juicy prey, and its Commander Gysae satisfied himself that it was an enemy vessel before issuing orders to attack. Two torpedoes sped on their way to the *Nova Scotia* mid-ships and a third was aimed at the prow. All three found their mark, penetrating the hull with devastating explosions that ripped a huge gash in the side of the vessel, which began to ship water as quickly as if a reservoir had exploded.

Many prisoners were drowned within minutes, but over a hundred were swept out of the hull and found themselves flailing about in the water. As the ship pitched forward, weighed by water pouring through the gash in the prow, it was a case of every man for himself, although some of the passengers managed to escape in the only lifeboat which was launched. The hull had been so twisted out of shape by the explosions that the pedestrian hatches covering access to the decks had been torn off, allowing some prisoners to escape onto the decks before floundering off as the ship continued to settle. It was fortunate that the *Nova Scotia* had been fitted with Carley floats, designed to detach from a sinking naval vessel, providing life rafts for all those who could swim to them. The Carley was an early twentieth-century American invention which was designed to float even in high seas. It comprised of a large copper lozenge frame fleshed by substantial round cork for flotation. The centre of the lozenge was a lattice, open to the water, so that swell and waves could pass through it without danger of it 'turning turtle'.

Vera and Ewan had grown accustomed to patrolling the upper deck before breakfast – a custom not discouraged by her parents, who had taken a liking to this young wounded airman. When the bow torpedo struck, Vera and Ewan were first flung against the railing, then lifted by the volume of water as the ship began to dip, its propellers still whirring as the stern lifted out of the water. That was the last Ewan saw of her. Some officers had managed to muster a mixed bag of crew-members and some Italians who had emerged through the pedestrian hatch, and succeeded releasing the lifeboat into the water. A British officer rescued Mrs Taylor's young daughter as her mother struck out vigorously to escape the suction of the sinking vessel. It was the last she ever saw of her daughter, with her little pink jersey, sitting on the edge of the lifeboat which later sank as a result of being far too overloaded.

Ewan struck out towards the nearest Carley float crowded by Italians, who pushed him away angrily until one of them spotted the small crucifix hanging about his neck and hauled him aboard. Mrs Taylor was also dragged up, the men helping her to slump, now prostrate, in the well of the Carley. In the distance, the submarine surfaced among drowned bodies, the hatch opened and two floundering Italians were hauled aboard. When the commander of U-177 established the enormity of his mistake, he radioed Germany which in turn alerted the Portuguese authorities in Lourenço Marques, then, unable to speak Italian, but able to speak a surprising Eton-English, a German officer shouted through a loudspeaker, "I am so awfully sorry. You cannot board my vessel because I have been ordered to retreat but help is on the way from Lourenço Marques. Please convey this to prisoners. You will all just have to hang on. We have left you a float with water and some rations plus emergency medical supplies." Then the figures on the conning tower disappeared, followed by the noise of a hatch being closed shortly after; the barnacled submarine sank, accompanied by the extraordinary bubbling and churning noise, which once heard, is never forgotten.

Mutilated bodies were surfacing, blood issuing from

gruesome wounds that soon attracted sharks, which dragged under many still half-alive men emitting shrieks that would haunt Ewan's nightmares for the rest of his life.

There were many survivors, Italian, British and South African – some on Carley floats, others pinned to flotsam, but when the frigate *Alonso du Albuquerque* arrived the crew realised that they were surrounded by a soup of floating mutilated bodies, relieved, here and there by people barely alive clinging to floats of one kind or another.

A day had passed before the frigate arrived, and during that time, Ewan drifted in and out of consciousness. His mind went back to childhood when his sister and he were given bicycles which led them to explore past the mission tree, an elderly relic, half-fallen, whose broken branches had sent numerous roots to aid its survival... past the Hirsts, until they reached the wood-and-iron shed of the Blourokkies, where they stole up to peek through rusty rivet-holes to watch a circle of grey-clad ladies dancing to their unique God... Past Mr McAlpine Rind's small old house, until they reached the edge of the known universe, The Whynot Tearoom, to guzzle creamy scones, smothered in butter, blackcurrant jam and cream, as they made sucking noises through straws plunged into chocolate milkshakes.

The saltwater enhanced the subtropical sun, and Ewan was conscious of his skin burning and reddening before the night brought Heaven-sent relief. The Indian Ocean is a restless god, permanently tormented by the westerly wind which drives in from the Atlantic, around the Cape of Storms, and parts, one part for Australasia with the other part driving up the Mozambique Channel. Further east, the seabeds are troubled by underwater eruptions. The result is a permanent swell with troughs and peaks, in bad weather, reaching fifteen feet or more. This permanent swell culminates in the crackle, crash and slump of giant breakers collapsing on Natal's beaches. This self-same swell makes clambering aboard any vessel dangerous, even for muscular seamen, and well-nigh impossible for exhausted survivors. These weather conditions were encountered by the Portuguese frigate. Clambering nets were let down, but members of the crew had to descend and almost carry survivors deckwards. The woman, Mrs. Taylor, was lifted first followed by the most exhausted-looking, Ewan being helped among the last. The saltwater had sloughed off the skin of some of them, in parts, but Ewan had escaped this ordeal. The last moment he remembered after being blanketed and vomiting up the proffered soup, before he passed out, was the woman's faint hysteria about the loss of her child.

The lifeboat and the small girl were never seen again, though her little pink jacket was eventually found washed up some weeks later.

Chapter Fifteen

The British Consulate in Lourenço Marques was a splendid, double-storey white painted building, with a deep verandah on the first floor. Generous sash windows allowed for cool zephyrs to work through the building and were sympathetic with the Portuguese architecture of similar buildings in the colony. It was sultry, and the lining of clouds rumbled with distant thunder that sounded like empty beer barrels being rolled down a cobbled incline.

Malcolm Muggeridge, Vice-Consul and Special Correspondent (although this title was explained rather vaguely by him as being the fellow who had to ensure that official letters to Britain were maintained to a high standard) was sipping his sundowner of gin and bitters on the upstairs verandah just outside his French doors, when the message arrived from London. It should have been passed on to his superiors, but the Consul and the Ambassador were away attending an end-of-the-season function in the garden of the Portuguese Commercial Counsellor, which Muggeridge had managed to avoid, claiming pressure of work. It had been decoded by the rather sultry Maria Dalgarno, who worked, as did Muggeridge, for MI5. It simply read "TOP SECRET. *Nova Scotia* sunk off Natal coast today. Provide best reception British and South African survivors likewise civilians. Ensure Geneva Italian prisoners. Meet Portuguese frigate Afonso de

Albuquerque LM. On no account reveal this source. Fabricate something if asked." On receipt of the message, Muggeridge resolved to invite the LM harbourmaster to join him for an overview drink on the terrace of the Polana Hotel, and invited Maria to accompany him – persuading her that she needed a break from all the extra work in which she was engaged over the weekend. She was not married, dedicated to work and her mind was occupied with what to do for the rest of the weekend.

The Harbour Master Miguel Rafael was already there when they arrived, and had already ordered a bottle of Dao. Malcolm enjoyed Miguel's company and they had formed an easy, casual friendship over the last year, during which the latter would unburden his complaints about his workers, their laziness and their thievery; he had also met Maria on other occasions and enjoyed the fact that he could communicate with her in Portuguese, if necessary.

"Hello, hello!" he said, rising and shaking hands with both of them. "I cannot stay long – there is a big (how you say) 'flap'. A British ship has been sunk south-east of LM... Lots of life lost, and one of our frigates has been sent out to help rescue hundreds of people in the water. They are mainly Italian prisoners of war; many arrangements have to be made for hospitalisation and general treatment. There are also some British and South African troops among them, so the flap is to keep them apart. Of course, they will all have to be detained until the end of the war. I'm in charge of co-ordination when they come ashore."

"Good Lord! How did you hear?"

"Germany radioed the naval base here – so I was alerted. You know how it is. We are neutral, so must be even-handed for both sides. There is an Italian ship in the harbour, for example, which we have forced to remain for the duration of hostilities. I will be alerting the Italian consul and you had better inform your authorities to be present at the dockside when survivors arrive. I suppose that someone from the German consulate will be there too. We would just ask everyone to be civilised and keep their distance."

All this, of course, was the perfect excuse for Muggeridge to have received neutral notification. What the Germans and Italians did not know was that all coded information passing between vessels of the Kriegsmarine had been compromised by the code being broken, and, likewise, cables exchanged between the German and Italian authorities in LM passed through South Africa and found their way to Bletchley Park, where they were being read. All this had to be concealed, so he was delighted to receive news of the event from a neutral source.

"And here I was hoping for a pleasant sundowner followed by a slow dinner which included somewhere in it a platter of Polana langoustine, joined by you and your lovely wife. When is the frigate expected to dock?"

"Late tonight – probably after eleven."

"Then there is still time! Maria, I am sorry to have to burden you with this, but your help at the docks would be much appreciated. We can at least eat a quick meal here after which we will have to drag our consul away to the docks. We'll be able to leave the ambassador there, although protocol says he should leave first... He'll sort it out."

The hull of the rescue frigate was floodlit, and lights ablaze on the superstructure signalled that it was a neutral vessel. The naval dockyard on Mozambique Island was likewise well lit – implicitly declaring that LM was not at war with anyone, although the reception groups on the quayside could suggest otherwise. The Italian group clustered about Umberto Campini and his aide Alfredo Manna; they might have otherwise glared at Muggeridge's small party. A German was also present at the quayside: Luitpold Werz, doing his best to placate the injured pride of the Italians. Also, seemingly out of place, were representatives of the Japanese consulate.

"Ho-ho," Muggeridge said to Maria, "there's 'Mussolini' himself – or he would rather like to think he is, complete with swirling his damned red and grey cloak around his shoulders. What a charmingly ghastly person. That little rat standing beside him is Manna, his chief spy, who spends his time monitoring our ships and transmitting details to Japan, with the help of those knee-high midgets standing close to him."

It was raining heavily again, and dock lights picked out the rain and the figures huddled together like penguins under whatever shelter there was. Coaches had been backed into the Customs warehouse which opened onto the quay, all set to transport the Italian survivors to a recuperation centre set up by the Portuguese.

Muggeridge had arranged for an independent coach to transport the allied survivors to the consulate and temporary accommodation. Blanketed Italian troops were the first to emerge, preceded by more than a dozen stretchered men, after the frigate was winched and secured. Only after the Italian consul was known to board one of the coaches loaded with the Italians did the harbourmaster give the signal for the allied troops to proceed down the gangway. There were only seven of them, including Ewan and Mrs Taylor, assisted by a doctor who had gone out on the frigate's rescue mission.

Holding on to the gangway railing and treading with uncertain footsteps to reach the dockside, Ewan found himself staring into a raincoated figure, strangely familiar, and said, "Have you stopped pulling wings off moths yet, Luitpold?"

Luitpold Werz started with recognition, and, extraordinarily, clicked his heels, the movement sending water drops flying off his raincoat. Then, after a long pause, he said, "Well, at least you are still alive. Are your parents well? And Miss Scobie? No, I gave up collecting butterflies and moths after I received some training for shooting the wings off enemy aircraft. I see you are in the Air Force, but I followed a career in diplomacy," upon which he turned on his heels and disappeared into the gloom. "You're going to lose the war, Herr Werz," Ewan shouted after him, and a distant voice came back, "But not the peace!"

"You do realise we have to turn you in, immediately you leave the consulate?" Muggeridge said at breakfast the next day, as the survivors were struggling to keep their food down. "Ewan, as the most senior officer here, I would like to have a quiet word with you, in due course. Mrs Taylor, I cannot say how sorry I am to hear that your daughter is still missing, and I assure you every effort will be made to find out where that lifeboat is. I do know that you were travelling on to Durban and I will see what arrangements I can make with the Portuguese authorities, to allow you to travel on to South Africa... But all this is for the future, and feel free to stay in the consulate, all of you, until you are fully recovered. And now you must excuse me – even though it's Sunday, work calls. The staff will attend to your needs; please do not leave the consulate premises. Officer Kirkwood, my assistant, Maria, will call down in about an hour's time and fit you in. Meanwhile, feel free to write letters or help yourself to reading material – there are plenty of *Punch, Picture-Post* and *Illustrated London News* lying about... even some worthwhile books in our little library. My dog's name is Wellington, by the way, and please don't feed him! The cat's name is Tabitha; she likes being petted...

"I have engaged a full-time nurse to help you; her name is Sr Rosa and she strongly recommends your resting for the next few days in the temporary nursing section we have set up for you. My wife, Catherine, will be visiting you a bit later on, and do please put any special requests you might have to her."

As Muggeridge talked, Ewan thought, illogically, of arriving home in Durban by tram in the twilight, and passing, sleepily, the Congregational church in Greyville, with its huge flashing neon sign, alternating between JESUS SAVES and JESUS RED. Never having been exposed to Afrikaans in his youth, he was always puzzled by the flashing -RED part, and wondered occasionally whether the church was suggesting that Jesus was a Communist. By this stage the neon English version SAVES had gone out, leaving the word JESUS to flash on and off by itself.

Then Ewan watched Muggeridge as he stepped up the winding stairs, past the official portrait of King George VI and the Queen, and disappeared into his office.

Chapter Sixteen

It was a foggy morning when Miss Wainwright came into Keswick's office carrying a roll of posters, so fresh from the printers that they still smelt of printer's ink, and asked Jardine, "What do they expect us to do with these? They arrived this morning from the Civilian Defence Unit."

The placards were emblazoned with the picture of a sinking ship and the slogan, 'DON'T TALK ABOUT SHIPS OR SHIPPING', at the sight of which Jardine chuckled, and said, "And how the hell do they think we are going to do our job in the harbour, with that in mind! I suppose you had better tell someone in Admin to distribute the posters about the area. The CDU's enthusiasm is commendable but somewhat misplaced. I see the notices going up all over the place, but with the town and harbour overrun with ships coming in and out, and transiting ships, the CDU is to be excused. Half the Royal Navy top brass was in my office here yesterday when you were at lunch, bombarding me with sundry requests covering maritime control – including all those bloody ships parked outside in the roadstead – sitting ducks for enemy attack. Thank God there hasn't been any, as yet. I tried to be civil, but the Navy seems to think that only they know all about the harbour and logistics... And that Walrus flying up and down watching out for submarine engines..." (the Walrus light seaplane was used as a submarine

spotter by being catapulted from Australian naval vessels.)
"It's noisy enough to frighten away the enemy – just to get
away from all that clattering noise! Trust the Australian Navy
to fly around in a contraption like that – dead give-away;
so many Australian ships have disgorged men to wander
around the streets for a few days. I can just imagine what the
AWB radio network is making of it, reporting to Lourenço
Marques! What we are doing is getting the whole lot in,
then docking them side-by-side like an out-of-work fishing
fleet – that includes an aircraft carrier which will only be able
to enter at high tide with about an inch to spare between the
hull and the seabed. As you can see, our tugs are having a jolly
time...Imagine what would happen if a mini-sub managed to
sneak in with them. Well, everything is underway, staff and
navy have everything under control and there is little more
I can do – you can do – but to sit here and bite our nails."

After a day's exasperation, Keswick said, "I think we
must take the rest of the night off – you have a household
to attend to, the night staff know what to do and all I can
think of is getting back to my wife and that flamboyant
tree – you must come up to the house again soon. Splendid
sight: the bougainvillea has even got into the palm trees and
is flowering, along with the jacaranda trees. As I was going
home the other evening, they were all set off magnificently
against a dark stormy sky. What a sight!"

In truth, Keswick, well past peacetime retirement age, was
finding himself to be weary all the time – whereas before he
could run up the stairs to his office two steps at a time, now
he found himself clutching banisters to aid his progress – and
time had not stood still for Miss Wainwright, either, though
her greying hair had been kept at bay by more frequent
excursions to Mrs McNabb, her hairdresser.

"Good evening, Jeeves. Is the missus there? Let me speak

to her, please," Keswick said, phoning home before leaving his office. When Cordelia came to the phone, he said, "Hello, darling; are you and the household up to my bringing home a couple of servicemen for a meal…? The whole of Durban seems to be doing it, so I suppose we had better do our bit."

"All right then, but they must go back no later than ten-thirty. I've been making sandwiches down at the Victoria League all day – incredible how many sandwiches these soldiers eat. Mabel drove me home – or rather, Tommy, her chauffeur, did. I wish she would get a car with a roof, instead of that fancy hood, especially designed NOT to keep out the rain. But you know how it is with rationing; I've no idea what we can feed them…but I've no doubt Jeeves and his wife could do something extra."

As Keswick was leaving, he spotted three young naval officers looking lost, and walking up towards the customs and security barrier; so he stopped, and said, "I am the harbourmaster, and you fellows are looking a little lost – it's quite a long walk to town, so I was wondering if I could give you a lift?" News had spread amongst visiting troops that Durban had opened its heart to them, so Keswick's stopping the car within the dockyard and inviting three young officers home was not as unusual as it might have seemed.

They jumped at the chance and piled into the car, saying, "We have no idea of where we're going, and what to do. Somebody warned us to stay away from the Playhouse, whatever that is, because the Australians have taken it over as their official drinking hole, so we decided to avoid that and find something else. Have you any suggestions?"

"Well, you are welcome to refuse, but I wondered if you could do with a meal up at our house – then we could run you back to the docks before curfew?"

They accepted with alacrity, after exchanging glances of

delight, and so it was that they found themselves winding up the Berea to the Jardine home. "I dare say you do get pretty good grub, but this could make a change from the usual diet. I warned my wife that I might be inviting some lost sailors home to our house, so she and the staff are going to do their best. Certain things are in short supply, like white bread, but there's plenty of other stuff to fill in the corners. Mind the coconuts," he said as they arrived and the men jumped out, pointing up at one of the coconut trees they were standing under. "This way… Onto the terrace. I'll just dart in and let my wife know. French doors – just stand clear them. If you need to wash and brush up you'll find the ablutions down the first passage on the right. By the way, my wife's name is Cordelia, and you will be served by Jeeves (he likes to be called that, Jeeven being his real name – but he's a Wodehouse fan) and his wife, without whom our whole household would fall apart, though we do have a couple of other employees."

It turned out that the men were from HMS *Eagle*, the aircraft carrier, which towered above the other vessels in the harbour. It had been constructed for the Chilean Navy, but purchased by Britain before completion and configured as an aircraft carrier, instead of as a battleship. It had seen invaluable service in the Mediterranean, facilitating the attack on Italian naval vessels and submarines, before its visit to Durban.

During drinks at the terrace, the men described with some amusement and awe how a small impi of Zulus had been invited on to the flight deck through arrangement with the mayor and the captain. In full traditional regalia, they had stamped and shouted their war dance, watched in fascination by the crew, most of whom had seen nothing like it before or indeed encountered black men in the flesh. At the end of the dance, which had the whole deck trembling from the exertions of the stamping feet, the impi was mustered onto the hydraulic lift platform and then lowered to the flight storage deck to be taken on a tour of the ship, and fed magnificently.

A sense of homely cheerfulness from a lone figure of a woman, dressed in white, singing farewell through a metal megaphone to troopships departing from the harbour for destinations up north. Her name was Pearl Siedle Gibson, and she was even there on the day she received news that her son had been lost in action. Allegedly, it started when a soldier shouting from an incoming troopship had asked her to sing, 'When Irish Eyes are Smiling'; and she obliged, and the tradition was born. She always wore a bright red hat.

Jeeves surpassed himself with pea soup, followed by roast chicken, potatoes, Yorkshire pudding and pumpkin smothered in gravy, which Jeeves had developed into a black art of deliciousness. It was rounded off by chocolate blancmange, and ice cream with wafer biscuits.

Keswick said, "We are not allowed to talk about ships or shipping, but as harbourmaster I can hardly avoid knowing that you three fellows are off the aircraft carrier. It was a tight squeeze getting you in – with inches to spare. I was there on the flight deck when that impi of Zulu warriors put on a war-dance – arranged between your captain and our mayor. Made the flight deck tremble."

"I thought I recognised your face, sir! I think the Zulus were as surprised as we were when they sank on the hydraulic lift to the crew's quarters and storage! I believe they were fairly awestruck being taken on a tour below decks."

While the port was circulating, and Cordelia had got them talking about home and undertaking to write to all their parents, Jardine said, "As harbourmaster, you'll understand that I have a pretty good idea of what is going on, though officially we can't talk about ships or shipping. I did pick up a rumour that there had been a nasty torpedoing off the Natal coast. Did you come across anything?"

The men glanced at each other and the one who seemed to have been elected to speak for the others, said, "We believe there's an enemy submarine in the area, and it torpedoed a ship carrying a lot of Italian prisoners of war, and a lot of lives have been lost. Nasty business, sir. That's all we know." Then, glancing at his watch, he said, "I'm afraid we must return, sir."

"I can confirm that loss of a ship, but mum's the word. Not good for morale," said Keswick. And then they piled into the car driven by Jeeves to be taken back to their ship, after expressing their profuse thanks and with much waving.

When Keswick and Cordelia walked out to the terrace, from which there was a view of the town, harbour and sea, not a vessel could be seen anywhere, except for a floodlit white-hulled hospital ship, making its way towards the harbour entrance.

"That's another shipload of wounded for Wentworth and Baragwanath," Keswick muttered to Cordelia, as they waved the men into the car. Wentworth had been set up as a fever hospital on the Bluff but was now converted to treat wounded servicemen. Other injured men requiring long-term care were taken by train to Baragwanath hospital, just outside Johannesburg.

When Keswick could be 'called away from his wretched harbour' as Cordelia put it, it had become customary for them to meet up with Donald, Prue and Emilia, when she could get away, at the so-called Country Club Beach, north of the other beaches; and separate from the other beaches, popular because it was beside the Lifesavers building. The approach to the beach was blocked off by barbed wire, but there was a zigzag passage through it kept open for early-morning bathers. It was 6 o'clock on Sunday, 30th November, 1942 – a beautiful silvery morning. The custom was to be clad in swimwear and then change for breakfast after bathing. The breakers were crashing and roaring that morning, with white horses appearing far out to sea.

"The sharks like this kind of water, so just be careful! Keep your eyes open!" – as if that would help if a shark attacked. Every time Donald went into the water, the scene of Zeno being attacked by a shark came to his mind. But floating in the foam and tumbling in the breakers were strange dark shapes that could have been thick logs of wood. Strips of clothing trailed from some of them. Washed up high and entangled with strands of seaweed was a small child's pink coat.

There was a strong backwash that day, so some of the bodies moved and rolled back with the receding water. A stray dog stood over one of the bodies and snarled when Keswick and Donald approached.

"My God, what a sight," Keswick said, gesturing to the women to stay away. "We must tell the authorities and get them to clear up this mess. Obviously, no one else has seen them yet. Well, no bathing today, and we had better get to a telephone as quickly as possible."

The women complied, got back into the car and Donald drove across the road up to the entrance of the Club, where Keswick got out, still dressed only in a beach gown, to ring on the doorbell. Being Sunday, early staff were preparing for a busy day of golfers and luncheons. It was freckled-faced Betty who came to the door and said, "We're not open yet."

"I must use your phone urgently, please."

"Are you a member, sir? And we can't let you in like that… Even if you are a member, we can't let you in like that."

"Bugger the dress code, and of course I'm a member – this is a matter of life and death, and let me in," he said. They pushed past her and rushed to the reception desk to look for a phone.

"Is that Salisbury Island? Put me through to acting Chief-of-Staff. Hello, is that you, Sam?" he said and went on to describe the discovery, asking him to tell the police, to close off all beaches and start mopping-up operations immediately – with any assistance required from the harbour authority.

The party then repaired to Chelmsford to eat a glum Sunday breakfast, as the Christmas beetles began to start up with their deafening screeching – first falteringly then with a permanent singing that made it almost impossible to hold a conversation near them. The insects, thousands of them, were clustered together in the golden oak trees – and 'ware any person that stood below the branches – a kind of sticky spit secreted by the beetles would drop on them.

Chapter Seventeen

It was Saturday, 12th December 1942, during a late breakfast at Chelmsford. Near Stalingrad, the German VI Army had launched an offensive in an attempt to break out of the encirclement in which the Russian army had them trapped, the BBC was announcing, when Frikkie Smidt, the local telegram boy, stopped his bicycle to wipe the sweat from his forehead. He wore a thick-woven, impractical khaki green uniform, trimmed in red, and was very overheated by the time he had reached Clarkson's corner, where Mount Argus Road branched off to the left at the start of Buttery Road. Here, the incline eased off, and the cyclist remounted to ride the rest of the way to Chelmsford. The dogs barked and the Shetland ponies lifted their heads and briefly stopped grazing to look at the stranger coming down the drive. Prue read the ominous telegram with a sinking heart: REGRET OFFICER EWAN KIRKWOOD PRESUMED MISSING AT SEA – NOVEMBER. LETTER FOLLOWS.

"Chi-Chinna-Chinnam-ma, g-g-ive the m-m-messenger some bread and jam and a m-mu-g of w-water. Curse you, Donald, I knew this would happen!" On the wireless, the BBC announcer on shortwave was giving more details of the offensive launched by the Soviet troops against the encircled German Sixth Army, in the depths of the freezing Russian winter.

"How on earth can he be 'missing at sea'? We know he

is up in East Africa, somewhere. Surely they have it wrong."

A huge void opened as both their minds attempted to come to terms with the news. Prue suddenly got up and left the room, ignoring the shattered plate – one of her rings had caught the embroidered tablecloth and pulled part of it, bringing her plate and cutlery with it. It was Spode willow pattern, and that particular plate had always irritated her to look at, because the pattern on the rim did not join properly.

Donald found her sitting in Ewan's study, in his favourite chair. She was staring, unseeing, through the wobbly old glass of the sash windows, past the giant fig trees and the glimpse of Red Hill in the distance. Ewan had stressed that his belongings should be left untouched, so that – when he did come home on leave – everything would be as it was when he had gone to war. Donald had managed to get hold of Emilia, and after he had joined Prue, he heard the crunch of her bicycle. She worked at the Y-station next door, so did not have far to come. She came into Ewan's study and sat with her parents, saying nothing. It was as if Ewan had just left the room... His sketches were on the walls...his drawing desk on its turned legs, with a slip of wood under one leg... the model glider he had built still hanging from the ceiling.

The servants' bush telegraph spread quickly and soon they were all sitting beneath the giant fig trees, from which one of its creaking limbs the children's swing was suspended. It had always been the children's favourite playing area, and even when Ewan had come back on leave, one of the first things he did was sit on the swing. The group sat silently, cross-legged. They sat there all day and dispersed only at sunset.

Cordelia sat with Prue and Donald in the dark for a while, before going out and closing the door gently. She joined Winnie and the two men on the front veranda in the dark, sipping whisky slowly, and staring out to sea. The

Jardines stayed overnight, and went to bed early, curled up like two foetuses.

"I suppose his name will appear in the 'Missing' column of the *Mercury* on Monday morning," Donald muttered. "I believe St Thomas's is holding a service tomorrow for, as they put it, 'Those that go down to the sea in ships' but I am disinclined to attend. I suppose all that mumbo-jumbo brings comfort to some of those who are left – but I am not one of them. It's too soon, anyway – people do turn up and neither Prue nor I are ready to face up to comforting words from church friends…Especially those who recall how so-and-so lost their lives. I don't care to hear about others at all."

Weeks later, Cordelia called her daughter Prue and prevailed upon her to join her in town in search of embroidery wool, which was now virtually unobtainable – using this device to lever her out of her sadness and lethargy. "Jeeves's wife whispered to me that embroidery wool can be found under the counter at Moosa's in Grey Street. Well, I can't possibly go there alone, and I fear being jostled in these wartime streets, so please persuade Winnie to join us upstairs in John Orr's tearoom, after which we can venture out to darkest Grey Street."

And thus they sallied forth, after arming themselves with tea and anchovy toast. The tearoom remained a ladies' 'sanctum sanctorum' into which defensive personnel never ventured. The jostling crowds thinned as they made their way up to an unfamiliar street, when Cordelia said, "I must sit down somewhere, for a while. Could we just go into the Catholic cathedral – never been into such a place before."

The grey colonnaded interior was cool and deserted, save for a few supplicants dotted here and there. A figure was lighting four penny candles, before returning to sit staring at a sculpture of the Virgin Mary. Coloured light shone in through the stained-glass windows, donated by the Empress Eugenie in memory of her son Louis-Napoleon, killed by Zulu warriors in 1879 in an ambush during the Anglo-Zulu War.

"Blimey!" Winnie muttered. "They do go in for a lot of carvings and statues – almost as if the congregation is illiterate and needs these reminders to keep them focused. All those Via Dolorosa carvings on the walls."

"Nevertheless, I find it peaceful and a place where prayer has meaning. I'm going to go light a candle and say a prayer for Ewan." The other two followed, in sympathy, fished for change to drop in the candle box and then, finding they had no matches, Winnie walked across to the candles burning before the Virgin Mary to catch the flame with one of their candles. They sat in the front row; then, impulsively, Prue knelt and closed her eyes in prayer, followed by Cordelia, while Winnie remained sitting silently in Presbyterian contemplation.

"Dear God, if you really do exist, and I have great difficulty in believing it, please find my son and return him alive and safe to us. If it is not your will, then help me to understand." An Indian priest entered at that moment by a door with a bucket, and proceeded to empty the candle coins into it with a disturbing jingle and rattle; but, noticing the three women, he came along and said, "Are you members of the congregation? I couldn't help wondering if something was troubling you?"

"We are not Catholics, Father, and came in out of the heat, but we were moved by the peacefulness; and my daughter has heard recently that her son, my grandson, has been reported missing."

"Then it is not certain, but he could still be alive. It is up to the Almighty to hold out hope; allow me to pray with you for a moment. There is only one Almighty; it's not for me to say that your prayers would not be heard. There are a million paths to the Great Architect, and ours is not the only one." Whereupon he knelt down with them and prayed, making the sign of the cross over them when he rose to go.

Chapter Eighteen

"Sorry it's taken so long to see you. All this bumph," Muggeridge said to Ewan, gesturing to piles of paperwork in trays. "Just imagine how much I would have to set fire to if we were overrun! One of the bigger bonuses of working in a neutral territory like Mozambique is enjoying the quality of the Portuguese coffee. Would you like a cup, or something stronger? You and your companions have had a very rough ride indeed. I hope you are beginning into recover... I expect it will take weeks. Ghastly business."

Muggeridge's office was large, and a muddle between officialdom and a typical journalist's: typewriter and a powerful-looking transceiver, a fireproof filing-cabinet and an expansive table beside his desk. They were sitting in easy chairs near the French windows.

"The reason I asked you was not only to enquire about your progress of recovery but to discuss ways and means of getting you and your chums back to South Africa."

"That sounds rather interesting – may I ask, is that the regular function of a vice consul in a neutral territory – I gather you told me you were the vice consul?"

"The answer is 'yes' the first, and 'no' to the second. In theory, I would have to release you into the arms of the Portuguese who would be obliged to keep you confined to barracks until the end of the war. But I have a plan which will make trouble if it is bungled. It should work according to plan; but if anything goes wrong, I could protest my ignorance and innocence. But before we go into all that, I have to swear you to secrecy and must warn you (this is the usual procedure) that betrayal of what I have to tell you to the enemy could attract the death penalty. So, at this point, I must ask you if you agree to the conditions, before we go on."

"Well, you know that, as an Air Force man, I'm sworn to secrecy anyway – so the answer is yes."

"Just to fill out the corners, I'm a journalist in wolf's clothing. Before the war I did a spot of teaching in Cairo before I was appointed by the *Telegraph* as foreign correspondent to Moscow. I was convinced that communism was the answer when I went there, but came back revolted by what I saw that monster Stalin doing to his country – nowadays I am in implacable opposition to all he stands for. The term 'Vice-Consul' and Special Correspondent covers a multitude of irregular things, and in fact I work for an outfit called MI5 – in other words British Intelligence, or at least a section of it. I see that you are wearing a small crucifix around your neck. Do I assume that you're Catholic?"

"No. Just a 'high days and holidays' Anglican – not sure if I believe in anything now – except that this talisman saved my life... I was trying to get on board a float with the Italian soldiers who angrily pushed me away until one of them caught sight of this crucifix and relented, pulling me aboard. I just wonder what happened to the priest... A harmless little fellow – I suppose he went west with the rest of them."

Muggeridge said, "That's a lucky talisman indeed... Better hang on to it. I confess I don't really want to believe – a friend of mine in Moscow once remarked, when I expressed my complete disillusionment of communism, that I was a libertine in search of God. But at the moment, I'm stuck halfway on the road to Damascus. By the way, I saw you greeting Luitpold Werz... How'd you know him?"

"Of course, he is much older than I, but he used to board at Chelmsford, my parents' house in Durban when he was studying law. My parents knew his uncle, mother and aunt when both parties were farming in Zululand. Luitpold was an amateur lepidopterist and used to go on butterfly hunts with a Miss Scobie, the sister of a scientist friend of my parents, Dr James Scobie."

"Well, you might as well know that Scobie always worked for us, and your parents did a lot of useful work for us over the years monitoring the von Weldenburgs, who were German masquerading as Swiss."

"That explains a lot of things... I overheard my parents talking about it. My father fought against the Germans in East Africa in the last war and developed a long-standing suspicion of their tactics."

"The husband has been the channel between Germany and the OBs, but is getting a bit long in the tooth, and since the family settled in Mozambique he has become a prosperous farmer of sugarcane, mielies and cashew nuts – those are some of his in this bowl. Drives around in an antique Horch which could be his downfall. I don't think his wife Frieda is involved – spends her time running a little school and welfare for the local indigenes with her ageing sister. Von Weldenburg makes the mistake of having his car serviced by our garage man, Harry Grimes – an appropriate name, that. By the way, did you participate in the invasion of Madagascar? Fantastic operation between South African and British forces... I don't think the Vichy French knew what had hit them."

"Yes, I flew Lysanders – just the job for that marshy territory. Short take-off and landing on a difficult terrain. A

French-speaking couple, originally from Durban, played a great part. He had developed a successful import and export business between Durban and the island (his parents were important farmers there – even marketed their own wines). Later he transferred his business to Mozambique and set up a similar operation servicing the Diego Suarez periphery. Got to know the Vichy naval people rather well, who took him on a tour of the naval dockyard and fortifications. Little did they know that his wife operated a clandestine transmitter in their attic, providing details to us in Durban. Despite receiving warnings that the Vichy were on to them, she went on transmitting up to and during the Madagascan invasion – despite the fact that her husband, Jean-Pierre, had been arrested and was facing trial and probable execution. As luck would have it, he managed to escape when the invasion took place and his jailers ran away. Truly, if anyone deserves a monument in Durban after the war, it's those two."

"Good Lord, I remember them. Great friends of my parents... He, Jean-Pierre, and my father used to sail a BRA (I think it stands for British Rowing Association) clinker-built dinghy in the harbour. Of course, they moved up to higher things, but still went sailing in the BRA occasionally for old time's sake. They used to make it plane, even though it wasn't designed to do so. His boat was a bit of a giggle at the club."

At this point, Muggeridge excused himself and went to the radio, saying, "Help yourself to a whisky... Might seem a little light-hearted, but I must listen to the beginning of this programme." A girl's voice talking in Portuguese came on, terminating in the Portuguese national anthem; then she announced, "Zees eez zee Radio Clerb of Mozambique," after which a distinctly South African voice said, "...And this is what we have all been waiting for, Lyon's Hits of Mozambique! What will be the top hit this week? Will

'Chattanooga Choo-Choo' still be on top? But first here's the answer to last week's question – in what state of America would you be served ham and eggs aboard the Chattanooga Express? We got over 1,000 entries, and, of course, the answer is the state of Carolina! And the prize goes to the first correct entry we opened, Sam Shuttleworth of South Broome! £50 prize will be posted to him from South Africa, along with a picnic hamper of Lyons Tea and other products. Congratulations, Sam, and to the family. Now who is going to answer the question successfully this week…? Listen very carefully. We'll ask it in the end of the programme." Muggeridge moved to turn off the set again, muttering, "Good, good." Then he explained: "Just indicates that we have managed to confuse the bloody Italians. Can't explain. But this leads me on to where I need your help. Another splash? Help yourself – and one for the road too. Okay? Here goes…

"Spying from a neutral country is a damn sight safer than operating inside enemy territory. It has risks… One could be arrested and imprisoned, but that would be as far as it would go. So we are all doing it, the Krauts, the Italians, no doubt the Americans too, and us – not only here in Mozambique but in places like Portugal-friendly Brazil, Switzerland, Ireland, Spain and Portugal. The Germans are particularly active in the Argentine and Chile – spreading rumours, nasty propaganda and attempting to sabotage Brazilian exports to Britain. Despite what you might see in the papers, it's nice to know that the Republic of Ireland is discreetly helpful behind the scenes. That applies to Portugal as well, though Spain is decidedly pro-German, but fortunately broke after their Civil War, so determined to stay out of the fray. Lots of Germans pretending to play tennis while overlooking the Gibraltar border, however.

"I was sent out here to get rid of that Italian, the Consul – but by that I don't mean slaughter him, but rather just to disable him and his shenanigans. That applies to his sidekick, Manna. The Italian is involved in some strictly non-consular business in a neutral territory. This involves sending reports of allied ship movements up-and-down the East Coast of Africa. He is harvesting reports from the Japanese consul in Cape Town, and right-winger reports from Durban and Pretoria. These are channelled through a powerful transmitter on the Italian vessel quarantined in the LM harbour to Germany. It is probable that he is indirectly responsible for the sinking of, not only the *Nova Scotia* but a lot of other vessels as well. Troop movements, from Australia and New Zealand, touching on Durban then heading north, are going to be huge in the months to come; likewise from South Africa, Rhodesia and Kenya. Although the Italians have been immobilised in East Africa, this does not affect continuing espionage by this bloody Italian. His sidekick spends his time at the Penguin club, near the docks, chatting to drunken sailors and extracting vital information. The bar girls are particularly attractive there – especially one of them called Rosa, who is in our pay. Our friend Umberto – who likes to swagger like Mussolini – also haunts the Penguin Club. Our man Harry Grimes will slip them knockout Mickey Finns after being enticed by Rosa and a friend into a car provided by Harry – at which point you and your friends will get in as well, and the girls leave. There will be another car to mop up the overflow and then you and the other driver will head for the Zululand border. Harry is a first-class mechanic, and although the largest-possible old American cars appear ramshackle, they will be in tiptop mechanical condition. We have an agent at the border who will 'magic' you through. You will have to drive as far as Empangeni, whence our agents take over, in conjunction with the South Africans. From that point you will proceed to Durban and go about your business. That's the plan and it should take place in about a week's time, allowing us to get everything in place. The Portuguese will be rather angry but I will deal with that – just so long as I am not associated with the disappearance of the Italians."

"What will happen to the Italians?"

"Oh, they will be kept under lock and key at Zonderwater – along with the rest of the Eyeties. No doubt they will be put into safe houses, perhaps by the Portuguese, who would see it as an intrusion of consular politics in a neutral country, but dear old Umberto will have no hope of release until Italy capitulates. On the other hand, Manna is a very good spy and I'm sure the South Africans will do their best to wring him dry of information and suggest that he works for them – after all, the Italians really are on a losing ticket... After this rumpus, I have no doubt that my enraged Ambassador will insist that I am called back to London...That will be the plan, anyway. Harry Grimes will remain in place. He is full of plans to flush paraffin through von Wellenburg's Horch's hydraulic brake system, so that next time the driver steps on the brakes, the tubes, weakened by paraffin, will collapse – but, I don't know, it might be just as well to leave him alone, as the Italian was the worst threat, and to leave the German in place means we can continue to monitor communications with Germany. Besides, we don't want to bump off his wife, by accident... and he does grow the best cashews in Mozambique!"

Chapter Nineteen

Although Club do Pinquine was in the downtrodden area close to the docks and was patronised by its fair share of sailors passing through, attracting in their turn the best of the bar girls, of all pigments from negro Shangaans through mixed-blood Mulattos to the palest of pale, it also brought in well-to-do foreigners out to 'slum it' – not least Umberto Campini and some of his German consul friends. The neon sign at the entrance had known better days, and fizzled alarmingly as it switched, naming the club by a graphic of the Penguin. Though down-at-heel, the club owner knew his business, and expanded it by employing a mournful fado singer and guitarist to attract Portuguese émigrés longing for home, while consuming in a dim light platters of prawns and crayfish laced with peri-peri sauce. The fug was thick with Portuguese cigarette smoke, the sweetish odour of dagga, of beer, and the whiff of cheap perfume.

Rosa and her friend snuggled up to Umberto Campini and Fulvio Manna at a table in the corner, devouring spaghetti (a concession to the Italians) and prawns enlivened with peri-peri, and accompanied by white plaited bread and goblets of Dao.

Rosa was beautiful. She was a pale mulatto who had been cut adrift when her parents had died in a car accident. She grew up in the poorest part of Lorenço Marques, and had been raped when young by a friend of her brother's. It had been inevitable that she would be lost to prostitution as the only means of survival. Harry Grimes had plans to extricate her from the downward spiral, though now she was to prove an irresistible decoy in the plan to get rid of the Italians.

The servants' entrance gate to the consulate garden had been left unlocked, allowing Ewan and the other South African survivors from the *Nova Scotia* to steal out to two beaten-up old cars, one green and one brown, parked opposite, beneath a street lamp-standard, where the bulb had been shot out by a catapult with a well-aimed stone. Later, Maria Delgardo, Muggeridge's assistant, would complain to the authorities about hooligans shooting out the streetlights.

The cars, driven by two of Harry's assistants, then slid away to the docks, to come to a halt just around the corner from the Club. There was food, water, a primus stove to heat water, and substantial cans of petrol in the car-boot. Ewan, who was to take over as driver in the lead car while one of the other survivors from the *Nova Scotia* was to drive the second car, was handed a bottle of chloroform and told to use it to knock out Fulvio Manna, with the caution to keep its use to a minimum, just enough to dump him unconscious on the outskirts of the city as they left it.

The drivers of both vehicles, with their South African passengers, proceeded to the Penguin Club, where they parked around the corner, the second brown car parking behind the green one. Grimes's men, waiting outside the Club to see the cars safely in place, faded away into the gloom of the night.

Campini and Manna were encouraged by Rosa and her friend Lucia to order yet another bottle of Dao. Both men were beginning to display signs of drunkenness, and Campini's eyelids were beginning to droop, as were Manna's. The Mickey Finns had begun to work, and on a signal from a man lurking at the bar (one of Harry's), the girls started persuading the men to accompany them to their rooms nearby. Two of Grimes's men sidled up to help the girls, after settling Campini's bill – a routine with which the club manager was familiar from other occasions, when men from the Italian Consulate would routinely settle the account. Manna had arranged a running bill with the management many months ago, so he was allowed to spend whatever he cared to.

There had been plans to push the captives into the car boots, but in the event it was decided to sandwich the unconscious prisoners between two other South Africans, posing as medical aides, on the back seats. The vehicles pulled off, after Ewan had climbed into the driver's seat in place of Grimes's man, who got out of the car and melted away. He had first outlined to Ewan the route out of the docks and to the border, backed by maps marked appropriately. After the two Italians were bundled into the cars, an unconscious Manna was thrown out very near the Docks Police Station, leaving him to be discovered and locked up for the night to sleep off his condition. He would never be able to recall what had happened to him that night.

"What will happen to the Italian?" asked Mrs Taylor, in the car with Ewan.

"Oh, he'll eventually be sent off to join his companion prisoners of war in Zonderwater. Meanwhile, I'm afraid you'll just have to cool your heels for a week after we arrive in Empangeni."

After the disappearance of the Consul, Rosa was able to convince the police that he had left her apartment, after he had satisfied himself, announcing that he had intended to hail a taxi.

194

There remained no link with the disappearance of the South Africans from the British consulate – whose escape had been duly reported by Muggeridge. As for the disappearance of the Consul – it took some days before it was reported, the Consulate being familiar with his repeated extended dalliances with Penguin Club girls. He would always show up a few days later. Only when a formal complaint was received from Italy was a full-scale investigation started. Some weeks later, a bloated body was spotted in the harbour, which had been in the water for so long that identification proved extremely difficult; it was assumed it might be him, but, exacerbated by wartime restrictions, it took many months to receive dental records from Italy, which led the police to realise that this was not the Consul; so they were none the wiser.

Roads in the African bush were rough affairs, mostly untarred and hardly maintained, just sufficient to provide the indigenous population of the area some relief from having to stride through untamed veld. In the middle of a moonless night, they were no place to drive at speed. Packs of wild dogs preferred to use these roads occasionally, as did many other nocturnal wild animals. The road to the border was also a highway for villagers staggering home from late-night beer-drinking gatherings.

Occasional villages would loom out of the dark, and one such settlement boasted a throbbing street-light outside the shuttered native store, which attracted the ubiquitous halo of night-flying insects. Between the next two villages, Salamanga and Manhoca, Ewan had to jam on brakes and slide to a halt in a cloud of dust when he encountered a herd of elephants, some of them standing on the road, and only persuaded to move on by the South African passengers winding down the door windows and thumping gently on the sides of the doors, while Ewan edged slowly towards them slightly revving the engine, and thus got safely past them. Angering them might only have provoked an attack on one or both of the vehicles, which would have been disastrous.

The border post was a modest affair – a flagpole, a solid-looking brick office, gates and wire fencing. There was no-one about – except for a bunch of baboons sitting on top of the roof and several going through the rubbish bins at the back.

Grimes's men had engineered false papers for the group, revealing that 'Hubert Campling' and 'Flora Manning' (Mrs Taylor, now disguised as the second patient) were suffering from advanced cases of sleeping sickness and yellow fever, respectively, and both required urgent specialised attention for treatment at the Empangeni Fever Hospital across the border and the Wentworth Fever Hospital in Durban; and, to that end, they were being accompanied by neutral Red Cross operatives – suitably kitted out with impressive-looking documentation and medical bags.

The Portuguese flag was hoisted on the border post at nine o'clock, so the occupants of the cars were able to have a bit of food and coffee from the supplies in the boot before the post opened, waiting in the darkness. Then followed a lengthy process of paper-stamping, inspection of the cars and the two very sick-looking patients lolling in the back seats. Reasons had to be given as to why the patients were assigned to separate cars, leading to the credible explanation that they were destined for different hospitals and required separate nursing staff to accompany them. The story was flimsy enough, but was accepted by the border control officer, who complained that he had a terrible headache after a late-night party – stimulating one of the 'Red Cross' attendants to dig into an official-looking medicine case and offer him some painkillers.

"Phew!" said Ewan. "That was a tight squeak!" after they had driven well beyond the border post and hidden around a corner, and Ewan had waved the other car to stop. "I know it's early but I think most of us need a stiff drink," he said while passing around a bottle of whisky, smuggled from Malcolm Muggeridge. They were watched with indifference by a giant marabou stork – staring at them with its left eye. One of the men, who had been a game ranger at the Hluhluwe game reserve in Natal before the war, pointed out that predators like cheetah and leopards (and humans) were equipped with eyes facing forward, whilst prey like that stork, zebra and impala had far better all-round vision where one eye on either side of the head did an efficient job of watching out for danger in all directions; "Even though that stork seems to be staring away from us, his left eye is watching our every move."

The party moved on, now in the no-man's land between Mozambique and South Africa, only to encounter a roadblock manned by what appeared to be army personnel; but turned out to be members of a tsetse-fly control unit, who proceeded to spray the cars – air intakes, wheels and underside – with smelly but efficient spurts of DDT, before waving them on.

They had been advised before departure that an officer at the South African border post would greet them by saying, "You're late!" and then, with a cursory glance at the passengers and general remarks about the conditions of the road on the Portuguese side, and how much better they would now find them in Natal, he waved them through, with a salute.

There was a military presence at the Empangeni police station where Campini, now a prisoner and on South African territory, still semi-conscious, was lifted out and carried away. It was the last that Ewan ever saw of him.

The men who had accompanied them from Mozambique

were being given Masonic Hotel vouchers, when James Bell, who was at the police station to pay his annual gun licence, spotted Ewan.

"Good Lord! How incredible – is that really you, Ewan? We'd given you up weeks ago as lost at sea."

"Hello, Uncle James. It was a narrow squeak, and makes a long story."

"Look here, Ewan, do your parents know you are alive?"

"I've been somewhat preoccupied over the last few days – and I doubt that any messages would have got through from LM…"

"Then look here, you must come home to the farm for the night – – I dare say your companions will be well provided for at the hotel (I'll make sure of that)."

And thus began the familiar drive to the Bell estate, and an astonished, delighted greeting by Edna Bell, the farm manager Noel Reed, and his wife Lucy.

"I'll book a trunk call to your family, right away," said Edna, striding quickly to the telephone. "We are still on a party line and you will have to shout like hell to be heard. I have no doubt the operator will spread the good news to the community… Have to wait about an hour or so, so sit down with us on the verandah, ahead of a good meal. Have you taken your quinine? No? Well, better do so – we're right in the malaria season and we can't be too careful."

The Kirkwood family, Donald and Prue and Emilia, still stuck to the custom of sundowners on one of the front verandahs; and were thus engaged when the phone jangled in a remote part of the house, answered by Chinnamama, who came through to say, "Missus Bell on farm must talk to Missus Dodo – quickly!"

"Prue, you'd better get yourself a stiff drink." Prue heard the excited tone of Edna's voice. "I have some very good news! Ewan is alive – and standing by the phone here to talk to you."

Prue shouted for Donald and Emilia to join her by the phone. Ewan's familiar voice, which they had all never expected to hear again, penetrated the clicks and whistles of the party line, so-called as any caller on the network could overhear a conversation simply by lifting the receiver. Naturally local news and gossip spread like wildfire.

After much excited chatter, it was arranged to meet Ewan at the main railway station in Durban the next evening, as the Zululand train did not stop at Umgeni on that particular day of the week.

When Jim Bell took him to Empangeni station the following day and they met up with other survivors who had just come from the hotel after a good night's rest, they arrived just as an altercation was taking place between the stationmaster and the men who, in keeping with the People-Rights principles of the Springbok Legion, were sitting on the benches marked 'Non-Whites / Nie-Blankes'. The stationmaster was also upbraiding them for being layabouts and a disgrace for not having enlisted. It was at this point that, at a signal from one of them, the unfortunate stationmaster was lifted bodily off the platform by the men who had been through so much, and carried through the building and dumped in a water-filled horse trough outside. The men returned just as the train from the Somkele railhead clanked into the station and pulled up at the platform. They clambered aboard thankfully.

Billboard advertising in South Africa was not permitted except on railway property, where it was an established source of income for the railways. As the train slowed on its approach to the Durban Main station, Ewan spotted, among the exhortations of 'Don't Talk About Ships or Shipping", several examples of a poster showing a splendid, ginger-haired man clad in striped pyjamas sitting astride a Bovril jar, afloat in a choppy ocean, with the slogan, 'Prevents That Sinking Feeling'.

Chapter Twenty

November nights in Durban are hot and humid – a paradise for mosquitoes to irritate sleepers. The Kirkwoods had removed all the blackout structures for the night and had to rely on window mosquito netting, never entirely successful in keeping out the loud whining and stinging little beasts. If one cast aside the bedclothes, one's entire body would be exposed to these night creatures: keeping the bedsheets on would result in a build-up of perspiration. Donald and Prue chose the latter path.

The Chelmsford species of mosquito seemed to be unique to the hilltop, in that they had black-and-white striped legs, rather like a minute football team. When the beasts stung, they would bite, then take off with a Stuka-like whine. Donald discovered that they bred in the leaves of the plants outside the bedroom windows, which had watery reservoirs at their bases, so he would routinely dose the plants with paraffin – extending this treatment to the underground wells. However, the battle against the mosquitoes was never fully won.

One morning at about four o'clock, the bakelite telephone in the Chelmsford hall started to jangle. At the time, Toby was a guest of the Kirkwoods, up on naval business from Simons Town in the Western Cape. In a guest room, he groaned and muttered again as the telephone kept on ringing. In the way of dreams, he was disturbed by naval ratings attempting to hammer barnacles off his official residence, but with a regular ringing sound.

Prue, half-awake, prodded Donald, who was a sound sleeper, especially so after doing the rounds of blackout duty. He was dreaming of riding his horse in Rhodesia, and could not understand why the bridle was emitting ringing noises. He was reluctant to let the dream go.

Prue nudged him again and said loudly, "You'd better answer the phone." When Donald stumbled his way down and picked up the receiver, it was Keswick's voice, saying, "You and Toby had better come down to the harbour and see a very unusual sight entering the bay – in fact, unique – and Toby should be there in his naval uniform anyway. I'll see you at the main security gate in an hour's time."

"Bad news?" asked Prue, who was now wide awake.

"No. It was your father summoning Toby and me down to the docks. Important duty. You know what he's like at this time in the morning – pretty abrupt; but I'd better go and shake Toby out of bed. Go back to sleep, Dodo. I'll phone later to let you know what it's all about, when I know myself!"

They met in the kitchen, where Donald was already frying eggs, brinjals and bacon when Toby arrived, kitted out in full uniform.

"We'd better fortify ourselves for a long morning ahead," Donald said. "Dodo gave me a large tin of Grant's porridge for my birthday…There's the tin; let me treat you to some. Know how to make porridge?"

"It stretches the perimeter of my cooking knowledge, but yes," Toby said sarcastically. "We'd better take my car. I don't have to worry about petrol coupons."

As they breakfasted they heard the clink of milk bottles, so Donald rose and opened the kitchen door, startling the barefooted milkman with a friendly "Sawubona", then shut the door again.

"Poor devil, I wonder what time he has to start work! He has to collect his supply from the depot, miles away, and deliver his milk all over the place."

They left in the early light, with Donald saying, "The storm-lilies are out on the back lawns – that means thunder and lightning in twelve hours. It will cool the place down." The laterite driveway glowed in the early light.

At the security gate, Keswick met them saying, "The password today is, 'Umgeni'. We are going down to the north pier to witness an extremely unusual sight." He would not be drawn to clarify his remark, so they just complied, with Keswick climbing into the naval car as a bright orange dawn broke out behind low-lying dark clouds. They joined a small group of men, including Donald's cousin, Gustaf Wilson, Durban's municipal police chief – his mother was Norwegian, hence his first name. She and Donald's uncle had settled in Durban several decades earlier.

From the south, cornering the Bluff headland, lit up by the bright early sun, appeared HMS *Jasmine*, escorting alongside it a large Italian submarine, with its high conning tower. What appeared to be the boat's commander stood beside a flagpole, with flags furled, the international naval symbol of surrender.

As the submarine neared the channel into the harbour, Keswick stepped forward.

"Well, it's not exactly 'The Fighting Temeraire' but I dare say if my grandson were here he would make a pretty fine painting of the scene. Italy has surrendered, and the Italian commander of this sub made contact with the *Jasmine*, applying to surrender officially at Durban. The sub. was in Japanese-held waters near Singapore at the time."

As the frigate passed the group, the ship let out a 'Woop, Woop' from its steam horn. Perhaps the captain had spotted Toby, in his splendid uniform. Unusually, Toby had donned his official Naval Officer's hat, which could be identified from a distance. Probably it was his headwear that had caught the eye of the frigate captain, who then instructed the horn to be sounded in recognition. Certainly, the submarine captain recognised the standing of the figure, and impulsively saluted. Toby, with great dignity, took the salute – a small cameo which did not go unrecognised by the other men in the group. Toby tucked his hat under his arm just as soon as the small flotilla moved away.

Returning to the security gate, Toby was handed a printed note, to which he reacted by saying, "Oh, Lordy, I've received a message from the Salisbury Island naval commander explaining he is unavoidably engaged in other business, and would I entertain the submarine captain and his second-in-command tonight – as a matter of courtesy, welcoming our new ally. Taking such a uniformed figure to a restaurant club packed with military personnel is not desirable, as it is felt that most men are bitter about the Italians, and will be for a long time to come. Donald, you cannot possibly invite them to your house, bearing in mind Dodo's expressed thoughts about any submarines almost killing your son."

Keswick immediately interceded by saying, "Well, I insist that we invite them to dinner at our house. Donald, try to persuade Dodo to come, and bring Emilia. As Italians love uniforms that look like something out of a comic opera, I am sure he will arrive fully kitted out tonight – so it's uniforms, for those to whom it will apply, including your daughter. Have

to alert Cordelia and the Jeeves cohort as soon as possible."
At which point he promptly left them.

Toby remarked, "I thought I would be able to escape this
bloody uniform for an evening, but it looks like I won't. I'll
have to take a snooze this afternoon – and maybe one for
Donald would be sensible. I gather it so happens that Ewan
will be home on seventy-two hours' leave; someone discuss
it with him. He may be intrigued to meet a real, live 'enemy'
submariner. He might well be able to persuade Dodo to
come along."

Upon his arrival from Mozambique, and two weeks'
restorative leave, it was recognised that Ewan would never be
able to get in and out of a single-cockpit fighter plane again
– his badly re-set leg would make this impossible. However,
he could fit inside a dual-control trainer, like a Harvard, so
he was posted as an instructor for fledgling pilots in the art
of combat against a merciless enemy. In fact, he earned a
particular reputation for his lecture on the Immelman Turn,
perfected by a German aviator in the First World War – and
how this technique of role-reversal could be applied in the
Second. After a period of training pilots, he was assigned to
co-pilot slow but highly effective Catalina amphibious craft,
deployed to patrol South African waters on 'seek-and-destroy'
missions against enemy vessels – including submarines.

One of the 'Cats' had been destroyed by a pilot attempting
to land on Lake Saint Lucia and encountering a hippo in
the water. The hippo and the amphibian craft were written
off, and the crew were severely injured. An extra Cat was
rapidly assembled, and was serviced with a scratch crew, one
of whom was Ewan.

During an earlier leave, Ewan had been introduced to a
Rosalind Orr, and their friendship had blossomed. Rosalind

stemmed from an 'ODF' (Old Durban Family), qualifying her to be acceptable to his grandparents, who were rather starchy in this regard, despite Cordelia's strongly-held liberal views concerning equal rights for the downtrodden.

"Perhaps Cordelia would countenance inviting Ewan's friend Rosalind to round out the numbers?" Toby suggested.

Tree trunks and other hazards had been whitewashed during the blackout in the town centre and main suburbs. For the same reason, Donald had instructed one of Layani's minions to whitewash and place demarcation boulders on either side of the drive leading up to Chelmsford. Even the trunks of the creaking old fig-trees had been disfigured with the same treatment.

The drive into town was painfully slow, inhibited by the hoodwinked headlights and the absence of street lighting. Ewan was accompanying Toby in the Naval car to fetch the Italians, who would be brought across the bay by launch from the surrendered submarine to the commandeered yacht club pier.

"Entertaining these Italians rather sticks in the gullet, Uncle," Ewan said.

"For heaven's sake, Ewan, stop calling me 'uncle'! I'm not your uncle, although your parents and I are such close friends. Call me Toby! You were saying…?"

"Yes, after talking to some Springboks who managed to escape from the Tobruk prisoner-of-war roundup, which was partly administered by the Italians; contrary to the behaviour of the Germans, the Italians spat at men's faces, sometimes slapping prisoners, and worse, and shouted abuse at the men. By comparison, the South Africans respected Rommel and his men's behaviour – following the Geneva Agreement to the letter on most occasions, in the same manner as the

Allies. Obviously, there were exceptions, but by comparison with the Italians, very few. The men I spoke to describe the Italians as dirty and disorganised – explaining how their carelessness had led to their managing to escape.

"Look at what the Italians did in 1935 and '36 in Libya and Abyssinia – bombing and mustard-gassing indigenous defenders. And look at the bombing of Guernica's defenceless civilians in the Spanish Civil War by Italian bombers – admittedly by some of the Nazis as well.

"I nearly lost my life after the torpedoing of the *Nova Scotia*, when I tried to clamber aboard a Carley float and I was attacked and pushed into the water by Italians who had commandeered the float. It was only luck that saved me and that crucifix about my neck given to me by a priest – for which I shall be for ever grateful! Believe me, Uncle – er, Toby – they are intrinsically nasty, nasty people."

"You think South African survivors in a Carley float would not have behaved similarly? An indirect ancestor of mine, Admiral Richards, was responsible for ordering the shooting of indigenous Africans at Richards Bay. Is this not as bad? Especially seeing he got the place named after him, as the ultimate insult.

"And how do you justify the British and French putting down the Chinese during the Boxer Rebellion, defenceless Chinese, just about, unable to resist modern warfare weapons – all so that the sale of opium to Chinese addicts could continue uninterrupted?"

"I must say that there is a certain admiration for the Italian Navy and its officers, during wartime, who did follow international agreements to the letter. Obviously, there have been a lot of exceptions – especially when armed vessels masquerading as trawlers were showing false flags, even false surrender flags, then opening fire on a trusting opponent. I think you will find these Italians a cut above the rest. Respect them for their endurance for days on end in a sweaty submerged cigar box."

Ewan lapsed into silence for the rest of the journey. True to the forecast of the storm lilies, a rain-splattered wind began to rock the car, followed by a bolt of lightning which struck a ship in the bay. They found the two Italians leeward of the clubhouse buildings, and Ewan, hoping he would not be struck by lightning, rushed across with umbrellas – part of the navy car's standard equipment.

Toby, the front seat passenger, turned to the visitors and extended welcoming handshakes, saying, "We are taking you to dinner at the Harbour Master's home, and can talk properly once we get there."

The Italians were carrying wrapped waterproof parcels for their hosts. The captain's second lieutenant spoke up and introduced his superior with, "Zis is my Captain, Mario Giannazola, and I am Enrico Abramo," explaining that his superior had limited English, but he, the sub-lieutenant, had enjoyed a prolonged holiday in England as a student before the war, thus explaining his better command of the English tongue.

Windscreen wipers seemed to be afterthoughts on most cars driven during the late war years, and functioned poorly. The combination of inadequate lighting, ineffective windscreen wipers and the buffeting wind carrying splashes of rain reminded Ewan of an occasion in Africa when his flight was forced to return to base with the onset of a sandstorm. He thought back to the sensation of battling with controls while his 'Glad' was being dangerously thrown about. It had been a huge relief when he landed safely.

"This is going to be an interesting little drive," he thought, and he was relieved when he turned into the Jardine driveway, where he slithered up the muddy drive to park at the top beneath the coconut trees by the entrance steps.

The arrivals were umbrella-ed into what the Jardines called the gun-room – more a place that smacked of wellington boots, galoshes and gardening boots and various coats for outdoor activities. Keswick was there to welcome them, and the first to discover that, true to predictions, their waterproofs concealed 'comic opera' uniforms. Jeeves was there to instruct an underling to clean and dry everyone's shoes in situ, before stepping into the drawing room where the rest of the party waited. The Italians clearly admired the warmth and setting of the room, splendid with books, seashells, marine memorabilia, a stuffed lemur on a window ledge, and the grand piano.

"I understand from my grandson that the drive up here was slow and hazardous. We had planned, weather permitting, to have sundowners on the terrace, but as you were delayed and the weather does not permit, I now suggest that we troop into dinner without further ado?"

Ewan had prevailed upon Prue to set aside her differences for the evening and she came, resplendent in a crimson dinner gown. Rosalind stood beside her, a trifle awestruck, surrounded as she was by such uniformed splendour. Keswick and Donald had elected to wear smoking jackets, Donald's complemented by his old Alleynian tie, and Keswick's similarly with his old Singapore Cricket Club tie.

Keswick welcomed everyone and introduced the guests, firstly to Cordelia, to whom the men presented their offerings – which turned out to be loaves of white bread baked in the submarine ovens that morning, a cluster of Italian wines and a bottle of grappa – apologising that they could not find flowers for the hostess; leading Cordelia to exclaim, "White bread! You must come here more often! We have not had white bread for years. It's a pleasure to receive these loaves

– far better than flowers. You can't eat flowers! We have had to put up with what was laughingly called ryebread, but tasted like doormats. Jeeves…" she said, turning to him and indicating that he should carry away the gifts.

As they sat down at the dining table, the polished gleam of the silver salt, pepper and mustard pots was highlighted with the gentle light of candles, in silver candlesticks around a central arrangement of bougainvillea blossoms. The Italian captain was placed to the right of Cordelia, opposite her husband, with the lieutenant to his right. Rosalind was placed away from Ewan, beside Donald (who could possibly end up as her father-in-law), with Ewan placed beside his mother. Before they sat, Keswick said, "Donald, would you do the honours…?" To this Donald responded by standing and saying grace, "Benedictus benedicat per Jesum Christum Dominum Nostrum …" which he had said so many times before, not least when Prue had dined at the Schnurr's remote Zululand farmhouse at Ntambanana, more than twenty years earlier.

When they sat down, the Italians were uncertain what to do next; and were relieved to see Cordelia lift her spoon and begin to eat her vichysoisse. The dry sherry which Jeeves poured to go with it loosened tongues, and soon the lieutenant was explaining that they were Sicilian, with many relatives in New York – one owning an ice cream parlour on Coney Island, another prospering as a barber in the Italian Quarter. The captain's family were milliners of many generations' standing, in the walled city of Enna. He had been sent to study opera at the National Academy of Santa Cecilia in Rome, when he was obliged to join the Navy – leading to his command of the submarine. The lieutenant's family owned a trawler, which plied out of a small fishing village called Mezameni. He too had been drafted into the Navy.

As the plates were being cleared, Toby, as the Navy

commander, stood and proposed a toast to 'our new allies', saying "I'm sure that together we shall win the war. Gentlemen, please be upstanding" – gesturing to the two Italians to remain seated while the toast in their honour was being said.

As Chardonnay was being poured, anticipating the next course, Cordelia said, "I am afraid you will be subjected to poultry, as beef and mutton are not available – except on the black market – the other option being whale-meat, which I would not wish even on my worst enemy." Realising just after saying it that she had put her foot in it, she hoped that the strangers would take it as some strange English joke.

While the main course was being served, the Italian Captain stood, holding a glass, and made an incomprehensible speech in Italian, but clearly showering thanks on his host and hostess and the opportunity to meet in the present gathering, winding up by holding his glass aloft – gesturing to the rest of the company to be seated, while prodding his Lieutenant to stand with him.

What the dinner party guests could not have known was that experts from the Pickering Street Irregulars, headed up by a man called Wiggins, entered the submarine and stole away the Italian naval codes, including those used to communicate with their erstwhile allies, the Japanese and the Germans. The entire codebook would be copied and returned to its place in the submarine before the captain and sub-lieutenant returned. An irregular, meanwhile, was admiring the unusual location of the aerial and transceiver. Since Marconi, the Italians remained dab-hands in radio development, as reflected by the state-of-the-art equipment in the submarine.

Another technician spent some hours immobilising the torpedoes, putting beyond use their triggering mechanisms, remarking that the sub could not be allowed to wander about the Indian Ocean like that.

At the dinner, Donald glanced at his small family with pride, noting that Ewan was abstaining and sticking to soda water. He was thus stone cold sober when he introduced the subject of equality of opportunity to Africans, Indians and whites.

It was customary to debate a relevant topic at all Jardine dinners, encouraging guests to join in. The Italian captain was at a distinct disadvantage, Ewan realised, but not so the lieutenant. Looking steadily at him he asked, "As a question for debate, should all South Africans – African, Indian, coloureds and whites – enjoy equal rights, and what might these rights comprise?"

"Ewan, I don't think our Italian guests are in a position to debate this topic – they have only been in the country for just over a day," said Donald quickly, anticipating where this debate was heading.

Ewan persisted, by saying, "Even though their stay has been very short, they will have noticed that there is huge inequality between the various races. At school, I have no doubt they were taught about the superiority of the Italian conquerors in Libya and Abyssinia, reigning supreme over suppressed indigenous people."

Diverting attention, Toby suggested that huge inequalities, admittedly, did exist in this country, but what would happen if the floodgates were opened? Perhaps qualified franchise would be the answer, setting down milestones of achievement that had to be reached before a member of any race could acquire the vote – on the assumption that all races could receive unimpeded standards of uniform education, and have similar living standards shaped to the needs of particular racial groups, and so on... A Bill of Rights could be considered after consultation with all groups...

"Well, a good start could be found in the principles of the Springbok Legion, which I joined along with many others while in Addis Ababa. The Legion offers equal rights to all servicemen, regardless of their colour – and I believe this idea will gain strength when the war is ended."

Rosalind was under Ewan's spell and listening attentively, but images were passing through her mind of her parents' reaction to sitting down to lunch with what they referred to as a garden boy, no matter what age the gardener was.

The discussion was headed off by the arrival of crème brûlée, with a good sauterne wine – the Italian captain tapping the custard crust approvingly and exclaiming, "Very good, very good!" It was followed by water biscuits and cheese. "Ah! Gorgonzola! My favourite, where on earth did you manage to find this?" exclaimed Donald, to which Cordelia replied, "You'll have to ask Jeeves."

Returning to the subject of equal rights, he said, "I'm impressed with your motives, Ewan, and, in an ideal world, things would be different; but your mother is correct recommending a 'hamba kahle' approach. However, we are all stick-in-the-muds and don't like change, so the Springbok Legion's manifesto, carried forward by so many ex-servicemen, could be the spark to inspire us to get on with it – as fast as our tortured minds can – with steadily introduced changes. Beware revolutions, which certain actions could bring about, destroying the very framework that we are constructing."

"Well, Ewan and Emilia, it's time to blow out the candles, I think…" Whereupon the two rose from their seats and, to the amusement of the Italians, Ewan blew out the candle close to him by saying, "When!" followed by his sister saying, "Who!" Keswick explained to the Italians, "The custom was developed to improve her pronunciation of certain words, when our daughter Prue was a child. It has become a tradition for the youngest members of the family to perpetuate the custom."

Returning to debate, Prue said, addressing Ewan in particular, "I think the ideals expressed have great merit, but are far too simplified to be applied immediately. Pursuing the ideal of equality in a climate of conflict might not be as easy to apply upon their return home to peacetime.

"We know so little, truly, about the other races at the moment. There's not even a discipline at university applied to African Studies, for example – and the same applies to the other divisions. Most of us, me included, go about with our eyes wide shut. For example, I came across a study in our library, the other day, investigating the existence and role of Zulu groups of youths who had moved to Durban from the bundu, bringing the traditional colourful practices and applying them to small societies of which we are just about unaware. These are loosely called Amalaaita – essentially mutual aid groupings which exemplify the propositions made by the anarchist and 'human geographer', Peter Kropotkin.

"Have you noticed that some of the young Zulus, often employed as gardeners in a particular area, all tend to wear what look like ceramic insulators in their stretched ear-lobes? Well, they all belong to such a self-governing society. Portions of their small earnings are pooled to meet sundry fines imposed on their members – for example, drunkenness at their beer hall leading to imprisonment.

"Another group, sometimes antagonistic towards outsiders, wear an oxtail around their heads… And so on.

"Who are we to suppose equality without years and years spent evaluating their needs? That Russian queried the need for any form of government, theorising that they should be replaced by self-governing groups of mutual interests."

Most of the party was listening intently, except for Toby who was doing his best to extract as much strategic information as possible from the Italians, who had revealed that, within a thousand nautical miles of Durban, there prowled about thirty-six alien submarines picking off solitary vessels, their job made easier by the allies' failure to introduce convoys in the Indian Ocean.

The Italians predicted the Germans would continue to wreak havoc at the entrance to the Mozambique Channel, with the Japanese focusing on ships servicing Burma, India and Ceylon.

Coffee was served in the drawing room where the Italian Captain was persuaded to sing for his supper – which he did with a surprisingly good rendering of 'Nessum Dorma' from the opera *Turandot* by Puccini. After he finished, Cordelia, applauding, remarked, "Well, he certainly has sung very well for his supper." He was not far off the scale of the scratchy Enrico Caruso recording, which was played on the turntable housed in the polished wooden cabinet where the breakable vinyl records were stored. "What are the words?" she asked the second officer, to which he replied, "It starts to say that no one should sleep, and ends by saying we will, together, win. He changed the original 'I' in the song to 'we', suggesting that as we are now your new allies, together we will win the war."

Speaking directly to the Captain, Jardine said, "Sub undis nuntius spei venit," at which the captain's face became wreathed in smiles.

"What did you say? Please translate for us mere mortals."

"I spoke in stumbling Latin, on the off-chance that he might understand – and obviously, he did. I said, roughly, that from beneath the waves comes a message of hope."

A bright moon was out when Ewan and Toby drove the foreigners back to the harbour. Ewan came back into the car after making sure that the Italians were safely returned to the waiting launch.

Toby said, "Well, that was quite an evening; that really was quite an evening! I was listening very carefully to your talking about the formation of the Springbok Legion, offering equality to all servicemen; and got to thinking, you know, all four of us have been in the frontline, in one way or another – your father suffering severe hardship in East Africa during the first World War, Keswick likewise in Belgium, I as a naval officer during the First World War and now you in East Africa. All of us have felt the need to make a better world as a result – and in fact a good number of reforms have come out of it – you know – with women getting the vote, and so on.

"Your father heard from Jim Bell about your escapade at Empangeni railway station. Frankly, we all found it funny, but realised the wider implications, if servicemen broke the rules all over the country during wartime. But gradually complacency and the struggle for existence take over, and further reforms fizzle out, as they did during the Great Depression, coupled with the fear that communism would bring down capitalistic societies, leading to the courtship of National Socialism in Germany. Radicalism in the west was more the plaything of the Arts, masking the rise of fanatics like Benito Mussolini in Switzerland.

"Excuse my rambling on like this, but know and be aware that radical reforms to bring about a golden age of equality can turn into fanaticism. But what I'm trying to say, in my rambling fashion, is don't let your radical ideas get you into trouble, bringing down with a crash the ideals that you were trying to pursue…we are, after all, still fighting to defeat the axis, so may I suggest that you hold your fire, until we win? Undermining the state, rightly or wrongly, could be seen as sedition in some quarters – especially remembering that you're a member of the armed forces.

"You know, we are all very proud of you – that includes being proud of Emilia – and believe that both of you have a great future."

"Thank you, Uncle – er, Toby – that's the best conversation we've ever had. You've really spoken a bit like a Dutch uncle, but thank you for the advice," Ewan said, starting the car. They drove back to Chelmsford in silence, with the morning star shining brightly in a rain-washed sky.

Chapter Twenty-One

Anglo-Africa House was an old building in Smith Street, and was accessible, by various arcades, from West Street, the main shopping centre. It was built by a developer who might have been inspired by Burlington Arcade in London, and while he probably had aspirations to emulate it, his comparatively modest budget inhibited such grandiosity; there were no Burlington cupids over the entrance as there were on the original. It had become rather shabby, and had been scheduled for demolition, but war had stayed the wrecker's ball. The entrance led to an extraordinary interior of several floors with doors and windows overlooking a central hall that reached the skylights.

It would seem that the entire building was built on a cladded steel framework. It made it possible to construct corridors with cantilevered walkways linking all the offices, with balustrades of cast-iron embedded with large 'Stars of David' as the main decorative element. Unintended was the feeling of mild vertigo for any visitor walking along the corridors, which swayed slightly underfoot.

Strips of muslin, crisscrossed and stuck on to the windows of small ground-floor shops which had gone out of business, remained in place, to prevent shards of shattered glass, as mandated by the authorities still bracing themselves for a possible aerial attack on Durban Harbour; but there remained a sufficient number open to create an atmosphere of business during weekdays, with customers walking about the tessellated paving, now working loose and the tiles clicking when trod upon; but on weekends the arcade became silent, with a haunting quality heightened by the occasional howls of a child issuing from the only apartment on the third floor, with an ornamental grill opening onto the arcade.

One of the survivors was a clock and watch repair shop, the owner styling himself as a horologist. Another was a bric-a-brac shop with a collection of old glass and silver ink wells in the window.

On the first floor was a dentist, who smoked and then thrust his tobacco-stained and smelly fingers into his victims' mouths.

All three floors took a sharp bend to the right at the end of the arcade. On the top floor, Ewan had taken a large room, at the far end of a corridor, to use merely as a studio and storage room for an easel, and an artist's 'donkey-stool' and materials. The studio became redolent with the smell of turpentine, linseed oil and oil paint. It was a convenient halfway-house between university visits, shoehorned between aviation duties and the art classes across the road from the Department of Architecture. He still lived at Chelmsford, and his bedroom and study there were very important to him, but the journey across town took quite a long time and reduced the time available between all his activities for whatever moments he could snatch.

Unbeknownst to Rosalind, he remained in touch with Masheila, who worked in the Natal Indian Congress offices in Grey Street. He managed to persuade her to pose over the weekends for a portrait, inspired by the paintings of Gauguin and Diego Riviera in the coffee-table books he possessed.

"You're looking at me as if studying a cabbage… right through me," she said.

"Actually, I'm studying the way light falls away from your left breast. To do this I have to look at you as an object, although doubtless what I render will contain feelings I have about you."

"What do you mean by the light falling away?"

"Well, look at that apple over there. See how the light falls mostly on the right-hand side, turning into shadow gradually. That's what I call the turning point. If you look at that shadow you will see it gets lighter further on from light reflected beyond the apple into the left-hand side of the shadow. All this shadow stuff is gradual, unlike the cast shadow of the apple on the table, which is dark and has sharp edges. My eyes were opened to these effects by an inspiring lecturer at art school. Brilliant! He drew like Rembrandt."

They rested the pose for a while; it was exhausting for Masheila to maintain it without any break. Ewan poured them tumblers of brandy and ginger ale. There was no ice to be had.

"I have told you about the Springbok Legion and its constitution giving equal rights to all, so tell me more about the Congress, which seems pretty ineffectual."

"Not in the least, since Dr Naicker took over. I'm not supposed to talk about this, but the feeling is that appeals for justice and delegations to Britain ran into a stonewall of indifference and refusal, so some more dynamic action is needed to break the impasse. Passive resistance is going to be introduced whenever strong rejection is felt in suppressive rulings by the administration. That means not only strikes, but a refusal to go to work."

"May I come along to one of your meetings?"

"It could be viewed with suspicion – even though Congress membership is open to all races, not least Africans.

I'll see what I can arrange. The meetings are held at night so I must warn you of other dangers, such as my cousin, Krishna Reddy, who has a liking for me which is not reciprocated. I can't stand him – one of the reasons being that he's a gangster and belongs to the Warwick Avenue Gang. He is usually high on benzadrine, which he gets from a pharmacy in Grey Street, under the pretence of alleviating his asthma. He has managed to gull some doctor into prescribing repeat prescriptions.

"About the gang...? They have nothing to do with the Congress. People there would be horrified to know that my cousin and most of the gang smoke dagga. They are a dangerous bunch of misfits with headquarters in an abandoned building in one of the back streets – never been there, but so I am told... They prey on sailors off the ships temporarily in port wandering around at night looking for a good time, and there are plenty of prostitutes to do just that – including the ones who lure solitary soldiers into the hands of the gang, who rob them or worse. The military police do their best, as do the local constabulary, but with the blackout you know how difficult it is."

They had a second brandy, and Ewan stopped painting, cleaning his brushes in turpentine.

"Let me see... When are you going to finish off my face?"

"When I get to it. Don't expect it to be a likeness. I'll never make a portrait painter. And I am not a photographer – my only hope will be able to enter it in our annual architectural students' Art Contest. No one will recognise it as you, be assured."

"What's that in the background?" Masheila asked.

"You should recognise it – it's a corner of the Chelmsford summerhouse. Remember those moments?"

"But there is no roof!"

"There never was, for as long as I can remember. The thatch was blown away in a cyclone many years ago and was never replaced – so that all that was left was the wooden framework and those curly cast-iron brackets in the corners."

She was close to him as she looked at the painting; her breasts brushed his shoulder, making him turn and kiss her. Instinctively they lay down beside each other on an artist's drape, making love as warmly and passionately as that first occasion in the Blue Lagoon Hotel.

"You and me," she said, staring into his eyes.

Ewan said, "I suppose this is what is called love."

"What about your little white girlfriend?"

"Nothing as deep as this. We have never 'made love', just a few kisses and fumbles."

They remained locked restfully, Ewan wondering at the beauty of her golden skin, with Masheila saying, "You're so sunburnt, you're almost the same colour."

"That's because I go sailing so much, when I can."

"You're lucky. We're not allowed on beaches... All we can do is sit in our cars and watch the white bathers and eat ice cream. There's no colour-bar in Mozambique, and the sky hasn't fallen in as a result...That could work for us. But you'd better do what's expected of you and marry your little white girl, and think of us as moments of innocence in a biblical Eden, where God is not staring at us through binoculars to see if we're doing anything against the law, but in Paradise, without security police and rule books."

Their child was conceived that day.

"What do you know about upland rice?" asked Sholto-Douglas. He and Donald were snatching a moment for lunch in Donald's office. "I don't know about you, but I'm sick and tired of this rye 'bread'. It makes everything taste of it. I had a call from someone in Pretoria, just before lunch, asking if we knew about the cultivation of upland rice."

"It's nutritious stuff, but unlike growing paddy rice, you can't drown the weeds by flooding the fields as one does with paddy rice. This means that the fight between hill rice, which must be soaked in water for a day or two before planting to help it germinate fast, and the weeds competing with it, can be avoided. The birds love the seed as well. I tinkered with hill rice at Ntambanana as the only crop left when we were forced to abandon the farm. Why the interest?"

"It seems to be a case of all hands to the pump, and any expert available – and that seems to be you, rather than any other person I can find, to help with starting rapid production of the stuff."

"Well, the best seed is 'Mountain Gold, Number One'. Believe it or not, it's likely to be preserved in the Mount Edgecombe Research Station Seed Bank. I don't know where else one could get a supply, except West Africa or the Caribbean."

"Do what you can to find out, will you – set aside everything else for the next couple of days? Yes, yes, yes, I know you're very busy, but that's a very special request from me. You could find yourself being put in charge of a development programme."

"Oh, God…I'm far too old for all that."

"Well, do your best. Otherwise we could have a riot or strike on our hands when the price of rice quadruples or more. Please give me your conclusions by Thursday."

Returning to the exhausted rice stocks: Sholto said, "Why the hell didn't Pretoria wake up in time, instead of leaving it until the last moment – I suppose they were far too busy staring out of the Union Buildings at their fancy new cars.

"By the way, how is the family?"

"Thank you for asking. Prue and her mother are busy doing 'good works', as usual, and my daughter is very happy doing some kind of hush-hush stuff. We see less of my son, Ewan, as he's busy flying Catalinas, hunting submarines. Doesn't say much when he is able to snatch some leave, and is preoccupied with his part-time architecture studies. Returning from up north and his torpedoing, he is greatly concerned about South Africa's perceived slide into a one-party state, dominated by Afrikaans right-wingers, if the National party gets into power at the next elections. He talks much about the opposition to this by the Springbok Legion formed in Addis Ababa by leading servicemen, including the head of the South African Air Force.

"It seems that the tide in Europe has now turned. Reading between the lines of a letter I received from a cousin of mine in England the censors didn't delete her mentioning that the place was swarming with American personnel. Something brewing, Americans building temporary airfields and so on. I suppose once we've beaten this dictator, the world will produce another.

"Well, best of luck on the hill-rice front. Do give your family best regards. I'm sure you're proud of them."

Unbeknownst to Donald, at the time, Prue was sharing sandwiches in Dr Scobie's offices, when he said, out of the blue, "They managed to catch two of the Angels red-handed, on the Bluff, near Wentworth. They had enough explosives in their possession to blow up the floating dock – the only installation capable of accepting a battleship for repair. Apparently, they gave themselves away by revealing their intentions on the Angel network which, as you know, was being read by us and Bletchley Park."

"Well, my daughter would have been monitoring those messages for some time... Never says anything, of course."

Prue had arranged to join Cordelia at the Wesley Hall for a session of preparing sandwiches and serving them to the servicemen who thronged the hall, from the hour it was opened in the morning until late in the afternoon. Before that, Cordelia had been to the Catholic cathedral, not to pray, but to discuss with the Indian priest charitable initiatives aimed at the most impoverished members of the Indian community.

"Do you remember encountering that Indian girl who attended Sonya's funeral?"

"Yes, very well: Masheila. She came to the house later, to join Sonya and me in making patchwork blankets for the needy."

"I came across her deep in cosy conversation with the Indian priest she'd come to see. They were so deep in conversation at the foot of the Virgin Mary that I quite startled them. I wonder what that was about; I thought she was Anglican. Pretty little thing."

Chapter Twenty-Two

"Are you going to paint my face today? If so, may I keep my top on? I feel a bit exposed."

"Better not... This isn't a paint-by-numbers exercise; chuck a towel across your chest and under your armpits to keep you warm, but leave your arms bare – do stop talking!

"I often paint over an old canvas. What you can see at the back was a painting of Chelmsford, but I didn't like it, and canvasses are difficult to come by. This portrait is being painted over another painting of some shacks at the head of the bay, behind the mangrove swamps. I got carried away by the market gardeners' simple dwellings amongst all those cabbages and cauliflowers they grow... I was touched when the women brought me out a cup of tea in a glass cup and saucer, on a tray, while I was sketching."

"I suppose she wanted to see what your drawing was like!"

"That was unkind of you! Now do stop talking!"

"Perhaps you will paint over me too."

During a break, Masheila said, "I saw your grandmother the other day in the Catholic cathedral – I think we were both as surprised as each other."

"What were you doing there?"

"I know your grandmother quietly helps the impoverished members of the Indian community seeking assistance from the church, and it seems it was the same priest I was talking to who was in charge of administering such funds to her satisfaction. I'm reluctant to tell you but, as a matter of fact, I am taking instruction, converting to Roman Catholicism."

"Oh, God! Why?"

"It is more embracing of all people. Anglicanism has served its purpose for me, but it seems to be the religion of the upper classes. Catholicism seems to be closer to Gandhi's philosophy of casting the net wide in pursuit of Indian-ness in this country. If you look at it, we Indians are a (how you say?) a mixed bag. The Hindus, Brahmins, Jains, are all jumbled up, with the caste system having broken down after crossing the 'Dark Water'. Some traders still like to think of themselves as Arabs, but Gandhi's concept is all-embracing, creating a new people of what you've heard people just call 'Indians', with not much insight... In pursuing 'Indian-ness' he enabled all local Indians to have a group negotiating power.

"But either way, you expressed an interest in meeting some senior members of NIC, so I spoke to Monty Naicker, who, on hearing about the Springbok Legion and your general thoughts about equality, invites you to come along to an informal get-together one evening. As the authorities are showing a keen interest in NIC, they meet in a backroom of Moosa's haberdashery – keep this information to yourself. I have to attend and take notes on these occasions. Monty took some persuading... When can you come?"

"I'll be on duty for next week, so I will let you know – and thank you."

Co-flying these seven-man 'Cats' was tiring, as patrols along the coast, over the south of Madagascar and further out to sea, could last up to twelve hours (although that length of time was generally exceptional). The crew had to be kept on their toes and cheerful, especially the blister gunners who had hours of boredom staring at an empty sea. The rest – the navigator, the engineer and the radar operator – were kept occupied with their tasks

Although he had not taken part in such missions, the Catalina he was co-piloting was painted black and had flown during darkness over the southernmost tip of Madagascar to establish by radar any activity, and observe the refuelling activities there of German and Italian submarines. It was dubbed the 'Black Cat' as, from that time on, the plane was left black for similar missions as they might be needed. With his gammy leg he had experienced difficulty in clambering up through the high entrance door, until the engineer devised a kind of 'Britches Buoy' to lift him aboard.

They were unable to talk about it until later, but one of their Black Cat's triumphs was the trapping of a U-boat 600 nautical miles off the coast of Durban, due to an inadvertent remark by the sub's radio operator with an uncoded message referring to a merchant ship. The Cat straddled the sub with depth charges, partially disabling it, although it kept on turning to avoid being hit. In the event the Cat was obliged to return to base as fuel levels were low, so dropped flares to indicate to another Cat where to finish off the job.

This was a secret world Ewan had to keep bottled up, that could only be shared with the Catalina command and his crewmates. Friendships shared at university paled against such bonds.... an experience common amongst many servicemen during and after the war. He began to realise why his father never talked about his First World War conflict experiences – the rest of the family would never understand such depths. Of course, Ewan remained unaware of his mother's secret life, the Pickering Irregulars, which she, in turn, could only talk about with people like James Scobie.

Ewan could never share his Catalina world even with

Masheila, and certainly not with Rosalind, who seemed more and more facile as his feelings for Masheila deepened. These thoughts flitted just below the surface as his conscious mind remained focused on the act of painting and observation – the cleaning off his brush in turpentine of bothersome oil paint, as he addressed another aspect of Masheila's face, the slight hint of blue in the shadows – should he dare touch his brush in dangerous Prussian Blue, or should he stick to safe Cobalt? How could he arrive at a shadowy flesh tone with these and Raw Sienna and Titanium White? And no, he wouldn't dip into Flake White: it was such a sluggish pigment.

"You're looking at me as if I were another cabbage, again."

"Well, it's the prettiest cabbage I've ever seen. And, of course, I am looking at you in that way because of concentration."

"That's a very smart watch you're wearing. Is it new?"

"It's issued to pilots and navigators. Anti-magnetic so can't be disturbed by the aeroplane engines, which are massive generators of magnetism. See – it's marked with a special arrow on the back, and my name."

"What are the numbers?"

"Just the model number: CK 2129. It's Swiss with an odd Greek name."

It was a lonely walk, away from the city centre, along blacked-out and shuttered Grey Street, and he had some difficulty finding his destination. He was admitted at Moosa's through a side entrance, in an alley-way. He was not in uniform.

"Whisky?" he was offered after the usual introductions, with Masheila sitting discreetly in the background with a notebook on her knee. One or two had glasses of whisky on the tables beside them, a few had cane spirit, and the rest were sipping Suncrush cordials.

"Miss Reddy explained your interest," said Naicker, "and talks about the Springbok Legion in general terms, and we understand that the principles of the Legion are similar to ours – no, ours is far more directed at our motley Indian population; but thank you for coming to listen to what we have to say. You must understand that this is not a general or council meeting, merely an informal gathering – but nevertheless Miss Reddy has been asked to be here to take notes of anything that may arise. Perhaps it would be a good idea to recite what we stand for – in general, actively seeking equal rights. Membership is open to anyone who cares to join and who shares our principles, and that, of course, would include a person like you."

"Could that include prominent natives?" – a question which set the little group stirring, some looking at each other, interrupted by Naicker saying, "In the past, the founder of NIC, Mahatma Gandhi, tended to regard natives as toilers of the soil; but, of course, all this is changed, and we are well aware of the growing strength of the African National Congress (as indeed is your white government).

"Returning to the points that need to be redressed they are – and I will spell them out: adult franchise; unconditional repeal of the Pegging Act; abrogation of the Housing and Expropriation Act – under this law the State has enormous powers to expropriate and demolish Indian-owned property on it, in the name of 'slum clearance'; removal of the provincial barriers that prohibit Indian residents in one province from legally moving to another; free and compulsory education up to Standard 8. We insist on equal trading rights without discrimination; and removal of the industrial colour bar. Also, there should be State subsidies for Indian market gardeners and farmers. Essential also are adequate civic amenities...And finally co-operation with other black and coloured organisations."

"Are you a communist? " Ewan asked, with Naicker replying, "No, certainly not, we are loyal to the British Crown and South Africa, but rather Gandhi-ists. But the time for beseeching is finished and the time for action has begun. Our plan of action is secret."

"And the war effort…?" asked Ewan.

"You can't fight a war on an empty stomach," said Naicker. "Have no doubt, we are loyal citizens – proved by many of us fighting up north; but all patience is exhausted. Thank you very much for coming. We had all better go home now – the streets are unsafe at this time of the evening."

There was a general scraping of chairs and some of the gathering left, including Ewan, at which point some men stepped out with him into the street, and Ewan was confronted by Masheila's cousin, saying, "Hey, white trash, I'm watching you. See this bulb?" He held up an electric light bulb, then smashed it and attempted to hold the broken shards up to Ewan's face. "You leave my fokkin' cousin Masheila alone, or I will cut out your eyes with this, d'ja hear me?"

Cartright Flats was a scruffy square on the left side of the main road to Umgeni, where Boswell's Circus was deployed in the season. In a side road leading to Grey Street stood an evangelical church, of simple construction, with a flashing neon sign on the roof, alternating between, 'Jesus Saves' and 'Jesus Red' leading to firebrands holding meetings on the Flats and calling it 'Red Square'. The bulk of Durban's population spoke little Afrikaans, so few passers-by realised that 'red' was the word for 'saves' in that language.

Leaflets began to appear wherever Indians gathered, in their workplaces, and in letterboxes, and under doors. Inevitably, some fell into the hands of the security police. Others were delivered to the newsrooms of local papers, the

Natal Mercury, the *Daily News* and, not least, the Indian paper, *The Leader*. Some had started to appear as far afield as Pietermaritzburg and Ladysmith.

They bore a black-and-white portrait of Monty Naicker with the simple message, "Rice Price outrage. Public meeting in Red Square. See you 11 a.m. on Sunday, 3rd December, 1944."

A sudden breeze fluttered the Naicker leaflet lying on the Mayoral parlour boardroom table. The windows were flung open and the air-conditioning had been turned off at five o'clock on the evening of Friday, 1st December.

"That puts paid to my weekend sailing, dammit!" said the Mayor, Rupert Ellis, to Col Gustav Wilson, head of the Civil Police, and Brigadier Tom Molineux of the Union Defense Force. The emergency meeting had been called by Wilson after being handed a copy of the leaflet.

"Wilson, how serious is this?"

"My informants tell me that the protest is designed to be peaceful, and any Indian stepping out of line will be dealt with by the community. The rice protest has been developed by the Natal Indian Congress to serve as a unifying initiative, and demonstrate to the powers the consequences of not entering negotiations into the bettering of the Indians' position. They dislike intensely being lumped together with the native population."

"So what will happen, in your view, after the meeting – and no doubt you have police deployed?"

"Nothing will happen."

"What you mean – nothing? Stop speaking in riddles."

"By nothing, I mean that all Indians will be encouraged not to report for work on Monday, 4th December – that includes docks, sugar estates, factories, cleaners – the lot, until the authorities address the rice price and supply, until it is satisfactorily resolved. But this is merely a device to demonstrate what happens when some of the other pressing demands are not met: schooling up to Standard Eight, access to technical training, adequate transport facilities and eventually equal rights; the end of the conflict in Europe is in sight (the British Home Guard is about to be disbanded, in this context), the return of serviceman is beginning – most of whom have joined the Springbok Legion, subscribing as it does to equal rights for all servicemen, no matter what creed or the colour of their skin.

"In Greece, the Germans have disappeared and the communist partisans are about to take over – against desperate attempts to restore the monarchy. I predict nasty business ahead."

"Tom?"

"I concur with Gustav, except to say that if you can find supplies of rice, to reduce the tension and introduce price control on it, bringing it down to normal levels, with the co-operation of the food companies; and publicise the fact that you are sympathising with them on the sky-high rice price, you could come out smelling of roses, as it were. A private meeting with Naicker should also take place here, with a sympathetic listening to their grievances."

Gustav chipped in by saying, "I've been in contact with a major importer and exporter, based in Pickering Street, by the name of Logan who, by the way, seems extraordinarily well-informed about the crosscurrents we are threatened with, and advises that a substantial shipment of American long-grain rice is aboard a Lykes Lines merchant ship due to dock in Durban early next week that could be our salvation."

"I'll call Jardine, the Harbour Master, immediately after this meeting and ask him to give that ship royal treatment, intensive docking and unloading."

"You may not have any Indian dockworkers, remember!"

"Tom, could you see your way clear for some of your men to volunteer to help unload?"

"Gustav, how do we get hold of Naicker?"

"As a GP, he has a practice in Grey Street and operates a clinic on Saturdays for patients who are too poor to pay. The public meeting being held on Sunday is in order, as his staff requested permission and my department has granted it – so he's certainly not breaking the law, and I cannot demand his appearance before you or a magistrate. This could change after the meeting, if he incites violence and lawbreaking. The best I can do is to invite him round for a chat, ahead of the public protest, but I suggest that his response will be that he will be too preoccupied for the next few days.

"Well, I know you will do your best. What do you know about him?"

"His father was a banana exporter and his son went to a junior school for Indians in Durban, before he was sent overseas to complete his schooling, after which he studied and qualified in medicine at the University of Edinburgh. He made a trip to visit Gandhi in India and I understand they got on rather well. On returning to Durban he was incensed, like Gandhi, at being treated as a second-class citizen and lumped together with our natives. He is an excellent orator – with abilities polished at Edinburgh University, where he shone as an outstanding member of the university's debating society. In public life he is driven to improve the lot of the Indians. Max Weber would probably have characterised him as a Charismatic Leader."

"Who is this Max person – perhaps we could ask his advice?"

"Unfortunately not; you may not recall that he was an outstanding political sociologist responsible for drawing up the constitution of the Weimar Republic. He posited that certain leaders possessed such exceptional charisma they could inspire the public to follow them – for example, Napoleon, Hitler, Gandhi and so on."

"History was not my strong point at university; as an accountant, I had little time for that sort of thing. Tom? You've been very silent. What should we do?"

"I agree with the efforts to lay a hand on that cargo and to suppress the price of rice very quickly – to which I suggest you brief the press about your efforts ahead of the meeting, but of course not the Indian papers; and remember, the Sunday press is produced on Saturdays. Also, tell the editors that you are open to discussions concerning grievances with the Natal Indian Congress. As for the Red Square meeting on Sunday... I suggest that you wait and see what transpires. If disruption is the result, Wilson will be justified in arresting and charging the ringleaders."

"All right, we have a plan of action; and we'll all be very busy indeed tomorrow and on Sunday, so I suggest we all go home and have a good rest."

"One for the road?" asked Ellis, going for the discreetly concealed cocktail cabinet and holding up a decanter of whisky, with eyebrows raised.

"Not for me," the Brigadier said, and made his departure politely, leaving Ellis and Wilson to settle back in their chairs for a while.

"What about Zulus?" Ellis asked... "You speak the lingo pretty well."

"Not as well as my cousin, Donald Kirkwood. He was a farmer for many years in the depths of Zululand – where, if you couldn't speak the lingo, you'd be lost. He's upcountry at the moment establishing a procedure for cultivating large crops of hill rice, which is an acceptable substitute for imported paddy rice."

"A bit late in the day, but I suppose it could all help – how long does it take to mature?"

"Donald told me that maturity could be accelerated by soaking the seeds for a full five days before planting."

"What about the African National Congress? Are they militant?"

"No, strictly declared passive in nature – more a platform for discussion, mainly comprising black religious leaders; formed in Bloemfontein long ago in 1912 to improve conditions through diplomacy and negotiation with the authorities. Membership is open to all races, although natives pre-dominate.

"The Naicker group are rather the ones to watch. He reportedly loves Tamil music…Reputed to be a good tennis player. He always had a charismatic quality about him – was even instrumental in the staging of the Tamil '6-foot dance' in the City Hall before a rather stuffy white audience of community leaders and their wives. It's a Tamil tradition celebrating the harvest time in Natal, usually performed by the Mount Edgecombe Indian mill workers, a bit high on cane spirit. A mixture of acting interludes, music and dance, where the workers – traditionally – donned women's saris to enact the small plays. Very bawdy and bold.

"I think you will agree that the municipal police are tolerant and go out of their way to respect the Zulu and Indian traditions and celebrations. But God help us if the Pretoria Security Branch people take it into their heads to muscle in. Naicker risks this – the security police have plotting Bolshevists on the brain…a communist behind every bush waiting to pounce and take over the country."

"Although I said Naicker was the one to watch – I meant,

here in Durban. It's a different kettle of fish amongst the African mine workers in the Transvaal, who predict there will be great trouble ahead. Even now, there have been strikes up there triggered by a new organisation, the African Mine Workers Association; they were suppressed after the workers had gone back to work, limiting the gatherings to twenty people in all of the mines, the keeping of workers in compounds, to prevent contact with Association officials. Sooner or later, I predict there will be a general strike – but for now, but we have to concern ourselves with the rice strike."

On Sunday, 3rd December, 1944, Donald, Prue, Emilia and Winnie were sitting on the front veranda drinking coffee after Sunday morning breakfast.

They were reading shared copies of the Sunday paper and mentioning pieces that struck their interest, and drawing the others' attention to them by reading the headline and first paragraph of the news item.

Emilia suddenly read out a headline, "Antigone *performed under Nazi eyes in Paris*". She continued to read, "*An escapee from Vichy Paris earlier this year reports a curious event which happened recently under Nazi occupation: a new play based on* Antigone, *the ancient Greek drama by Sophocles, right under the eyes of the Gestapo. The play was first performed in Paris at the Theatre de l'Atelier on February 6, 1944. Jean Anouilh's play* Antigone *is a tragedy inspired by Greek mythology. In English, it is often distinguished from its antecedent through its French pronunciation, approximately 'an-tee-gon'. It was produced under Nazi censorship, but the play is purposefully ambiguous about the rejection of authority (represented by Antigone) and the acceptance of it (represented by Creon). The parallels to the French Resistance and the Nazi occupation were clear…but perhaps the Nazis are too arrogant to see it.*"

Suddenly, Emilia exclaimed to Donald, "Daddy, you are in danger of being attacked by an Archispirostreptus Gigas. Look at your left foot!"

"Oh…a shongololo," laughed Donald as he bent down and touched the centipede, which immediately curled up into a tight spiral. It triggered a thoughtful reminiscence of when he was distracted on a visit to the Von Wellenburgs, many years ago in Zululand. At that moment he had been fascinated by the pattern of behaviour by black ants emerging from a hole near his feet, engaged in activities and completely oblivious of the giant human staring at them. Other worlds have existed from time memorial, and would continue to exist after humanity had become a mere Anthropocene: as such was the innocent world of the centipede, which he slid, coiled up as it was, onto a piece of paper, and tossed into the nearest flowerbed, to go about its business unharmed by warring humans.

"What's it called?" asked Donald.

Repeating the Latin name, she said, "I came across it in one of our Children's Encyclopaedias, and was so bewitched by such a long-named little beastie that I have remembered it ever since."

Chapter Twenty-Three

Red Square began to fill well ahead of eleven o'clock, the number of Indians swollen by a marked police presence, supported by several 'Green Mambas', as the green police vans were known. At about 10h30 a lorry pulled up and a makeshift wooden platform was unloaded on the far side of the square. An Indian was seen to run out a long lead and connect it to the electrical supply of a shop. Just before eleven, Naicker and other prominent Indian leaders appeared, accompanied by Masheila Reddy, demure in the background. Some white supporters stood to the left in a group, which included Ewan.

Gustav Wilson, part of the police presence, drifted across to him and said, "Ewan, none of my business, but are you sure you should be here? There could be trouble ahead…"

"Oh, hello, Colonel Wilson," Ewan said. "Thanks for the warning; used to trouble… I just came along to hear the speaker – with my defence force friends here."

"Keep an eye out. It could be thought that you're mixing in the wrong circles."

"Thanks for the tip, Gustav."

Ewan moved away as he was interrupted by a burst of Tamil music from the speakers, as Naicker took to the podium with a few supporters and said, "Fellow Non-Europeans, thank you for coming today. What I have to say is short and to the point... And it is this... You're coming together to protest the high price of rice, and even its unavailability, is really a signal that we are unified in our refusal to accept our second-class citizenship, demonstrated by neglecting to protect access to essential food, causing starvation amongst many of us. What we are asking you to do is to unite in further passive protests to the right authorities in order to bring about change, and show the power of unity in the non-European community.

"The last thing these protests could be described as is violent – that is not the way to go. The way I will describe is 'passive resistance' – the power of doing nothing. By that, I mean not going to work – on the sugar and tea estates, in the factories, in the cleaning departments and everywhere else where you, my brothers, are employed.

"But what the white repressive government has done by calling us all 'non-Europeans' is exactly the opposite of what was intended. It has brought us all together to struggle in a common cause – be we Hindus, Christian, Muslim, believers in tribal religions, Communists, or nonbelievers.

"Let us borrow the motto you see on the crest of the Union government, which is 'Unity Is Strength', or in Afrikaans, 'Eedrag Maak Mag', and use them in our favour. By demonstrating unity in the Non-European community, Indian, African and Coloured, we can hasten change and bring equal rights to all South Africa's citizens.

"So from midnight tonight please do nothing, don't go to work until the price of rice is brought down and supplies are made available. As soon as this happens we will tell you to go back to work. Before you go, please enjoy the food and tea our kind ladies have been setting out in the tables behind. Remember – unity is strength and peaceful resistance is the answer.

"Thank you."

"Bloody churras!" shouted a white youth from a small group of them, as they kicked one of the trestle tables over; but were prevented from doing any further damage by Ewan's group who anticipated what might happen and moved quickly to wrestle them to the ground.

"We'll break your bones unless you pick up every cup and apologise to the tea ladies. Right away!" Those youths who could melt away did so quickly, seeing members of the police joining the confrontation.

"Do you want to lay a charge?" asked one policemen, to which Naicker replied, "No... They are just disturbed children. No real harm done."

Monday was strangely quiet, although, as predicted, the papers were full of it; but distribution of the editions ran into trouble because there was a complete absence of Indian newspaper boys on street corners and van drivers to deliver the papers further afield. White staff were asked to volunteer, and it was an unusual sight to see the General Manager of the *Natal Mercury* driving a newspaper van along Essenwood Road. No papers reached the periphery, and the public had to depend on muted wireless reports. As few whites were present in Red Square, rumours ran riot – ranging from the death of the King to an attack by Japanese at Isipingo.

Strangely, the Indian paper, *The Leader,* was circulated efficiently amongst the Indian communities in Durban and Johannesburg, with scant space given to the declarations of Rupert Ellis. Ewan was back on Catalina patrol duty for the next fortnight, so had no means of seeing Masheila.

The Indian community went back to work when rice supplies reached the market at pre-crisis levels, thanks to the efforts of Rupert Ellis. There were repercussions, however, when the Security Branch took Monty Naicker, Yusuf Dadoo,

Masheila and some others into custody. These were the days before the Nationalist government, which would be voted into power in 1948, had introduced the '90 Days without Charge' and all were released except Masheila, after seven days. Masheila had mysteriously died in custody – allegedly through falling down a flight of stairs.

After much protestation, her body was released to a remote relation who arranged her cremation. A close relative accompanied by the cathedral's Indian priest (although the priest was not permitted to see the body) reported that he had seen strange burn marks all over her body – as if caused by some kind of torture. Her neck had been broken, allegedly through the fall.

With no idea of what had befallen her, upon finding it impossible to make contact, Ewan decided to visit her home, the evening after he came off duty. It was only then that he learnt about her from the family who lived in the next door flat. The occupants were the friendly family with whom she supped regularly, the wife being secretly privy to Ewan and Masheila's relationship. He nearly stumbled over a young child sitting on the floor with an array of coloured paper, glue and scissors.

"That's little Julie, you remember? We sometimes call her Juliet. She is being very good. She loves cutting out little stars and placing them into her school jotter… Become quite skilful, ever since we ran out of stars from the stationer."

She explained that one night the police came and took Masheila away, after searching her flat and carrying out all sorts of books and files. The family could not find out who had taken Masheila, but the police who came spoke Afrikaans amongst themselves. They were not the municipal police, she said. Much later they learned that she had died. An inquest was held after which the body was released when the coroner recorded a finding of 'Accidental Death from Natural Causes'. The priest was asked to hold on to her ashes until the relatives had decided whether to bury or scatter them – bearing in mind that she had converted to Catholicism.

A distraught Ewan left with a stony face, barely looking where he was going, only to be confronted by Masheila's unstable cousin, Krishna Reddy, who encountered him in the dark half a block away as he was walking back to the main street.

"Hey, white trash, I told you to leave my fucking cousin alone. You're a spy for the police all along. Why didn't you stick to your own kind?" So saying, he plunged a short knife into Ewan's chest, then slashed his throat, and, after Ewan fell, kicked and stamped him repeatedly, then dragged his dying body into a reeking alleyway where he searched his pockets for belongings and wrenched his watch off, before making his escape.

Blood flowing from the body attracted a stray dog, then rodents.

Gustav Wilson came into Donald's office at the Cane Members' Association one morning several days later to discover Donald stamping out a flame in his waste paper basket, having accidentally set alight a crumpled memorandum with a discarded match he had used to light his pipe.

"Good Lord, Gustav, what brings you here? Excuse me while I make sure the fire is out. Come in, come in – I'll order some tea for us both," he said reaching for the intercom.

Wilson was in mufti, suggesting that this was not an official visit. The small paper packet which he was carrying he placed on Donald's desk as he sat down.

"Donald, I have what is likely to be terrible news. We

found a body resembling Ewan in the Indian quarter, several days ago, and have been struggling to identify the remains; but now it seems there is no other alternative but to conclude it must be the body of Ewan. I won't go into details, but it seems he was murdered. For the last fortnight there has been intense police work to establish the location of the probable culprits, leading to our raiding an abandoned house used by the so-called 'Warwick Avenue Gang', led by a murderous lout called Reddy. We searched his bedding and belongings and came across cash and this watch," at which point he opened the brown bag with two small cellophane packets, one containing Ewan's aviator watch.

"You see on the back, this belonged to Ewan. Strictly speaking, this is part of the evidence and I have just taken it unto myself to 'borrow it' to show you – and I must return it, to the police evidence-collection.

"Donald, I cannot say how difficult it has been to cause you so much distress – but I thought it was most appropriate to let you know first. Also, I must ask you to come to the central police station, to identify the body, when you're up to it."

"Have you told Prue?"

"No – what if we were wrong? I'm afraid the body is not in good shape and positive identification by you is necessary, I suggest, before breaking the news to her. If we have to break such news, may I suggest that you alert Prue's mother to be with her when you tell her?"

"But it seems so entirely out of character of Ewan, to drift around the Indian quarter in the middle of the night. If so, what on earth was he doing? All right, I'll come along with you – but give me some time to compose myself. Our whole world will have been turned upside down if this is true."

After the positive identification at the police station,

Wilson said that he would do his best to keep news of the discovery out of the press, and that it was fortuitous that paper deliveries were seriously disrupted due to the rice strike.

There was a numbness in Donald's heart when they parted. After establishing that the Jardines were home, he drove up to the house, explaining over the phone that he had received some most disturbing news and would like to discuss it with them. They were sitting out on the verandah patiently when he arrived and parked under the coconut trees. Thunderstruck, it took a little while for them to absorb the news, after expressing doubt about its veracity, as it was so completely out of Ewan's character, when Donald suddenly realised that he hadn't told the office where he was going – he had just walked out of the building, as if he were sleep-walking, struggling to accommodate the realisation that he would never see his son again.

Prue was in the front gardens supervising several of Layani's minions thinning out the agapanthus. The dogs and cat were there too, as they followed her everywhere. Winnie was writing letters, as best she could, on a front verandah, within sight of the party toiling in the garden. The Christmas beetles were in full throttle among the golden oak trees when Prue saw Donald and her parents; and felt great foreboding.

Donald took Prue aside to break the news, which she seemed to receive with composure, saying to the workers, "Layani, I have received bad news. No more work today, and tell your umfaans I will pay them a bonsela for the day's work – it's not their fault we had to stop. You had better have some bread and tea and bietjaan nyama." She then walked away from Donald and her parents to sit on the summerhouse bench, staring into the valley.

When Cordelia joined her, she said, "We will have to tell Emilia, but she is on duty." There were no tears when Donald joined them; the pain was too deep. Donald felt appallingly alone. The tears came later when she and Donald were left with their grief.

Several days later Cordelia got a call from the Indian priest she knew at the cathedral, saying that he had news of Ewan's reason for being in the Indian quarter so late in the evening, which would put his parents' minds more at rest. A Dr Naicker wished to talk to them; and thus it came to pass on a particularly humid day in the otherwise deserted cathedral, they met him.

Donald had never been inside a Roman Catholic church before, so his eye wandered over the Stations of the Cross and figures of the Virgin Mary and Joseph. He felt uncomfortable, and was ambivalent in his attitude to talking to two Indians on an equal footing – and this was especially so just after the rice protest had been resolved.

Dr Naicker was direct, saying that Ewan had become friendly with the girl who helped in the offices of the Natal Indian Congress of which he was the president, and had expressed an interest in meeting members of the Congress after joining the Springbok Legion in East Africa. This suggested similarities in the creation of the Indian congress. It helped to explain his presence in the Indian quarter when he was killed by Masheila's jealous criminal cousin, part of a murderous gang which terrified law-abiding citizens. It appeared that he was particularly unhinged by being high on cane spirit and illegal drugs.

Before he left, Donald thanked Dr Naicker, but said, "I sympathise for the poorest of Indians, but are you not playing a very dangerous game, leading to losing any ground that the Congress has gained?"

Dr. Naicker replied, "Although the Virginian Thomas Jefferson had some very strange ideas about equal rights, affecting indigenous native Americans, and controlling 600 or more slaves on his estates, he did utter some memorable words – particularly that (to paraphrase) when unjust laws are made, resistance is a duty. And yes, it is a dangerous game. Some of us were taken into custody as a result of the rice protest, and to our great distress Masheila lost her life while she was behind bars. The circumstances are suspicious and we are doing our best to find out what really happened..."

On saying that, he departed, leaving them to the priest, who said that the girl's very distant relatives showed reluctance to receive her ashes, and had left them to the priest to deal with.

They sat in silence with the priest for a while, before Prue asked, "How close was my son to this girl?"

"Very close. She was carrying his unborn child."

"Then her ashes and Ewan's should be buried together," said Prue – glancing at Donald, who reacted with surprise, then compliance.

She said to the priest. "Please come to the funeral service at St Thomas's Chapel. I know you will understand that we will not explain your presence, only indicating our pleasure that you are attending. It will require your presence afterwards, at the graveside, when you can scatter – Masheila's, you said the name was? – ashes and those of the unborn child into the grave. We are not Catholic, but I am sure that God doesn't care."

"Kissimus Nimzaan! Kissimus, Umkkosikazi" pleaded a raggedly-dressed native, squatting outside the cathedral, who had lost one eye and was wearing a bedraggled army jacket. His left leg was missing just below the knee. Donald stooped and asked, "Where did you serve?"

"First Infantry Support Regiment, in Africa, sah! It is

abulala abaningi bethue," he said, making a fruitless attempt to rise.

"What is your name? Where is your home?"

"Freddie Punyaan, sah. The priest allows me to sleep in a room at the back of the church."

"I will see what I can do. Isosha elikanye naye," Donald said quietly, emptying his pockets of loose change.

Chapter Twenty-Four

"Strange to think that elephants and even lions wandered here just over a hundred and fifty years ago," murmured Donald to Prue and Emilia.

"Well," said Prue, "at least we still have bushbuck roaming the hilltop at Chelmsford – although, God knows how long they can survive in this tiny fringe of bush; but for now, it remains our link with an ancient past." Then she wept at the significance of what she had said, dwelling upon the children's Chelmsford childhood and all that had been lost for ever.

They were sitting in the little overgrown graveyard in the grounds of St Thomas's Chapel on the Berea. They had left Layani and Chinnamama in the chapel accompanied by the Jardines – Ewan's funeral in the Chapel had been set back, to allow for Zululand friends and relatives to travel down by train, accompanied by the Minister who had not only married Donald and Prue but christened both the children, the Rev Robin Short and his Australian wife, on whom age had smiled kindly.

They sat in silence, struggling to come to terms with the fact that their future had changed for ever.

"Well, we had better go in," Donald said. Nearby was the freshly dug grave, and on a bench beside the back wall sat several native workmen, eating sandwiches. The chapel was full except for the front pew places kept for them by the Jardines. At the end of the row sat Jeeves, Layani and Chinnamama. Dr Naicker sat beside the priest from the cathedral. The splendid organ, built by the same people who had made the one for the Albert Hall in London, surged and thundered as the Reverend Short went to the nave to welcome Ewan's coffin, bedecked with bougainvillea blossom, which was carried in by members of Ewan's squadron and led by the Minister carrying the processional cross.

"I am the Way, the Truth and the Life. Whosoever believeth in me shall never die; thus saith the Lord," intoned the Minister – now from the pulpit. "We are gathered here today to remember Ewan Keswick Kirkwood, son of Donald and Prue and brother of Emilia, grandson of Keswick and Cordelia Jardine – and commit his body to his final resting place. Never was there such a tale of woe... Grief is the punishment of love, and I can see, looking about me, the grief and love shared in all your eyes – for certainly Ewan was loved by all who knew him, for his integrity as an airman, and his sense of fair play in his relationship with fellow human beings, regardless of how grand or humble they were, unrestricted by the evils of prejudice.

"I remember christening Ewan so well; there was no pomp and grandeur, just simple and moving. It was an outdoor affair beneath a spreading old tree on Donald and Prue's remote Zululand farm called 'Yonder', named thus, simply because was it was just that... Very, very yonder indeed. The baptismal font was an enamel basin from Prue's kitchen, but with a depth of meaning as great as any ceremony held in a cathedral.

"Ewan served his country well, and endured not only a plane crash in Africa but a torpedoing of the ship on which he was coming home, when hundreds of people lost their lives. Fate intervened – some would say God – and he was rescued by a Portuguese frigate and landed in Lorenço Marques. Escaping internment, he managed to reach Empangeni, then to Durban and into the arms of an incredulous family, who had been told that he was lost at sea. During that time in East Africa, he, like thousands of other South Africans, joined the Springbok Legion, whose manifesto declared the intention to build a better life for all South Africans, offering equal rights to all servicemen, of whatever creed or colour.

"Allow me to digress for a moment... As part of my ministry I am charged to care for the educational needs of children of my Zululand congregation.

"Yesterday, a Durban colleague and I visited a native school for young pupils in the Valley of the Thousand Hills to assess what could be done. Yes, the schoolroom had a roof, a very old and very rusty corrugated iron roof that was so full of holes that every time it rained classes had to stop. Yes, there was a blackboard, but no chalk; yes, there were schoolbooks, but only seven to share with a class of thirty; ink, but few pens... You get the picture.

"In the afternoon we visited a private boys' school up the hill – not far away – and encountered impeccable classrooms, a magnificent chemistry lab, a swimming pool of almost Olympic proportions, manicured playing fields and a group of inspired teachers. I asked myself, how on earth can we build a better society, a more equal society, when such dichotomy exists? Ewan and thousands of his fellow-servicemen had been fighting against a Nazi tyranny intent on crushing millions of people under the fascist boot, in the hope that when these evil forces were overcome, they would return home to build a better future for a more equal and just society, with opportunities for all, regardless of racial origin. These are the ideals Ewan carried with him to the end. The best we can do to repay his enduring service is to live up to the ideals he believed in."

At the graveside, it was Layani who broke down and wept, setting off others, covered by much blowing of noses.

As the coffin was lowered into the grave, the Indian priest, at a signal from Donald, emptied the ashen contents of an urn onto it. The coffin was still smothered in Bougainvillea blossom, while, with impeccable timing, Harvard planes, in "Missing Man" formation, led by the Black Catalina, circled low over the chapel several times before the Catalina peeled away and flew off to the west. Donald found out from one of the Air Force members present that it would have been impossible to stage the flight with Catalinas, as they were all either on duty or being serviced for their next long flights. As Ewan had spent some months training suitable pilots in two-seater trainers, it was entirely appropriate to fly a 'missing man' formation. The black-painted Catalina was the very one co-piloted by Ewan in search of enemy submarines.

There is much more to tell, but that would be another story – save to say that the Jardine family was eventually decreased just to Prue, and, when Donald and Prue died, both houses were left to Emilia.

She and her architect husband Neil lived in the Jardine house for a while, and Chelmsford was put up for sale. It was purchased by a Doctor Alfred Newton, an ornithologist, who developed the base of the cliff into a bird refuge, with an artificial waterfall cascading down the cliff. All went well until the Umgeni River came down in flood, so great that it swept away most of the sanctuary, although many of the birds were rescued and temporarily housed in a structure thrown up close to the summerhouse.

When Newton sold the property to capitalise on the post-war building boom, and Emilia got wind that Chelmsford was about to be demolished to make way for redevelopment; she raced there only to find that the old house was already destroyed. She did manage to save, however, wooden timbers from the summerhouse, the cast-iron main fireplace, and one of the wooden bell pushes.

While she was making arrangements to get the heavy timbers and the fireplace transported, an African labourer showed her some rags found in the rubble, which turned out to be the remains of a soft children's ragdoll in the form of a dodo.

By this time she and her husband, Neil van der Bijl, had set up a successful architectural practice in Pietermaritzburg where they lived in a Neutra-style house cantilevered over a little valley on Town Hill, where the Dorpspruit chuckled and rippled on its way to find the Umzinduzi.

Emilia loved Ewan's painting of Masheila, and she had it framed in the wood rescued from Chelmsford. It was titled 'Masheila in the Summerhouse'.

THE END

Epilogue

Neil and Emilia remained completely apolitical and concentrated on their thriving architectural practice, though Neil became side-tracked for a while when he opened a curry restaurant close to Pietermaritzburg's flourishing legal practices – the city, being as it was, the capital of Natal, it was the focus of Supreme Court cases. He named the restaurant 'The White Elephant', alluding to the Zulu name of the city, Ungungunhlovu – 'The meeting-place of the white elephants' (as opposed to Ginginhlovu – 'the meeting-place of the black elephants'), alluding to that Zululand area being regarded as a gathering place of Zulu influence.

Emilia insisted on keeping her maiden name of Kirkwood after her marriage, and for a while, both Neil and Emilia's telephone number could be found under 'Kirkwood-van der Bijl'; but it proved to be such a mouthful that it was reduced to 'Kirkwood-Bijl (pronounced as 'Bale'). So the Kirkwood surname survived, though somewhat transmogrified. Their three children were David, Andrew and Phoebe, the latter being a somewhat wan beauty, not very strong, who tragically died at sixteen. Their eldest son eventually chose to drop the 'Bijl' tail.

Neil's restaurant proved to be a 'white elephant' indeed, and closed down within a year.

After the war, Luitpold Werz was appointed as German

ambassador to the Argentine. He remained a practising Catholic, and it was rumoured that he had links with certain Vatican priests and functionaries who assisted the escape of senior Nazi war criminals to that country. This was never proven.

Toby Strafford never married again, but he was helped in the upbringing of his children by a loyal and motherly Cape Malay woman. He left the Navy again after the war and pursued a successful career with the Pegasus Vacuum oil company.

Hubie von Weldenburg and his wife Frieda remained in Mozambique after the conflict, and he became a leading figure in the production and export of high-quality cashew nuts. He and his wife extended their business empire by creating a luxury hostelry for tourists in XaiXai, which was managed by Frieda's sister Anna, Luitpold's mother.

The Bell's sugar estate likewise prospered greatly, and they were eventually buried on the farm beside their daughter Emily's grave.

Dr Monty Naicker was imprisoned for his efforts several times and then eventually banned, after a final release. He was arrested again along with Nelson Mandela, but released without charge.

The Springbok Legion became a force to be reckoned with after the war, and turned into the Torch Commando, leading to mass marches in Johannesburg, Cape Town and Durban, demonstrating resistance to the Nationalist government's intention of taking the Coloured electorate off the Voters' Role.

The Nationalist party, through gerrymandering, succeeded in getting into power in 1948; this was the start of Apartheid-proper. South Africa left the British Commonwealth in 1961, and became a Republic, during which time African, Indian and Coloured communities were uprooted in the name of slum clearance and 'Separate Development'.

Layani's son went on from Adams' Mission to Fort Hare, and graduated to become absorbed in the political struggles of the time. His mother spent the rest of her days at Adams' Mission.

Overwhelming circumstantial evidence convinced the court that Krishna Reddy had murdered Ewan, and he was sentenced to death; but this was commuted to lifetime imprisonment in an institution for the criminally insane. This took into account that the prisoner was out of his mind on drugs and liquor when the crime was committed. He was released after twenty-five years and went to live in Ladysmith, where he was employed as a cleaner in the Lord Vishnu Hindu Temple.

The wounded soldier whom Donald and Prue had encountered outside the Catholic cathedral was found a position as a gardener at Marian Hill Monastery, not far from Durban. Sister Pieta spotted a talent in him for carving wooden pieces, and encouraged him to carve the Stations of the Cross for their nuns' little side chapel.

Farming was redeveloped at Ntambanana, except for the private development of a reserve, Thula Thula, dedicated in the 1990s to rescuing orphaned elephants, not very far from the original path which led to Yonder. The Kirkwoods would have liked that.

Ivan Cohen's musical instrument shop continued to prosper, strongly supported by members of the Durban Symphony Orchestra and the town's music teachers. Joelle, his wife, remained a leading light at the Durban Jewish Club which was renowned for its theatrical productions.

The U-177 which sank the *Nova Scotia* was destroyed near Ascension, an Atlantic island, by an American Liberator bomber dropping depth charges. Many of the crew survived and were picked up by the USS *Omaha*. An officer who claimed to have been aboard the U-177, when she sank the *Nova Scotia*, settled in Durban after the war and was employed as the manager of a powdered soup factory. After a retirement party, he went home and shot himself. A black granite gravestone marks his final resting place in New Germany – a suburb near Durban.

Umberto Campini was released when southern Italy surrendered in 1944, and faded from view. He was last seen attending a performance of Puccini's *La Bohème* in the sweaty old Durban Criterion Theatre, shortly after the war, when the opera was performed by a visiting La Scala cast.

Jeeves and his wife stayed on after Keswick and Cordelia died until Emelia settled them in a retirement village near Stanger, established by the Cane Growers for frail senior Indian employees. Needless to report, their little cottage was called 'Blandings'.

Layani never returned to Mozambique, but was settled by the Kirkwoods to join his wife at Adam's Mission.

Chinnamama spent the rest of her life with her extended family at Phoenix. She took pride in serving visitors from a Chelmsford tea set presented to her by Emelia.

Glossary

The glossary serves all three volumes of the Kirkwood trilogy.

Compiled by Anna Baggallay
who also edited the manuscript.

ABULALA ABUNINGI BETHUE   Zulu. "They killed many of us"

AFRIKAANS – Two meanings:

Nationality: Descendants of early Dutch, German and Flemish settlers, whose language and customs blended into a new culture, plus French (after 1688 when Huguenot refugees from France arrived to settle); now less than 10% of the South African population.

Language: It evolved from many influences, as above, plus words from the San – the indigenous bushmen – and Khoi, the Hottentot farmers who had brought agriculture and livestock herding from central Africa; also Malay slaves brought from Batavia (Indonesia) to the Cape by the Dutch East India Company. The first Afrikaans grammar book appeared in 1876, and a bilingual dictionary in 1902. It was officially recognised as a new language by the South African Government in 1925; and is spoken as a first language by at least 14% of the population, including many coloured (mixed-race) people.

AFRIKANDER Cattle breed evolved to suit southern African conditions, of the Sanga type (humped), with lateral horns sweeping upwards.

ALLEYNIAN Eng. An Old Boy (former pupil) of Dulwich College, a private (known as 'public' in Britain) secondary school in South London – founded in 1619 by Edward Alleyn, an Elizabethan actor.

AMANZI Zulu. Water

BIETJAAN NGAMA Zulu. A small piece of meat

BILHARZIA Afr. Medically called Schistomiasis: debilitating disease carried by a small host snail in certain rivers and streams in southern Africa, the organism enters the bloodstream, causing physical and mental weaknesses. It can be treated if diagnosed. The name derives from T. Bilharz, the German physician who discovered the parasite and by whom the genus schistosoma was named in the nineteenth century.

BLACKJACKS The hooked seeds of 'Bidens pilosa', an alien from South America, now a widespread strong-smelling weed, known as khakibos. Seeds about 70 – 80mm. long, cling to clothing and animal pelts and are thus distributed.

BOER Dutch. Farmer; later used as a term for those of Dutch/German ancestry who defied the British attempts to take over the country and trekked (q.v.) north .

BOEREWORS Afr. Farmers' sausage. Mixed meats and spices, usually cooked at a braaivleis (barbecue).

BONSELA Afr. Tip, bonus.

BOOMSLANG Afr. Tree snake; very venomous.

BOREEN Irish. Lane, path – diminutive of road (bóthar, a road)

BOSBERAAD Afr. Bush Meetings – usually held in secret, e.g. by the Broederbond.

BRAAIVLEIS Afr. Barbecue. Literally, 'braised (braai) flesh (vleis)'.

BRINJAL Afr. The vegetable known as aubergine in Europe and eggplant in the USA and Australia, botanically the berry of 'Solanum melongena', a member of the nightshade family; thus related to the tomato and potato.

BROEDERBOND Afr. 'Brotherhood' – powerful secret society, founded in May, 1918, (as 'Jong Zuid Afrika' – changed its name in 1920) of male Calvinist Afrikaners dedicated to the advancement of Afrikaner interests and the erosion of British dominating interests. By 1948, all the members of government and apartheid supporters were members.

BRÖTCHEN Soup, broth.

BUCHU Zulu. Medicinal plant, 'Agathosma betulina', native to western South Africa; known by Africans for centuries, used for urinary tract infections, inflammation and intestinal ailments.

BUNDU Wild bushveld, wilderness.

CEILIDH Gaelic Social gathering with Irish or Scottish folk music and dancing – a party.

COILLE Gaelic. Wood, woodland; dense trees and undergrowth.

COLOURED People of mixed racial ancestry, specifically white and black, white and other races imported as labour. NOT used for indigenous black people of pure tribal ancestry. Mostly Afrikaans speaking, and mostly found in the Cape Province.

CONDY'S CRYSTALS Potassium permanganate – "the

most useful survival chemical"; purifies water for drinking, and is a healing agent for skin lesions, rashes, bites, etc.

DAARONDER Afr. Under there

"..DIESE DEINE GEBEN" "these thy gifts"

DONGA Zulu. Dry water course, eroded ditch; often dangerously and deceptively deep.

DRAY Flat wagon, usually with narrow sides which can be let down for loading.

DRIEDAGSIEKLE Afr.'Three-day sickness'; i.e. the second wave of the Spanish Flu, a mutation of the original.

DRIFT Eng. Fording place across a river

DUBH Gaelic. Black

DUIKER Afr. Literally, a 'diver': a small, shy, mainly nocturnal antelope that dives into cover if it is disturbed.

ERHEBUNG A survey

ERSATZ Grmn. A substitute, replacement, usually inferior, for something else. From German Ersatzen = to replace.

FADA Sct. Possibly borrowed from the Irish, "long"; but has many meanings in Gaelic. "Fada Farm"- a long, extensive but narrow piece of land.

FAHFEE Ch. Chinese gambling game/ numbers racket, played illegally by Chinese indentured immigrants, but also by Africans and even some Europeans who get sucked in hoping to 'get rich quick'.

FECK Irish. Originally, to steal or to throw; now used as a mild swear word, to avoid the similar English word which is far stronger.

FECKLESS Irresponsible, useless

FLUCH UND BELASTUNG Curse and burden

GEBRUIK Afr. Used, made use of

GRAND MAL Fr. "Great sickness" – used to describe the worst type of epileptic fit, when the patient becomes unconscious, often with violent muscle contractions, and can injure him/herself in the process, which lasts several minutes and is due to an electrical disturbance in the brain.

GRÜSSE Grmn. Greetings, regards

H. HAKKE Afr. Hocks (of an animal)

HAMBA Zulu. Go; go away (imperative) – ekhaya Go home

HAMBA KAHLE Go well – widely used by all Nguni (q.v.) speakers.

HAMBA NGO KUCOPHELELA Farewell, ride with care

HARTEBEEST Afr. Large antelope species; can run fast.

HERRSCHAFT und KNECHTSCHAFT "Lordship and bondage", Master and slave, as labelled by Hegel, a German philosopher.

HILL RICE Eng. A variety of rice grown in S-E. Asia and Africa carried thence to America with slaves, thought to be extinct by the early twentieth century. until rediscovered in Trinidad in about 2016. Doesn't require a watery field, so helps save the growers from malaria.

I.I.D.B. {Acronym) Illicit Diamond Buyer

IMPI Zulu. A regiment in the Zulu army

INDUNA Zulu. Official functionary of king or chief; the Head Man of a district; "great advisor". Now somewhat derogatory.

INSPAN Afr. To harness, or yoke up beasts (oxen) to a wagon.

INVAL Afr. Invasion

ISILWANE Zulu. Animal
ISIGODI Zulu. Valley; district
ISOSHA ELIKANYE NAYE Zulu. A fellow soldier
IZIMPUNGUSHLI Jackals
IZINGANE Zulu. Young children

JUKSKEI Dutch. Old (at least 270 years) Dutch boeresport; trying to knock a peg out of the ground by throwing other pegs, akin to tossing the horseshoe.

KAFFIR Arabic. Originally an infidel, unbeliever, not a follower of Allah; thus in South Africa came to be applied to black people. Now a word of great racial and political sensitivity, a slur, the use thereof punishable by law.
KHAKIBOS Afr. Bos = Bush. See BLACKJACKS
KHAYA Zulu Home, dwelling
KLEINE HŰGEL Hillocks
KNOBKERRIE Swahili. Club with a knob at the end; fighting stick.

LATERITE Eng. Rock / Soil, clay-like, usually orange colour, with iron and aluminium; found in hot, wet tropical climates. Used for road and path-making.

MADODA Zulu. Boys or men (collectively)
MIELIE/ MEALIE Maize, sweet corn; white or yellow.
MOGE ER IN FRIDEN RUHEN May he rest in peace.
MOMPARA Dutch. Fool, idiot – disparaging term, but not unkind. Originally an unsophisticated country bumpkin.
"MONKEY'S WEDDING" Phenomenon when the sun shines through rain, refracting it and producing a rainbow. Strangely enough, many languages and

nations have similar expressions for this oft-seen rainbow – in Afrikaans, a Jackal's wedding; in Zulu, Monkeys, as in English. Seen also at waterfalls when the sun shines through spray.

MOOCHIES Zulu. Loin cloths; beaded or animal skins.

MUTI Zulu. Medicine, sometimes plant-derived, but sometimes animal or human, involving barbaric practises and removal from a living creature.

MYNAH Asian bird, of the starling family, which can be taught to talk and thus was often caged as a pet. Imported to South Africa via trading ships calling into the Cape of Good Hope, and gradually spread northwards during the twentieth century; now almost a pest in much of S. Africa, outbreeding native birds.

NAGANA Disease, usually fatal, of cattle; a parasitic virus, which spreads quickly, carried by tsetse fly.

NAGMAAL Afr. Communion service in the Dutch Reformed Church in South Africa.

NATIVE Term used for an indigenous black African person, as opposed to an Indian or a Coloured person (one of mixed race).

NGOSI Zulu. Hereditary Chief

NGUNI Zulu. A breed of native African cattle, remarkable for their varied coat patterns, by which they are individually known.

Also a group of similar African languages, including Zulu, Xhosa, Shangaan, Ndebele, Swazi, mutually comprehensible.

NUNU Afr. Bug, insect

OPSAAL Afr. Saddle up; used as a rallying cry to Boer forces in times of conflict.

OPSITKERS Afr. "Courting Candle", lit where a young couple are permitted to sit together but know they must part when the candle burns out.

OUMA Afr.   Grandmother, grandma

OUTSPAN Afr. Unharness – oxen from wagon; a rest, a pause in a journey.

PADKOS Afr. Literally "road food" – picnic food for a journey.

PANGA Zulu. Long-handled slashing blade.

PANJANDRUM Indn. Powerful person; important, influential, often pretentious, official. Invented name for a character in a work by Samuel Foote, playwright, in 1755.

PASOP Afr. Beware, mind out, take care...

PHUMANI KAHLE BATHANDEKHAYO. Rest well, beloved.

PICCANIN Young Zulu child

PUTU Zulu/ Xhosa Pap. A stiff porridge made by cooking maize meal with water to the consistency of mashed potatoes.

QUAICH Sct. Shallow two-handled cup, often of wood, used in Scotland.

RIDGEBACK Br. Breed of large dog evolved in Rhodesia, originally for hunting lions. Bull mastiff type, bred with older hunting breeds, with distinctive ridge of hair along top of spine.

RONDAVEL Afr. Round hut of wattle-and-daub, widely used in southern Africa, conical with thatched grass roof.

ROOI Afr. Red

ROOINEKS Afr. Slang term for British, who tended to get sunburn on their necks.

RUCK Br. Used in rugby when the ball is on the ground and players of both teams are contesting it, using only their feet, and when it gets pushed to the back, the nearest player can grab it by hand and run with it.

RUSKS Br. Hard-baked dry biscuits from a sweet bread mixture, traditionally eaten with coffee early in the morning; now often flavoured with buttermilk or muesli.

SAMP Afr. Dried, stamped corn kernels, mixed with beans (usually sugar beans) and cooked slowly till soft.

SAWUBONA Zulu. "I see you" – greeting.

SEBENZA Zulu. Work (noun)

SGIAN DUBH Small single-edged knife worn as part of traditional Scottish dress, usually carried in the sock.

SIKHONA Zulu. "I am here to be seen" – response to greeting.

SITKAMER Afr. Sitting room

SKELLUM Originally Scottish, from Old German and Dutch, "schelm", a ne'er-do-well; a rogue, rascal, scoundrel, and archaically, a corpse; now only commonly used in South Africa.

SLEEVEEN Irish. Sly, untrustworthy person

SLIM Afr. Clever

SPAN Afr. Team of oxen; originally the yoke which couples them in harness.

SPRUIT Afr. Stream, brook; tributary to a river. Cf. English word 'Sprout', an offshoot. Used in many place names, indicating the importance of water as the trekkers went north and founded settlements.

STEAMELA Zulu. Train, drawn by a steam engine

STERRETJIE Afr. "Little Star". "–tjie" is a diminutive ending in Afrikaans.

STOEP Afr. Verandah, porch

SWAHILI Language used mainly in Kenya, Tanzania, eastern DRC and Uganda – a mixture of African and Arabic influences, which had many different dialects; eventually standardised in 1928 from that spoken in Zanzibar, used by most races including colonials of European origin.

TARN Scot. A small lake, usually at high altitude

TICKEY Afr. Old name for a very small silver 3d. coin.

TICKEYDRAAI Afr. Boer dance, where couples "turn on a tickey", i.e. make tight turns. Favoured by car salesmen to describe a car's wheel lock.

TOFF Br. Slang used derogatorily for an arrogant person assuming a superior air.

TOPPIE Afr. Nickname for a commonly-found bird, correctly a black-eyed bulbul.

TREK Afr. Verb: To pull. Noun: an arduous journey, often on foot, but associated with oxen pulling wagons; as in the Great Trek, the movement of Afrikaners (q.v.), northwards away from British-controlled territory near the Cape from 1834 onwards. (Cf. 'Star Trek', a modern usage from the 1960s, and adopted by operators of walking trips in the foothills of the Himalayas).

TSONGA Bantu tribe found in South Africa, on the borders of Zululand and Mozambique.

UDANSA Zulu. Danced.

UFUNA USAWATI Do you want some salt?

UKHAMBA Zulu. Clay pot, kept to offer drink to the

spirits, or to test drink is not poisoned before giving to a chief or visitor.

UKUTHI Zulu. That.

UMFAAN Zulu. Young boys.

UMKHUHLWANE Zulu. Fever – used for Spanish Flu in 1919.

UMLUNGU Zulu. White man (originally the white foam that collects on the beach).

UMNUMZANE Zulu. Head of a household; lesser chief; respectful term for old man.

UMUZI Zulu. Individual householders, in a cluster or extended family kraal.

UMVITHI Zulu. Tree of the bushveld, Boscia Oleaides or B. Albitrunca; Shepherd's Tree in English. Zulus say it prevents lightning, so protect it. It has the deepest roots of any known root system.

USHUKELA Zulu. Sugar.

UYAPHI Zulu. Where are you going?

VELD Afr. Open countryside. (Cf. English, "Field")

VELDSKOEN 'Field Shoes', i.e. outdoor footwear, usually short boots of tough skin or suede.

VÖLKISCHER BEOBACHTER The official paper of the NAZI party, from December, 1920.

VOORLOPER Afr. Forerunner, precursor, person leading the way, e.g. ahead of a span of oxen.

VRYHEID Afr. 'Freedom'; capital of the Nieuwe Republiek in northern Natal, established 1884, after King Dinizulu gave the land in exchange for a promise of protection; but absorbed by the Transvaal Republic, the ZAR, in 1888. Now a town in KZN on the way to Durban from Johannesburg.

VRYSTAAT Afr. Free State (usually ref. to the Orange Free

State; could be applied to southern Ireland. The Irish and Boers were close allies, both anti-British.)

WAT 'N GEMORS! Afr. What a mess!

WELLIES Br. Short for wellington boots – named after Arthur Wellesley, first Duke of Wellington, who popularised a boot of leather, adapted from hessian, which then became rubber and waterproof; and is widely worn by gardeners, farm workers, etc.

WELVERDIEND Afr. Well done.

WOZA Zulu. Come!

WRAGTIG Afr. From Dutch "Waaraglig" – Really? Truly? Surely... Expresses surprise, emphasis, used as a mild expletive.

ZOPF Ger.-Swiss. Traditional plaited loaf of bread; a plait

ZULU Zulu. The arch of heaven in which clouds float and birds fly, the source of lightning and thunder. King Shaka used the word to unite tribal elements under his rule. The Zulus emanated from the Ngunis who inhabited central and Eastern Africa. Over the centuries they migrated, mainly, to Natal, southern Africa. In 1879, the British fought a war against the Zulu kingdom in the northern regions of Natal. They resisted bravely and were only defeated after a series of bloody battles that remain prominent in the annals of colonial warfare. Zulu is one of the official languages of South Africa.

9 781399 942867